Love's Promise

Stories

By

Opal Palmer Adisa

The Following Stories were previously published:

God's Child, Small Axe Salon 16, July 2014

"Mother Mushet," XCP Cross Cultural Poetics, 2007, pp. 92-110

"The Living Roots," So Long Been Dreaming, eds. Nalo Hopkinson & Uppinder Mehan. (Arsenal, 2004), pp. 230-242.

"Conscience is the Same as Do Right," The Caribbean Writer, Vol. 17, 2003, pp.121-133.

"Mattie and Night's Sister," Crab Orchard Review, Volume 2, Number 2, Spring/Summer 1997, pp. 3-10.

Published by Plumeria, an imprint of CaribbeanReads Publishing
Text and Cover Image © 2016 Opal Palmer Adisa

ISBN: 978-0-9978900-6-8 (Paperback)
978-0-9978900-8-2 (Hardcover)
Library of Congress Control Number: 2017932934
All Rights Reserved

CaribbeanReads Publishing
Fairfax Station, VA 22039
info@caribbeanreads.com

To Gem, my childhood friend, and others who laced my childhood.

Acknowledgements

Special thanks to my daughter Shola for her keen insights and editorial eyes, and for sending me back to the drawing board to re-look and search out some of the stories more deeply, and also, to Karen James Cody for helping me to see the larger place and world where these stories belong.

And thanks too for time passing, and me delaying these stories until they matured and developed, and more ready to step out into the world.

And thanks to the editor and publisher who understand the merit and are willing to give these stories an audience.

And thanks to you, the readers, for taking the time and going on the journey with these characters.

And special thanks to all these characters—people who decided to come and visit me, and sat patiently inside my head until I sat down and gave them voice, after years of carrying them around with me.

Thanks to writing... a blessed release...

Other Publications by Opal Palmer Adisa

Look! A Moko Jumbie, children's, 2016

4-Headed Woman, poetry, 2013

Incantations & Rites, poetry (with devorah major), 2013

Painting Away Regrets, novel, 2011

Caribbean Erotic, anthology (co-edited with Donna Aza Weir-Soley), 2010

What a Woman Is, poetry, (with paintings by Shyam Kamel), 2010

Amour Verdinia, poetry, chapbook, 2009

Conscious Living, poem, chapbook, 2009

I Name Me Name, poetry, 2008

Playing Is Our Work, children's, 2008

Until Judgment Comes, short stories, 2006

Eros Muse, poetry and essays, 2006

Caribbean Passion, poetry, 2004

The Tongue Is a Drum, poetry/jazz CD (with devorah major), 2002

Leaf-of-Life, poetry, 2000

It Begins With Tears, novel, 1997

Tamarind and Mango Women, poetry, 1992

Fierce Love, poetry/jazz recording (with devorah major), 1992

Traveling Women, poems, (with devorah major), 1989

Bake-Face and Other Guava Stories, short stories, 1986

Pina, The Many-Eyed Fruit, children, 1985

Introduction

Love's Promise is sweet respite from the often publicly-displayed hate that has become a staple of public discourse. Stories of innocent childhood love, of couples meeting up again after years of being apart and finding each other still with the passion of earlier days; older women finding time to enjoy body and companionship and sex, parents ensuring that a daughter was prepared to rekindle past connections; a wife whose love for herself takes her to another zone of self protection. This is Love's Promise which refreshes our faith in humanity, a way of being naturally in the world, flaws and all; full of gains and losses.

The stories offer a logical sequence from the childhood love stories which begin the collection to the more mature and sexually explicit themes and situations "Love Bush" is about teenage desire and adult fulfillment in which a local weed is endowed with meaning. But one can just as easily begin reading any story in this collection for there are many different types of love presented. "Bus Stop" is ostensibly about teen attraction but it is also about a mother's love for her daughter and the necessity she feels to offer protection until she gets signals that her child will not be hurt. What we get in the entire collection is a gradual unfolding from childhood affection into more sensual narratives with some wonderful surprises along the way.

The title story "Love's Promise" contains all of these unfoldings. It begins with childhood best friends who climb trees to share their art and spend pleasurable hours in each other's company, only to be thwarted by the residues of colonial educational. In this case, the publishing of the list of those who have passed a Common Entrance exam (also called 11+) in the middle of adolescence, marks one for success or failure. A young boy who had had the stigma of failure becomes nonetheless a celebrated writer who is honored in that same country for a collection of stories called "Love's Promise." With his childhood girlfriend, an artist, creativity is the glue of their friendship which also brings them back together again.

What is noticeable is that for Opal, returning home in each case brings with it a bonus of reconnection; a reversal of the migration paradigm in which the joy of a better life is the promise sometimes unfulfilled at the proposed destination.

And in this case, the promise of further unfolding and the return to a childhood tree climbing passion ensures that the creativity is sparked even further.

My favorite is the magical "The Living Roots" which gives us an opening line that titillates with the sweetness that runs through the entire collection: "Dusk skipped in like a woman in haste to meet her lover." The rest of the story offers us Caribbean realism with its magic of shape-shifting or transmogrification. A community which can make itself invisible as it lives literally underground, in Piliferous Layer, has characters who can merge into tree trunks, and remain still within reach but elsewhere. It is a different take on maroon communities right in our midst, and takes the logic of in/visibility to a wonderful conclusion. Occasional visits to the "enslaved world" reveal us as encumbered by so many levels of enslavement from clothing to the inability to see; hair that is not allowed to be free. The sensual language which is used copiously in this story is a bonus. A description of a lover: "He tasted like roasted sweet potato." But so too is the sense of freedom that runs through this lovely story.

Opal Palmer Adisa crosses from magic realism to the creating of New World mythologies. Beyond the narrative of Ibo Landing narrative which has been mined by films like Daughters of the Dust to novels like Paule Marshall's Praisesong for the Widow, is another possibility of imagining those who found a way to break free and live underground:

"I cannot tell you how we did it, except that once the ship docked and we were relieved of our chains, we each ran, and to keep from being detected we buried each other, and in our desperation to be quiet, to keep from being captured, our bodies transformed and we found ourselves being pulled more deeply into the earth, as if through quicksand, until we sank to a latitude that had a floor."

Stories of spirituality and knowledge of the non-western sciences and magical rituals also appear as in "Conscience is the Same as Do Right." Here an unwilling healer/herbalist who in her daytime occupation is a street vendor, has a gift and training passed down from her father who still returns after his death to bring messages or offer protection and to right a series of wrongs. Another story, "Mattie and Night's Sister" takes it further, this time going into the being of a woman for whom "the only thing she loved more than her own company was the night." An odd child with peculiar passions reveals a certain different gender non-conformity, as she becomes a woman "whose independence caused men to doubt themselves and women to grow mustaches" But for her, the self is sufficient as she moves beyond human levels of sexuality to a relationship with Night itself. In this interesting story, the narrative shifts between the real and the magically real in which an actual child is produced from her encounter with Night but who becomes the village's child.

"Matrimony" though its title suggests a different unfolding offers the familiar "Bake Face" who has to defend her daughter from predatory child sexual assault which she had also experienced herself. The sensuality of food, of taste, of self assurance of familial relationships and the promise of love partnerships are possible only through the reclaiming of inheritance.

But get ready for "Trio" told as a conversation between two women in which a life story unfolds a technique used by Zora Neale Hurston in *Their Eyes Were Watching God* (1938). I suppose this is what some would call 'slackness' because though it reveals an older woman enjoying her sexuality, the price she pays for this pleasure is really too much.

Following her daring poems about life and love, motherhood and politics, her novels about marital dissolution and community's failures, Love's Promise presents a refreshing mélange of joys and sadness, carelessness and certitude, a Caribbean potpourri that engages the senses at every level.

Carole Boyce Davies, Cornell University
Professor of English and Africana Studies
Author of *Black Women, Writing and Identity: Migrations of the Subject* and
Left of Karl Marx: The Political Life of Black Communist Claudia Jones, among others.

Table of Contents

Love-Bush

The flame of love rode around with her throughout her adolescent years and lingered in her early adult body in the hula-hoop she twirled and kept balanced above her waist until it danced up her neck and her fingers grasped it ever so tenderly.

* * *

The first time she saw him she was fourteen, and he was playing the lead in a musical at the Little Theatre on the same bill as her dance company. His presence so distracted her that during her dance routine she fell, and another dancer almost stumbled over her. Although she managed to spring up and get back in step, embarrassment burned in her, pungent as stinking-toe.

He never spoke to her, but he always smiled, warm and enchanting as yellow hibiscus. She observed that he chatted with some of the older dancers closer to his age who flirted shamelessly with him. She hated being fourteen.

"You might have a woman's body, but you're still a child," was her mother's daily reminder.

She was tempted to ask him to be her beau, though she was not yet allowed to have a boyfriend and he was reportedly twenty years old.

He was the color of cane-juice, with light brown eyes and nappy brownish hair that always seemed to need a comb raked through it. Tall and lanky, his smile caused her to smile too, foolishly, and a wobbly feeling shimmied up and down her body. Throughout the three-weekend rehearsals, she stole every opportunity she could to regard him, watching his every move. Her obsession more than once caused her to miss cues, unleashing the wrath of Ms. Nance the dance teacher, who took tremendous pleasure in berating them for their poor posture, their sloppy executions of the steps, their distractedness, and their general lack of grace.

Ms. Nance shouted and pointed at her, "You of all people shouldn't have the audacity to be late and miss cues. Do you know why you're in this production? Do you? Because you've been with the company for over six years and I feel obligated to cast you. I don't think you have what it takes to ever be a professional dancer." She would have walked out, but to do so would have been to chance being punished by her mother for impertinence. So she had to suffer through Ms. Nance's tirade and suck in her tears until the end of the routine. Then she ran, exiting the theatre half blinded by tears and exhausted from holding her breath for so long. Why did adults have to go on and on like that, constantly pointing out what you did wrong? She would never be like that when she became an adult.

Shoving the door open, and being stabbed by the bright sunlight, she crashed into him, spilling his soda and causing him to let out a curse as he looked quizzically over his shoulder at her running away. Doubly mortified, she kept running, to find a tree or a car in the parking lot behind which she could hide.

If only she were eighteen or seventeen, or even sixteen, the age at which she could be allowed to have a boyfriend, she would approach him boldly. But, if she were that age, she wouldn't have had to approach him; he would see her. He would pursue her—chase her down the way she'd overheard her mother telling Miss Dorothy that her father had done—chasing down her mother until she agreed to marry him. If she were sixteen, she imagined dreamily, Hansford would pursue her relentlessly.

She looked up in alarm to see that he had followed her, crept quietly to where she squatted between two cars, doubly embarrassed by both being singled out by Ms. Nance and then gracelessly colliding with him. Her chest heaved and she erupted into fresh sobs, the tears flowing like the river spilling over Flat Bridge, as she replayed both humiliations in her mind. She felt a hand on her shoulder, warm, light, tingling; and she turned to see him offering her his handkerchief.

"Don't take it so personal. Teachers love to make their best students feel like dirt. Man, you're good!" he said bending slightly down towards her.

Squinting into the sun, tears on her cheeks, she looked up at the kind prince before her. She was shocked by his praise. To awaken herself from what she was sure was a dream, she shook her head. Her lips parted, but her tongue would not move—and at that instant she became conscious of the snot dripping from her nose. Another wave of humiliation washed over her and she abruptly turned away. But she reached back and took the hanky. She needed it. She blew her nose several times and finally turned to thank him. To her astonishment, he was gone.

She cleaned herself up, brushing aside the tears and pulling her bun tight again to the crown of her head, re-entered the auditorium and slipped back into her place in the squad as if nothing had happened. She tried for the rest of the rehearsal not to look at him; but whenever she caught his eye he winked. His eyes revealed understanding and made her feel warm inside, like a hot cup of Milo before bed.

The dates for the recital came and went, and although she tripped on stage at the final performance Ms. Nance said they did very well, and that she was very proud of them, all of them; this Ms. Nance said looking directly at her.

She didn't see him again for a very, very long time. Every time she went to, or even walked by, the Little Theatre to a performance or to dance rehearsal she would crane her neck in some vain hope of catching sight of him, but she never once did. She still had his handkerchief, embroidered at the corner with his initials—HJ. She fantasized about the two of them together: married with children; acting and dancing and singing in plays together; traveling. She wrote his name and hers and crossed out the letters that matched and convinced herself that the two of them were compatible. She picked the roses from her mother's garden, and petal by petal she would declare, 'He loves me, he loves me not' and if the petals were all gone on 'He loves me not,' she would begin again.

One day when her family went to the country to visit an aunt, she spotted a wild growth of Love-Bush on a fence. Looking about surreptitiously lest her parents should see, she pulled up some and wrapped it in newspaper. That night when they got home, pretending to take out the dog, she tossed the Love-Bush into the hedge in front of the vegetable garden. If it took root and grew there, she told herself, it would mean he loved her.

A week later she went to peek at the planting, but it had dried up; it seemed dead. She was heartbroken. She slunk into the house, crept into bed, turned her face to the wall, and determined never to resurface. Swept up in her own melodrama, she imagined her heart in pieces like the crystal wine glass she had once dropped onto the tiled floor of their kitchen and shattered into shards. At dinnertime when called to set the table, she pretended to be asleep; and when her mother came to wake her, she claimed to be ill. Her mother sat on edge of the bed and asked what was wrong. She lied that her stomach hurt and her head ached. Feeling her forehead, her mother declared her free of fever, and said that all she probably needed was some cerasee tea, her mother's cure-all, a bitter brew that even with several spoons of sugar made her want to vomit.

She did not have the strength to object. Since she was going to die anyway from the lack of his love, she would suffer the cerasee, she reasoned. Up until that moment she had thought her mother knew everything. But clearly she did not if she could not see that her youngest daughter, whom she claimed to love more than the immense blue sky, was dying from a broken heart right before her eyes.

Alarmed by the absence of protest about her having to drink the brew, her mother wondered out aloud,

"You must really sick for true. If you don't feel better in the morning I might have to take you to Doctor Moody."

She drank the warm cup of cerasee in one gulp—which, as a compromise, her mother had sweetened with condensed milk—and then slumped back into bed, prepared to wither away until she died. Her mother patted her shoulder, kissed her on the forehead, and left. Eventually she fell into a deep sleep.

In her dream she was falling. From way up high, and out of nowhere, Hansford appeared and caught her just before she crashed to her death on a rocky hillside.

"Don't ever doubt my love," he declared, beaming his beatific smile down at her, snug in his arms. Then he carried her to a boat where he sat her down ever so gently, and they sailed off in the deep blue-grey moon lit sky, the ocean tranquil as a stream.

She woke in shivers the next morning and could not get out of bed. Her mother let her stay home from school that day, and took her to the doctor in the afternoon. Dr. Moody used his cold stethoscope to listen to her breathing. He pulled down her lower eyelids, peered into her eyes and up her nostrils, and told her mother she was fine—probably just adolescent changes. She decided in that moment that Dr. Moody—who had been her doctor since she was a child— didn't know his arse from his elbow. She didn't know whom she hated more, her mother, Dr. Moody, or Hansford.

Yet the next morning, everything was different. She awoke about ten o'clock, well after the sun's rays slipped through the half-parted curtain. For some reason the sun appearing like it did every morning melted her resolve to stay in bed until she died. She knelt on the bed, parted the curtains fully, and looked out at the day, inviting as a promise.

Beside her bed on a tray draped with one of her mother's starched embroidered doilies were a peeled orange in a saucer; a glass of guava juice; and a cup of cocoa tea with nutmeg and oil floating on top, with lots of milk like she liked it. Covered on one of the Sunday plates were two Johnny-cakes, three slices of plantain, and callalloo with salt-fish—but mercifully without onions, which she detested. All of her favorite foods, prepared exactly as she liked them. She smiled shyly as she pulled the tray close to her bed and took the knife and fork in her hands. Perhaps her mother might be right that some people didn't always know what was good for them. This was obviously true of Hansford Jones. She would have to wait until he came to his senses. She was prepared to put off dying and live just a little bit longer.

Eating everything on the tray, she was stuffed, but got up, showered, then walked bare-foot into the yard, and although the sun had dried away all the dew, she wiggled her toes in the stubby grass, spread wide her arms, and sang out, "He will love me one day." Her mother always told her that she was a love child, and people couldn't resist loving her.

A few months later, Hansford turned up again.

She was half asleep at one of her mother's Red Cross concerts and there he was standing alone on the make-shift stage set up on the lawn, singing proudly, his voice like bamboo vines blowing in the wind. She stood with the tray of triangle sandwiches that her mother had left her to serve the guests, mesmerized by his voice and lost in seeing him so unexpectedly. She forgot that she resented her mother for always dragging her to these charity affairs. Hansford, handsome in a white shirt buttoned up to his Adam's apple and navy blue slacks, seemed to be singing to her, just to her.

So engrossed was she in the moment that she didn't see or feel the stray dog that had crept up and was eating the sandwiches off the tray. She started and, in her confusion, tipped the tray and watched in dismay as the rest of the sandwiches fell to the ground.

Her mother shot her a look from way across the lawn that made her quail up like a wilted hibiscus petal. She looked down at the spilled sandwiches at her feet and at the dog quickly swallowing them, then realized that the singing had ended. Glancing towards the makeshift stage where Hansford still stood amidst applause, her eyes locked with his and she felt her stomach flip-flop, flip-flop. He did not smile or wink and she knew he was as embarrassed for her as she was for herself. However, something in his eyes told her not to fret. No matter that her mother was going to bawl her out all the way home.

Surprisingly, her mother never mentioned the accident with the sandwiches. On the contrary, her mother was quiet. But she could see in her peripheral vision that her mother would glance over at her every so often; and she thought she glimpsed a smile brush across her mother's lips. At home again, still mum, she strode to the side of the yard to pick some guavas and that was when she saw it.

The Love Bush had not died. It had grown—wildly, with abandon, along the entire side of the house. "I knew it," she thought triumphantly. "I knew it." She danced, leaping over the cabbage, carrots, onions, and pumpkin vines, forgetting about the guavas she had come to pick. "He loves me." She pulled free several strands, placed them on her head and over her shoulders, and took a handful to her room, where she placed them in her panty drawer beside his handkerchief.

A day didn't go by the rest of that year without her thinking of him.

Yet a few months later she came home from school to find that all the Love-Bush had been cut out from the freshly trimmed edged. She cried when she saw the heap, mixed in with the weeds, grass, and other garden cuttings.

"Why did he cut down my Love-Bush?" she hollered, tears streaming down her face.

"Why are you going on like it's the end of the world?" her mother asked, reaching out to wipe her tears. "Hush. It's just a weed; it will grow back. It's a parasite you know!" Her mother laughed, and that made her cry even more.

The following Sunday Hansford's picture appeared in the papers as one of the winners of a scholarship to study in Britain. He would be leaving in a matter of weeks. Her tears flowed unchecked, almost daily, until one day, several weeks later they dried up, when a boy with the unusual name of Vergard, touched her elbow, said she was pretty, and asked if she would be his girlfriend. She had stared at him, doubtful that he was speaking to her, but realizing how nervous he was under her scrutiny, it suddenly dawned on her that he was caught by the womanly charm her mother always told her she possessed; and even though she was six months shy of sixteen and did not have permission to have a boy-friend, she surprised both herself and Vergard by answering: `Yes.'

Vergard hung his head and smiled, and even though he inspired no strong reaction in either her body or her mind, she dated him until she graduated from high school, at which point she dropped him abruptly, realizing that she would never love him and did not want to marry him. He was really too nice to string along; he deserved a girl who really cared for him. She did him a favor, cutting him loose, and she knew he would see it that way in time.

Although Hansford crossed her mind often enough and she wondered if he still sang and was as handsome as she remembered, thinking of him no longer pained her. She had only seen him once since that ill-fated Saturday afternoon with the dog and the sandwiches, but since that time she had not heard anything about him. She suspected that like most people who went away to study, he remained in England. Contrarily, when it came her turn she insisted on attending UWI, rather than going away as her father had suggested.

And it was in her very first class at UWI she met the man she would marry. And she would love him, if ever so slightly, and they had an uncomplicated marriage because he adored her, as her mother often said, adding that it wouldn't hurt if she were to shower him with more affection.

Six years into marriage, on a leisurely Sunday afternoon, while sitting on her veranda feeling contented and satisfied with her life, yet wondering if she had married prematurely, she unfolded the newspaper in her lap, opened to the entertainment section and there was a photograph of him, handsome as ever, with the headline that read, "Island Son Returns to Give Concert." She choked on the cracker and gundi on which she was nibbling, the paper falling to the floor. At that same time her husband walked out, yanked her arms above her head and patted her back. She buried her face in his stomach as he stood in front of her, his hand soothing the top of her head, and he whispered, "I am so grateful for your love."

The following week, Monday, Tuesday, Wednesday, and Thursday she thought about buying tickets for the concert, but told herself she was being foolish. Handsford had been puppy love and she now had the real thing; still his memory nagged at her. Friday, when she finally made up her mind to get tickets, she learned that all three nights were sold out. Relieved, she told herself it was just as well. She arrived home late to find her two favorite flowers —bird-of-paradise and anthuriums—in a vase on the dresser, courtesy of her husband. Next to the vase was a card that read, "Just because you make my life happy; Forever, Bert…" And on her side of the bed was an envelope. When she opened it she saw that it contained two tickets for Handford's concert the following night. Tears smarted in her eyes, and her heart pulsed.

After ensconcing their daughter with her mother until Sunday evening, she dressed carefully. Admiring herself in the mirror, she wondered for whom she was dressing—Bert, Hansford, or both? Would she insist that they wait around and greet him? He won't even know I am there, she thought sadly. I'm all grown up now. She took one last glance at herself before switching off the light and sashaying out to where Bert waited. He whistled and kissed the back of her hand fervently.

Imagine her surprise when she discovered that their seats were dead center in the first row. Then, just as the lights dimmed, Bert shocked her further when he whispered: "We have invitations for the reception, so we'll get to meet Hansford." Her breath caught and her heart rate accelerated as if she had just run a race. During the intermission, unable to contain himself, Bert told her that the first time he saw and fell in love with her was at a Red Cross concert when he was fifteen years old. His mother had dragged him to that concert; but because he was not feeling well, he had sat in the car. Hansford had played at that concert, and she had been serving sandwiches on a tray. He had watched as a dog took advantage of her inattention, poaching several of the sandwiches off the tray, and had been much amused by the chain reaction of events that followed.

"You were there?" she said, astonished. He had never mentioned it before. He nodded. "That was when I fell in love with you," he said, "and I have loved you ever since."

She looked into her husband's eyes and his love warmed her body and made her shiver. The first time she remembered seeing him was when he walked in late to her literature class that first semester at University of the West Indies, and how he smiled confidently as if he had a right to be late. At the time she couldn't help staring at him, noting the self-satisfied assurance that he exuded, then and even now. He was his own man—not arrogant or prone to bragging, but secure, very able, no matter what he undertook; and in him she always, always found a shelter, a place safe from all the chaos of the world. Now, standing beside him, her heart swelled renewed. She caressed his back and snuggled closer to him.

Hansford had developed into an amazing soprano, and the diverse range of his songs, from European classics, to African-American spirituals to local, Jamaican folksongs thrilled the packed audience. They responded to him with thunderous applause, demanding an encore at the end of the concert. When he came back and said he wanted to do a song he had been writing for thirteen years and had just completed when he signed the contract to return home to do this concert. A hush fell over the crowd.

"This is for a passionate, young dancer I met at the Little Theatre almost fourteen years ago. The last time I saw her was the day before I left the island; she was walking by the theatre and I invited her for a milkshake. This song is called Love's Promise for Arleen."

"He could be talking about you," Bert whispered in her ear, his arm draped through hers, hooked at the elbow curve. She patted his arms, finger trembling. When she didn't answer, he asked, "Is he talking about you? Do you know him?" Bert's voice rasped in her ear.

"Ssshh," she whispered, her full attention on the stage.

The song was playful and spoke of childhood friendship and love, suggestive but also open-ended.

The concert ended on that crescendo, and she found herself patting away tears at the corner of her eyes as the lights in the theatre came up and the audience began to file out. She and Bert headed for the reception, Bert clutching her hand and glancing at her surreptitiously.

At the reception, she disentangled herself from Bert and managed to get Hansford to herself.

"Thanks for the song," she said beaming at him. "I am truly honored that you remembered."

"Thanks for the inspiration," he replied kissing the back of her hand. "Are you still dancing?"

"Yes," she replied, " but mainly as a hobby. I gave it up…" She stopped abruptly, thoughtful. This was neither the place nor the time to fill him in about all the details of her life.

She fished in her purse for a moment, feeling for the handkerchief with HJ embroidered at the corner. She handed it to him.

"This is yours and I don't need it anymore, but thanks; thanks for whetting my desire."

Bert arrived then with her wine. She introduced them, and the three of them chatted for about five minutes before Hansford acquiesced to the other fans who vied for his attention.

She was surprised to realize that by then she was anxious to leave; and on the drive home, she nibbled on Bert's ear and crooned that she was ready to try for a second child.

The little girl she had been had finally walked away so she could be fully the woman for whom every day was love's promise. Besides, both sides of her yard were overgrown with love-bush that Bert had tossed and had forbidden their gardener to uproot. Their love had long been planted and tended.

Conscience Is the Same as Do Right

"You have to carry on now. Me go as far as me can go," he said stretching his back. He had insisted that she accompany him to the field and they hadn't spoken while he dug the yams and chopped off the heads that she piled for planting later.

"Memba ears need nose fi listen." They were heading home when he said this and although she didn't understand what he meant, she hadn't asked for an explanation as she knew what he would say:

"Understanding come later; just let de words settle in you body."

So she walked in silence with him, his words running around in her head. Just before they went through the gate that led to the house, he held on to the pinky and ring fingers of her right hand, fished his free hand in his pocket and gave her a trupence, a whole nutmeg in its hard shell, and a small black stone shaped like an uppercase L.

Two weeks later he died at the field near the yam heads piled for planting.

He hadn't come home and her mother sent her to get him. She found him face down in the dirt and Sampson, his dog, curled by his cold body, howling softly as she approached. He never told her what she was to do with what he had given her or what she was expected to carry on.

People came to see her from time to time. Many of them seemed ashamed, as if they wanted to run and hide but couldn't. Often they left empty-handed, and she would see the look of doubt and fear plainly written on their faces more clearly than their eyes. But a few left laden with herbs and other things that she had helped her Papa to collect.

She remembered that she was not yet four years old the first time Papa took her with him to collect herbs. They were out all day. She became tired and he carried her on his back. Her mother had fussed at him when they came home in the dead of night, a crocus sack filled with bush slung over his shoulder.

"You can't mek her into nuh obeah woman. She is still picknie. Look how she tired and hungry. Nuh drag her into your madness."

Her mother had taken her roughly from him, fed and bathed her, then put her in the bed to sleep between them. Another time, when she was seven years old, her mother and Papa played tug-o-war with her. Each pulled at one arm, her mother insisting that she wasn't going to the bush, her Papa asserting that she had to learn to find the herbs and he couldn't teach her at home. Her mother won that battle; but a week later, her father crept into her room at night, picked her from the bed she shared with her two sisters, and slung her outside, where he dressed her hurriedly and they stole away with Sampson at their heels. They were in the bush for three full days living on bush tea and fruits that Papa picked along the way. When they returned, her mother flung a stone and hit her Papa on his left knee, giving him a limp he had until he went to his grave.

"You can't take me gal picknie and tun her into nuh obeah oman. Is education she getting; she gwane turn nurse; she nah go be no obeah oman like you."

Saying that, her mother had grabbed and dragged her to the bathroom where she scrubbed her from head to foot with the loofa sponge to wash away all the knowledge her father had taught her. From then on her mother watched her like an enraged lioness, but still her father managed to steal her away and take her on excursions.

Once it was for an entire week to Port Antonio, where many men and women like him were gathered, chanting songs and making different packets of herb, and where she was made to drink nasty-tasting bush tea. For the entire week, she had no food, had diarrhea for three days, and danced and sang until her feet ached and her head spun. Mostly she was scared when she realized she could look at the people at the gathering and know what they had done to others.

When she returned home, she was sick for a week, and from then, she banded with her mother. She hid whenever she suspected Papa was coming to steal her away to go on one of his expeditions. She did not want to hear from looking. She was eleven years old then, and started her period a month later, and that was the last trip she took with her Papa.

When he died she watched his coffin being lowered into the ground. She tossed a handful of dirt into the hole like the others and an overwhelming sense of loss engulfed her. In that moment she knew she hadn't gotten what she needed to continue on her own without Papa. The tears that streamed down her face weren't for him—although she loved him dearly and always defended him when others spoke ill against him—but for what she knew she had to get on her own. She felt quite alone.

The night of Papa's nine-night he came to her. She had fallen asleep at the kitchen table. He woke her.

"Get up, Big Sista. Go ah yu bed."

She had rubbed her eyes, forgetting for a moment that he was dead, buried in fact, and had answered obediently,

"Yes, Papa." She had stumbled out of the chair. She felt his hands on her elbows, guiding her to the room she still shared with her sisters.

"Always memba," he admonished her. "You can only do wha you can do but you mus do dat well. Don't ignore wha you know. Tomorrow after de rooster crow, get up and me will tek you to bush."

Then he was gone. But she somehow knew his words had to do with the trupence, the nutmeg, and the L-shaped stone he had given her exactly two weeks before he died. She was fifteen years old then and the next morning she got up when the rooster crowed and began walking.

They found her four days later, frothing at the mouth.

Her mother shook her fist at the sky, and screamed at her dead husband, "No you don't." That same day they went to a healer to get protection from Papa. It worked, for it would be five more years before her Papa would come to her again.

She felt his presence during those five years, but always she pushed him away.

Then she became pregnant with her first child so dropped out of nursing school.

Papa was annoyed with her. She knew it even before he said anything. His left eye twitched when he was upset and he took on a slight stutter.

"A. . .ah didn't give it to you fi sit on. Is not me decide it must go from fada to oldest dawta. . .Is not me, but you can't sit on it. You is de right one. Do what you know."

Then, just like the other times, he was gone like mist dissipating in the heat of the day.

She hadn't told anyone, not even her mother, about the trupence, the nutmeg, and the L-shaped stone; but now she felt the need to tell someone. She had been keeping the objects in a pouch made out of his work pants. She carried it with her most times, but she didn't know what to do with them. Pregnant, and feeling her Papa's spirit tugging at her, she sought out Aunty Matty who lived down the path that led to nowhere, and who was rumored to be a duppy-witch who flew on the tale of night, cast love potions, and perched on trees like an owl. Aunty Matty laughed as she approached and asked her why she took so long to come.

"Chile, you is one of me now," Aunty Matty cackled, tears trickling out the corner of her eyes but drying before they reached her cheeks. "You Papa used to come knock back a rum with me every fortnight. We would talk and help each other help others. Ah don't suppose you bring a bottle, now did you, child?"

"No, Aunty Matty," she replied. She stayed with the old duppy-witch until way into the night while the woman cooked her a dinner of boiled cornmeal dumplings and susumba with cod-fish. They ate mostly in silence. Every so often

Aunty Matty would ask her a question, but then would answer it herself. When she finally got up to leave the old woman said to her:

"Dat trupence you papa gi you, keep it. Bore a hole and wear it round you neck fah protection and fi help you ears open. De stone is fah you son you will ave—and de nutmeg, well…you will find someone fi gi dat to." Then Aunty Matty reached across and pulled on her ears, and she heard the sound of the wind rushing through. "Now you will be able fi ear wha you already know."

She never went back to the old witch-woman after that day, but ever so often they would run into each other on the same path. On these occasions Aunty Matty would cackle as if someone had told her a joke.

One day, shortly after she had her first child who she named Hortense after her deceased paternal grandmother, she and Aunty Matty had almost stumbled into one another. They each mumbled 'beg pardon,' and she continued on her way. But she heard Aunty Matty stop and her voice was like a hot iron on her back.

"Me did tell you Papa dat you nuh mek fah dis line of wuk. You want stay blind to life. Me hope you will prove me wrong, but anyway, me done bless you baby wid eyes and ears."

She had glanced back, but Aunty Matty had turned the bend in the road and only her scent, like burnt cane, wafted on the air. But she never forgot what Aunty Matty had said, and shortly thereafter she began to see through her ears.

By the time she was twenty years old she had learned that a gift could be as much a blessing as it was a curse.

She dropped out of nursing school in her first year because she couldn't silence all that she heard around her—without anyone speaking a word. Her Papa had stopped visiting, because she would pretend not to see him whenever he appeared to her.

Although she fell in love, she would never marry, hearing more than she wanted to hear, especially the lies, as useless as shame-old-lady bush that Hortense's father kept telling her never to up-root. Shortly before Hortense was born she broke off the relationship with the baby's daddy completely. Two years later she met another man, and just when she became pregnant, he took off for Canada. She gave birth to a son, whom she knew when he was born that she would bury him.

Her Papa visited her again right after her son was born. The infant was only a day old, and she was still in bed.

"Big Sista," he said, using his pet name for her, "de worse ting about gift is when it can't help you save you own, but dats not you job. We mus always love like it gwane last." He patted her arm, kissed his grandson on the forehead, and was gone. In that instant she decided to name the son Seymour, after Papa. And also she accepted her gift, placed it on her head like a scarf.

She spoilt Seymour, and as he got older, Hortense would accuse her of loving him more, because he was a boy. She couldn't bring herself to tell Hortense that she knew the two of them would bury her brother and that she Hortense would inherit the gift.

Over the course of her life she never worked for anyone else. After Hortense came she built a little stall by the side of the road and sold escoveitched fish, bammy, fritters, and roasted sweet potato. That was how she supported herself and the children and paid to send them to school, even the boy whom she knew she would bury. She tried to pretend that he would out-live her, and most times she succeeded; but more times than not, awareness was an unshaded light bulb.

Even before Seymour was a month old, people began to knock at her door, people she didn't know and had never seen before. Mostly though, people would come to her as a result of stopping to buy fish and bammy or fritters and the roasted sweet potato she grew on her Papa's land. Their conscience spoke loudly even before they asked,

"So is how you sell de fish?"

The first person she helped was a young lady in nursing school who aborted a pregnancy without telling her boyfriend, fearing being trapped without a profession. But she loved the boy and felt guilty, and was seriously thinking of confessing.

She handed the young lady the fish, but did not give her the change. Two other people were waiting to buy fish. She waved the young lady to a bench and went to serve the other customers. When she returned she took the young lady's hand and said, "Not every news come over radio."

The lady faltered and stepped back.

"What you saying?" she asked, alarm written on her face.

"Is you one know. You head don't rule your heart, nor your heart rule your head. Common sense is de same as wisdom. Come by tomorrow and me will have some herbs to help strengthen you woman space."

She didn't know where the words came from or how she knew but she knew. That night she went gathering bush in the dark. Her children were asleep when she returned to spread the harvest on the table, sorting and combining. She didn't know what she was doing, but her hands moved of their own accord, making small bundles. She fell asleep still sorting. The next morning she awoke to find the bundles of herbs in neat piles. Hortense, four years old, smiled and handed her a small bundle of herbs.

"Grandpa say dese for de lady."

The child turned away, and it was only then that her daughter's words sunk in. She grabbed the child.

"Grandpa who? Your grandpa dead before you born. Which grandpa?"

Her daughter looked at her as if she were stupid.

"Your Papa been dreaming me long time now. Him say you to stop gwane like you blind. Deaf ears can't see."

She spilled the tea and burned her thigh.

Then she chuckled to herself. Papa always did know how to steal away a child; no matter how watchful the Mama was. I guess I shouldn't be surprised.

By the time Hortense was ten years old, she was responsible enough to be left alone to run her mother's house and care for her brother. On weekends Hortense went into the bush with her grandpa, who taught her where to find all the herbs and how to combine them. But it was her mother who taught her to administer them, writing out the formulas and instructions.

Her gift did not always sit light upon her shoulders. She never got over feeling uncomfortable about the ease with which she read people's consciences in order to prescribe her remedies. The man who repeatedly beat his wife then came for fish and bammy because he knew she loved them and would forgive him when he returned home with the treats. Four times in two years he came to her. The first time, his hand was swollen from hitting on his wife so hard. Sweat caked the shirt to his body that first night, and his fear and shame were like hot, red coals tossed on the ground. Even as he stood before her, pointing to the fish, not able to talk, she smelled the beating on his body and she had to turn away and spit, her anger at him alive.

"Me no have anything fi sell you," she shouted and fanned him away to another vendor. He moved off, head hung.

"Good," she hissed. "Is not me gwane help you." But ten minutes later the man, bowed head, sweat dripping from his forehead, was back in front of her stall.

"Ah don't know why ah do it," he mumbled.

"Ah don't give a blast, you damn wife beater!" She kissed her teeth and averted her face.

"Ah love her, but she just mek me feel. . ."

"You betta shut up while you still have teeth cause me is not you wife."

"Help me nuh. Dem seh yu can help me."

Despite her feelings, she sold him the fish and made him a mixture of herbs that was to help him remain calm. She supposed it worked, for at least six months, then he was back. The fourth time he came back, she was through. Later she learned that he choked on a fish bone and broke his right hand in three different places and was never able to make a fist again. He never came to buy fish anymore, thereafter.

Then there were the half-hearted thieves, the husband stealers, the church backsliders, the cheaters, the big-mouths, the envious. They all ended by her stall, always thinking they were coming to buy fish or fritters, when they were really coming to unload. From 6 p.m. until well after midnight on Friday and Saturday nights she was by the stall selling and prescribing, often to the same people. She didn't know why people refused to do what they knew was right and give up guilty feelings.

The young lady, her first customer, came back twice. She knew on the second visit that Cordela, the young lady, was the one to inherit the nutmeg that her father had given. She told her to keep in her underwear drawer. Cordela had married the boyfriend and they had two children, but then she had an affair with a doctor at the hospital. Then there was the time she stole medicine and sold it to get money for her daughter's tutoring to pass the common entrance exam for high school. She told the young lady that she was a simple woman who sold fish and gave away herbs, and not a priest in a confessional. "Yu have to forgive your own indiscretions and do right." That was the last she saw of her.

Then there were those love sick women who naively thought taking a piece of their husbands' or lovers' clothing to the obeah man would solve the problems of a wayward man. One woman had gone too far, and found herself trapped with a man who grew deadly ill. She had gone back to the obeah woman begging her to reverse her charm, but still her husband was failing in health. She didn't want to be responsible for killing him. She laughed at the woman before telling her to go home and beg her husband's forgiveness and for seven days make him tea to drink from the herbs she gave to her. A year later the man divorced the woman; but shortly thereafter another man shot him dead for sleeping with his wife.

Then her Papa, who hadn't appeared to her since Seymour was born, began to visit her again. He came the night she was the only seller on the road. It had rained hard early during the day and she was undecided about going out, but since she had roasted a large amount of sweet potato and cooked fish, she went. She was there for two hours before anyone stopped, and she only sold two small fish and a bammy. She was weary and felt herself dozing off when she heard her Papa's voice firm and clear.

"Wake up, Big Sista. Someone coming to rob yu. Why you not wearing dat trupence me gi you?"

She jumped awake almost tipping over the covered tray of sweet potato on a box by her feet. She looked around, but her Papa wasn't there. She felt her neck, and remembered that earlier in the day the chain had broken and she had placed it, along with the trupence, on her dresser. Then the bright lights of a car blinded her. For a moment she panicked, but then she sensed her Papa standing behind her. Before the car came to a stop a man jumped from the back seat.

"Gi me four of yu biggest fish and some fritters and roast sweet potato."

She knew he had no intention of paying for them. She tried to search his face, but he kept pacing back and forth in front of the stall, his neck twisting like a frightened hen. She wrapped the fish slowly in foil and added onion and vinegar soaked vegetables on top.

"De woman you knock on her head not dead, but if you go back in dat car tonight you gwane have accident and mash-up bad-bad."

"Ah wha yu a talk about, oman? Yu know me? Just gi me de fish dem and shet yu mouth."

"Ah tellin you, she not dead. She know you face, but she nah gu turn you in if you ask her pardon and promise to work for her."

"Me look like gardener to yu. Me's a town bwoy. Me is pretty bwoy wid plenty gal."

She handed him the fish and roasted sweet-potato. "Town man and pretty man can meet in accident and mash-up same way. De driver is a mad man, racing round corners and speeding like death a chase him. Mek sure death nuh catch up with you." He grabbed the fish and sweet-potato from her hand and turned to go, but she felt a rush of wind and he stumbled but did not fall, catching himself.

"Is obeah oman yu be?" he asked turning to her.

She smiled and his shoulder slouched under her stare. He fished into his pocket and tossed a handful of crumpled bills on the top of the tray and jumped into the car, which sped off almost immediately. She heard it come to a screeching halt about 200 yards away, and decided it was time to turn in. Just as she was through packing up her things, she smelled the young man, and turned to see him, hands in pockets.

"Ah didn't mean to hurt her. She was supposed to be at church. We did just want the money. Times hard," he said by way of explanation.

"Times hard fah who?" she asked; disgust edged her voice.

"Nuh wuk nuh deh bout," he said firmly.

"Pretty bwoy can't get him hand dirty, but him can steal from an old woman who work hard fah more than forty years," she said, hands akimbo, looking at the young man squarely.

"Is why me talkin to yu?"

"Cause you don't turn harden criminal yet, but if you keep hanging wid dem two, you bound to end up in jail." He stood digging his shoes into the moist ground and she watched him in silence.

"Ah beg yu a fish and a sweet-potato. Me jump out de car when it nearly crash into a van and dem neva gi me fi me share of de money." She thought about not giving him anything, then decided to be generous. He would eat the fish and go to the old woman's house whom he and his friends had robbed and he would ask her forgiveness and work for her until he had earned her trust. She turned to her basket and wrapped three large fishes and a sweet-potato, then handed the packet to the young man before she bade him 'walk good.'

Life continued without many successes. People kept on stopping to buy fish and relieve their consciences, and she offered them food and remedy. Most people who came to her never heeded her or mended their ways. The failures piled high, but she kept her focus, dwelling on the ones she helped to find the right path. She felt her Papa's presence almost daily, and whenever she was out alone selling, he would come and keep her company, always asking her the same question, "How yu coming wid de herbs? Hortense know way more dan you."

And always she replied the same, "Well, she neva have Mama scrubbing away her knowledge."

It happened one Saturday night when the road was busy. She made the most money she ever remembered making in a single night, just selling fish. In fact she sold out before midnight, and not one of her customers needed her help. She got home to find that Hortense wasn't home and neither was Seymour. She had told Hortense that she could go to a dance, but Seymour was to have been home studying. She went into his room and saw the L-shaped stone on his bed that she had warned him to carry with him, no matter where he was going. Back in her room, she found the note he left her saying he had gone to a party the cricket team was hosting. He rode his bicycle. She bathed and sat in bed reading, determined to have it out with Seymour whatever time he came home. She went over in her head exactly what she would say to him. "If is man you tink you is, den you best find you own place cause me nuh wan nu man in fi me house." She fell asleep reading and was awakened by Hortense.

"Mama, is five o'clock and Seymour nuh come home. Me know something do him."

She came awake slowly feeling as if her body had been dragged through the streets. She couldn't get out of bed no matter how hard she tried. Hortense made her tea, then helped her to get dressed. It was six o'clock by the time she was ready to go out the door; Hortense held her by the hand. Just as she stepped over the threshold of the door, her Papa stood blocking her way. He seemed to be crying. She had never seen him cry before. Hortense held her mother up to keep her from falling. She clutched the door frame and opened her mouth to let out the scream.

Seymour's body was discovered at 5 a.m. It had been dragged almost a mile. All the skin was scraped off his back, as well as the hair from the back of his head and his scalp. Cause of death: hit-and-run driving.

"Mostly likely another Saturday drunkard," the police inspector said. "Unless someone comes forth, we might never find the person. There was no eye witness."

She buried her son, and went with Hortense into the woods to find herbs. For three months she stayed home, making packets of herbs and writing out remedies that Hortense sold.

Then one Friday, she found herself frying fish and roasting sweet potato to sell. Hortense insisted on accompanying her. The night air was cool and the sky heavy with stars. The other vendors greeted her and she smiled at them. Not many cars were on the road; a few zoomed by but none stopped. About eleven p.m. a lone car with a broken headlight stopped and a man limped out. She could tell he was tipsy. Even though he didn't approach her stall, she watched him. She could smell the rum oozing from his pores. He asked for roasted sweet potato, and the vendor whose stall he had stopped in front of said she had no sweet potato, and pointed to her. The man looked at her; and in a flash she knew him. She leapt up, knocking over her tray, and was pounding the man on the ground before Hortense could restrain her.

"Is him same one kill Seymour. Is him drag him body more than a mile scraping off all de skin off him back and head. Is him!"

The man had managed to sit up wobbly, his head bleeding where she had pounded it into the ground. The other vendors surrounded him.

"Is yu kill dis oman's one son?"

"Is yu de drunkard driver dat run down people and left dem fah dead?"

The man tried to get to his feet, but he was inebriated. A foggy memory crept over him. He had not drunk for the last three months because he felt there

19

was something he needed to remember. He remembered driving, then hitting something, then dragging it along for a while. He assumed it was a dog or goat. The next morning when he woke and saw the fender of his car all damaged and bloody, he had straightaway washed the car, and kept it locked in the garage for more than a week. He told his wife that it wasn't working, that the mechanic was waiting for a part to arrive from Miami. Two days later, after dinner, his wife had read the report of a hit-and-run that occurred about five o'clock Sunday morning, and remarked that it was around that time he came home, but he told her she was mistaken; he was in bed by three o'clock, and he had not been drinking that night. But it was a lie that he could not swallow, and he promised God that if he gave him a second chance, he would give up drinking. And he had, until this night.

He felt the women closing in on him, and knew the loyalty of street vendors to each other. He found his voice; he was a member of the comfortable educated class.

"Lady, you are mistaken. I am sorry to hear about your son, but I assure you, I had nothing to do with his death. Now if you will allow me to get up, I'll be on my way and won't press any charges."

The women froze mid-stride and looked at each other. They had been taught to acquiesce to educated voices. If the man had murdered Seymour, why would he stop to buy fish from them? It had been in the papers and on the radio for weeks. He was on his feet now, brushing off his pants, patting at his head, the fish scattered on the ground. Two carloads of young party-going people drove up and immediately in loud voices asked:

"So how the fish tonight? Who has the best fish?"

The women looked at her, still restrained in her daughter's arms. This was her first night out. She was still grieving. How could she be sure this was the man?

"What's going on here? Oonuh selling or praying?" one of the young party-goers asked.

"We sellin," a vendor replied and moved back to her stall. By the time the carloads of party revelers were gone, the man had quietly crept away. Hortense packed away her mother's stall.

She returned the next night, and the night after that, her heart beating fast every time a car stopped, but the man never appeared again. The police had closed the case as yet another unsolved hit-and-run. But she knew what she knew, and her Papa reminded her, "Time longa dan rope. Whoeva drag Seymour body to death must hang demselves."

Exactly a year and a day after Seymour's death, the man's wife stopped to buy fish. She recognized her immediately. She saw that the man had given up driving and drinking and had the shakes. She saw also that her Papa had been visiting the man, messing with his mind. She covered her mouth. She should have known. With shaking hands she sold the wife the fish then told her how she could help her husband: she had to bring him to the stall early in the morning, around five o'clock. The wife agreed. They decided on a date. The man could hardly walk when the wife brought him to her. He did not remember her, but she knew him, smelled the rum oozing from his pores, felt the cool morning air on Seymour's back as he rode home, jubilant after partying all night with grown men. He was whistling and didn't even feel when the car swerved, knocking him off the bicycle and catapulting his body into the air before it landed on the bumper and rolled off, his shirt caught, causing him to be dragged until it was threads. She witnessed it all as the man sat before her shaking like a coconut palm dancing in the face of a storm. She could kill him and no one would know.

But she couldn't. She didn't.

"You gwane rot in jail," she said, dashing a cup of rum in his face. "Yuh gwane rot a jail. You murder me son."

His wife looked alarmed and started to protest, but the words sputtered; she spit bubbles from her mouth.

"Just leave, galang. You conscience is de same as do right."

A month later, the evening Star carried the story of the man who confessed to a hit-and-run murder that had taken place more than a year before, and the article reported that his trial date had been set. She moaned deep in her womb for her dead son, and tossed the paper aside. She would not be going to the trial. He was a man of stature with connections, and very ill. More likely he would not be sent to prison, but it didn't matter; her Papa had already given her justice.

She stopped selling fish. She and Hortense opened a little herb shop in Spanish Town. She kept cotton in her ears and wore dark glasses all the time, but still all the guilty ones came to her for help. No matter how much she protested, she couldn't refuse them.

Bus Stop

Wayne remembered the exact moment he met Carlene, the first day of First Form at Excelsior. She sat in front of him, hair parted into three even triangles, one to each side of her head and one in front. She wore brown ribbons at the end of her braids, which he could not resist pulling. In fact he pulled her braids and loosened her ribbons all the way through third form.

But he did not fall in love with Carlene that first day. That day he fell in love with Miss Brinsome, their form room teacher. It was instant. Seeing her walk through the door he could feel the weight of his shirt pressed against his chest and a lump instantly grew in his throat so that he could scarcely breathe. As was customary, the class stood and greeted her in unison, "Good Morning, Miss." But he could not even mumble those few words.

Miss Brinsome had looked each of them over, her face softening in a smile; then she replied, with laughter in her voice, "Good morning soon-to-be men and women. Let every day we greet each other be a good one." Then, instead of taking her seat in front and sitting at her desk like other teachers normally did, she strolled among them, touching their shoulders or arms, scrutinizing them as if inspecting them and trying to read their brains. Then she ordered them to get pick up bags and form two lines, girls in one and boys the other, and stand in the back of the room. After they were so organized, she strode up front and, climbing onto the platform on which the teacher's desk sat, she stood adjacent to it, unloaded her folders unto the desk and turned to address them; her tone was somber, her face as inviting as a red hibiscus to a humming bird.

"This year you begin a new period in your life. This year you are walking out of girlhood and boyhood and entering adulthood. That journey is not to be taken lightly. Your parents have made a wise decision by sending you to this school, a school that understands that young men and young women should not be separated at this crucial stage in their development, but rather must study and learn together and grow into adulthood with an understanding of each other. Thus, when they decide to mate, it will be as equals. If you plan to be wives and husbands, fathers and mothers, then you need to learn to be with each other as friends first. Single sex schools are passé. Co-ed schools are the way of the future."

It was only after Miss Brimsome said this that Wayne had been able to let go the disappointment he had been harboring because he did not get into KC, one of the top boys-only high schools. Although he didn't understand all that Miss Brinsome said, the cooing lilt of her voice and the beam of her face assured him that he was in the right school. Next she assigned them seats, boy, girl, six rows across and five tiers deep. Carlene was in the front row, the closest one to the front door of the classroom, and he was seated behind her. Miss Brinsome told them to introduce themselves to the classmates beside and behind them and learn something about each other. She then looked in her roll book and randomly called a name. The student stood up and said, "Yes, Miss," and she told that student to introduce not him or herself, but rather his classmate, one either in front of or beside him.

Wayne was almost the last student to be called and he was asked to introduce Carlene. Sweat pressed his shirt to his body, and as he stood up and looked into Miss Brinsome's eyes, Carlene's name vanished from his memory. Everything vanished. His mind went blank, but he managed to address her properly, "Here Miss." She prompted him, addressing him by his last name.

"So Mr. Sullivan, you are not able to remember the name of this beautiful girl in front of you? Look at her. You can see she is loved. Her hair is nicely combed; her uniform is starched and pressed, her shoes are shining, she has lovely teeth— and you can't remember her name." Then, addressing Carlene she said, "Sweetheart give him a clue, tell him what letter your name begins with."

Carlene had turned to face him, and with one hand on her hip like she was a big woman, and her face "just nuff," she said to him as if she were speaking to a servant,

"It begins with C, but is not Carol or Carmen."

Sweat formed on his forehead, and he could hear some of the other students snickering. By now his tongue was a ton-weight in his mouth. He didn't even try to guess. Miss Brinsome sensed his distress, and after a few seconds that felt like hours, she said,

"Sweetheart, tell Wayne your name again; he is obviously overwhelmed."

But Carlene did not do as instructed. Instead she turned to Miss Brinsome and said,

"Miss, I don't want to tell him. I remember his name. He ought to know mine. I really don't want to tell him. Do I have to?"

"Okay Carlene, you make a good point. I will do the honors. Wayne Sullivan I would like you to meet Miss Carlene Reed. Now you both may be seated." From that moment on Carlene was labeled teacher's pet and he was nicknamed 'Can't talk.'

That was his first and most enduring realization about Carlene, that she often, even with the strictest and meanest teacher, got to do things her own way, and she was never afraid to challenge a teacher, although she always did this respectfully. But Carlene was not on his mind the first few years at Excelsior; it was Miss Brinsome.

He didn't realize what was happening until a week later when he was telling his older cousin how every time his teacher walked in his classroom he felt as if his breath stopped and Donavan, his nineteen year old cousin, playfully slapped his head and said,

"Youth, look like the arrow pierce your heart."

He could sense that Donavan was making fun of him, but he still didn't understand.

"What arrow!" he had asked skeptically.

"Boy! Is what you learning in school? You don't know one thing. Cupid, spar, cupid. You have the hots for your teacher, but I hear you not the only one." Wayne had looked incredulously at Donavan, kissed his teeth, and walked away, feeling both embarrassed and betrayed. He had walked over to the stadium not far from where he lived, but he did not join his friends in soccer. Instead he had sat thinking about what Donavan said and he realized that no other teacher made him feel this way. He thought Miss Brinsome was the prettiest woman in the world, and he would close his eyes and just listen to her speak, and she always made him think of a Doctor bird hovering around a red hibiscus.

Although Miss Brinsome was their form-room teacher for only first form, he still saw her around and found himself staring at various parts of her anatomy. She caught him once, and cautioned him appropriately.

It had been lunchtime, and he had spotted her talking to another teacher near the staff lunchroom. His eyes had bored into her. She must have felt them, because after the other teacher went inside, she turned, caught his eye, and called him over.

"Young man, it is best to save that kind of scrutiny for girls your own age. An innocent crush is one thing, but obsession can be dangerous. Turn your attention elsewhere." She spoke precisely as always, and stared at him until he hung his head. After that incident he was not able to look at her eye-to-eye.

By then he and Carlene had become friends, if somewhat grudgingly. She helped him with math, he helped her with biology, knowing by then that he would study one of the sciences; although he had no desire to be a doctor despite his mother's insistence that he was smart enough and could be the first doctor in their family.

In fourth form he and Carlene were placed in different classes. Also, he was beginning to gain a name for himself as a soccer star. His lanky body was turning to muscle and he was finally "stretching," growing tall, as his mother said with pride. From habit he would speak to Carlene whenever he saw her. Then one day after school, while he was fooling around on the soccer field with some of the boys, Carlene and a few other girls strolled to the periphery of the field, their arms folded and their noses stuck up in the air as if they weren't there to check out the boys. They began to giggle and point. She was across from him, and he realized that she now had breasts that were pushing out her white school blouse, and, although she was still skinny and short, he saw that she had a behind pushing out her straight-cut school skirt. Her hair was no longer braided like a little girl's, but was pressed and slicked back. Wayne had been so surprised that he had walked straight across to where Carlene stood and stopped in front of her.

"What you looking at, Mr. Wayne? You forget my name again?" she said loudly, pushing her face closer to his, haughtiness in her voice. He was on the verge of asking her when she started to grow breasts, but instead, shame and embarrassment conspired and he said,

"Is when since you start press you hair? You did look better with ribbons."

His hand had involuntary reached out to pull her hair. But in a deft response she slapped his hand away and swung away from him. The field went wild with laughter and he had walked away feeling defeated, especially when a boy he didn't like shouted, "What happen, Can't Talk? You should know by now Carlene too nuff fah you."

More laughter and hooting. He avoided her at school after that. That is, until half way through the first semester of their fourth year; one morning as he caught his regular bus to school she came on two stops after he did. He had managed to secure a seat in the middle of the bus, and she stood up front, hanging on to the vertical rail as she was unable to reach the bar overhead. When the bus turned suddenly she lost her balance momentarily, and a man helped steady her. That's how their eyes locked and he nodded and motioned with his fingers for her to come where he sat. At first she cut her eye at him but the bus jerked again, sending her lurching, and the passengers hollered almost in unison, "Wha appen driva, is buy you buy you license? Drive good, mon!"

After some maneuvering, Carlene stood beside him. He rose and gave her his seat and she held his school bag on her lap. They did not exchange one word, just gestures, and for the next two years if he secured a seat he would relinquish it when she came on the bus two stops later. Once they got off the bus at school, they almost never spoke and quickly separated, as if they didn't know each other.

Often he wanted to say something to her, but he feared her quick rejoinder. Alone, and especially at nights, he found himself fantasizing about her, and he had his first wet dream as he imagined their lips glued together and his hand on her breast. When he came awake, still erect and with his pants wet, shame bore into him. He didn't want his mother to know so he hid his shorts under the mattress.

Girls at school were boldly giving him the eye, even girls in sixth form; but every day at school, especially at lunch, when the boys mostly hung together and bragged, he found his eyes searching the school grounds and the benches where the girls sat eating lunch, just to see Carlene. Sometimes, he would walk by where he saw her sitting or leaning with her friends, but pretended as if he did not see her. Those times his heart burned, and he walked on the side of his shoes. It was torture either way, seeing Carlene or not seeing Carlene. He often wished he was bold and confident like those actors who always got the woman.

As far as Wayne could tell, Carlene didn't know he existed. And to make maters worse, when he hung out with his boys, many of them said how they liked Carlene, how they were going to get with her, even though she had a big mouth and acted "like she nice." At such times Wayne was beside himself, and often found something smart to say to make whichever boy was talking about Carlene shut up. Once he even punched a boy for no other reason than that he bragged that when Carlene was going to class he'd patted her on the bottom, which was firm and plump like a breadfruit. He got detention, and perhaps the only reason his mother wasn't called was because when asked why he, an honor student and supposedly a gentleman, would stoop to such behavior, he replied with water stinging his eyes,

"Junston always talking badly about girls, Miss, and trying to ruin their reputation." And since Junston had in fact gotten detention several times for inappropriately touching girls—two of whom had retaliated by ripping his shirt and scratching his face—Wayne got off with just one day's detention.

Somehow Carlene heard about the incident, and to Wayne's surprise, as he walked to the bus stop after his detention she walked up behind him.

He slowed his pace and they walked together, but no words passed either of their lips. They sat together too, and when she rang the bell to get off two stops before his, Wayne found himself getting off the bus early and following her. Just before she turned unto what he was to learn was her street, she stopped, looked him up and down as if assessing him, and with her familiar big-woman attitude that made him feel as if he were a naughty puppy, she said:

"This is my street, so you can turn back now. Mama says I am not allowed to have a boyfriend and I don't want one either."

He had stood there, his tongue literally hanging out, and looked pleadingly at her, just like Discovery, his dog, sometimes did when Wayne was eating something he wanted to taste. It worked. Carlene took pity on him. Her eyes smiled at him and she said, "See you tomorrow morning on the bus, and thanks for walking me home." Then she turned and never once looked back, but he stood there long after she had opened and entered what he assumed was the gate of her home.

Wayne strolled the rest of the way home, Carlene sitting on his heart. He was certain his mother would be worried and her anxiety would come out as a threat, "So you think you is big man. Well think again. Me is the only woman living here and me know school and soccer practice done longtime." But to his surprise, Wayne entered the house to find his mother talking with his father, whom he only saw about twice yearly.

He had vehemently hated his father since the previous year when he had asked why he didn't come to any of his games and his father had replied with shock, "Come to you games! Take you out! What am I suppose to tell my good family?" It was only then that Wayne had learned the truth about his birth—that his father was married to another woman and had another family in St Elizabeth.

He had gotten Wayne's mother pregnant when she was in high school, shipped her off to Kingston to stay with an aunt, then had helped to get her a job in a retail store with a family friend. He came to visit only twice, sometime four times, in a year. He had now come to tell his mother that he and his "good" family were migrating to Canada, but that he would continue to send her a little something whenever he could.

Wayne was so angry, and still feeling the sting of Carlene's rejection had gone into his room, punched his mattress, then crawled into bed and bawled like a baby—he refused to be consoled by his mother. That was the first and only time he did not do his homework, and he deliberately missed one, then two, buses, not wanting to face Carlene.

So imagine his surprise when, as he sat at the bus-stop undecided about whether or not he would go to school, a shadow fell across him and, looking up, he saw Carlene standing before him.

"You know you make me late for school and I have a perfect attendance record for the last four years."

He could smell her. She was right in front of him, and all he had to do was reach out his hand and touch her, grab a hold of her. He felt his hands tremble and made fists and tucked them to his side. He wanted to embrace her, to feel her in his arms, to cry on her shoulder, and wash away his father's rejection.

"See bus coming here. We will miss first period but will make second period. Come, and I will go with you to the movies Saturday." She reached for his hand. He followed her onto the bus.

They sat near the back and her fingers played with his. As usual they did not speak, even when they exited the bus and hastened to school. At the gate they were greeted by Mr. Henchford, a teacher known for being mean; but Carlene just smiled at him, and in a voice that would silence an angel she said, "Good morning Mr. Henchford! We are so glad you are at the gate to greet us. This has been such a difficult morning. See how I am sweating. I have a perfect attendance record—and the buses this morning! Three went by before we were able to get on. Mr. Sullivan and I are so upset. Please sir, can we just go to our second period classes so we don't miss any more important lessons?"

Carlene spoke softly, but rapidly and with assurance; and without giving Mr. Henchford a chance to reply, she squeezed past him through the partially open gate. As she hurried to class, seeing Wayne still standing by the gate, she called out, "Mr. Sullivan, I suggest you hurry to Miss Dancy's class."

How did she know he had Miss Dancy for second period? But he had no time to ponder this as Mr. Henchford chimed in, "Mr. Sullivan move and get to your class before I send you to the office."

Wayne pushed through the gate and headed towards the classroom, but for the entire day his head raged between his hatred for his father and his desire for Carlene; and the fact that she had waited for him and then come to get him.

Although he had planned to skip soccer practice, when he saw Carlene in her PE clothes with her tennis racquet, he went, but every so often he would run off the field to make sure Carlene was still on the other side where the tennis courts were.

Afterwards, as he leaned on the street light near the school, his eyes glued to the school gate, he bit on his bottom lip and twisted his shoes to the side thinking he might have missed her. Although he did not have a watch, he was sure he had been waiting more than thirty minutes. His throat was parched, his skin itched. He was beside himself by the time he finally he saw her pushing through the gate with two of their classmates behind her.

Wayne had to grasp the light pole to steady himself. He kissed his teeth, vexed with the girls for interfering with his plans to walk Carlene to the bus stop.

He had hoped she would allow him to stop and buy her a soft drink and patty, or candy, whatever she wanted. He was prepared to spend his whole week's allowance if necessary. Then they would take the bus together and he would hold her hand and walk her to her street, and stand at the top of the road until she went through her gate so her mother did not harass her. Though she wasn't allowed to have a boyfriend, he was hoping she would agree to be his girlfriend anyway.

Emboldened by these thoughts, Wayne pulled himself straight and slung his bag over his shoulder just as Carlene and her two friends pulled up to him. Carlene smiled at him and he found his tongue.

"Let me carry your bag," he said, reaching for it.

She stopped and handed him the bag, then staring directly into his eyes she said, "Jeanne and Tanya, you know Wayne? He's my boyfriend."

Wayne's face cracked into a smile so deep you could plant seed in it. Then regaining his composure, he retorted, "Yes," and he paused for effect, "Carlene is my girlfriend." He moved boldly and grabbed hold of her hand.

All three girls were visibly surprised, but they continued walking, Jeanne and Tanya a few paces ahead of Wayne and Carlene, who held hands but did not speak. As they approached a shop that sold refreshments, he turned to Carlene, "Let me buy you a soft drink to quench your thirst after your tennis game." She turned and smiled shyly at him. Their faces were close, closer than ever before, and Wayne was thinking, 'What if I was to just kiss her here?'

Jeanne interrupted the moment. "Bus coming!" She and Tanya began running; but Wayne and Carlene waved to them and turned into the shop.

It was after 7 p.m. when they disembarked the bus at Carlene's stop, and they walked hand-in-hand towards her street. There Wayne stopped and handed her bag to her.

"So you not planning to walk me to my gate."

"Last time you said your mother said ..."

"So I thought you told Jeanne and Tanya that I was your girlfriend," Carlene stated and kept walking down her street without taking her bag. Confused, unsure, Wayne hesitated, then ran to catch up with her. Before they got to her gate, he saw a woman standing there and instinctively knew it was Carlene's mother looking out for her.

"Good evening, Mama," Carlene sang out.

"You mean good night. You know what time it is? I just now planning to come and look for you. Don't I tell you not to let dark catch you on the road."

"I had tennis practice Mama, and that's why Wayne agreed to walk me home."

Even in the semi-dark, Carlene's mother's eyes bored into his like a torch, and he felt as if his body was being sponged down with a damp cloth. To steady his hands he put them in his pockets.

"So Wayne, who you be? Thanks for walking my daughter home."

Wayne didn't know what to say, so he said nothing. Then Carlene stepped back close to him and said all excitedly,

"Mama, Wayne has something to ask you."

Wayne felt like he might pee his pants. What did he want to ask her mother: could he kiss her? No, that would be too bold, and her mother would probably chase him with a broom—or worse, a cutlass. She looked as if she had a sharp cutlass just waiting for any boy who got feisty with her daughter. His brain scrambled as he wondered what Carlene wanted him to ask his mother—oh, maybe about taking her to the movies.

"Boy, if you have something to say you best get on with it cause it late and you should be getting home."

"Yes, ma'am," he mumbled but he still wasn't sure what to ask.

Carlene whispered, "Ask her if I can be your girlfriend."

Carlene was well mad, he thought. She wanted to get him killed. But since this had started off as one of the worse days of his life and had ended up being one of the best, Wayne squared his shoulders and found his voice.

"Mrs...." he hesitated; he realized that Carlene never spoke about her father so he didn't know if her mother was married or like his mother—anger and sadness washed over him again as he thought of his own father. But he sensed both Carlene and her mother's impatience at his in-articulation. He plunged. "I am asking you to allow Carlene to be my girlfriend and for me to take her to the movies on Saturday."

Carlene's mother laughed heartily, but with surprise "But see here now. What this me hearing? No sah you can't ask me this in the darkness. We have to go inside under the light so I can look in your eyes." And, so saying, she pushed open the gate and waved Wayne and Carlene inside.

His shirt clung to his back like it did in the middle of a hot Saturday soccer match where he had just scored a goal. He climbed the steps to the veranda behind Carlene, feeling her mother at his heels. He paused at the door, unsure whether he was invited in, even though Carlene had skipped ahead.

"Go on in and take a seat," Carlene's mother said pushing past him. He found himself in a small but neat living room, crowded with a piano pushed up against the window on which were many pictures of Carlene from babyhood to her present age, a sofa set with a center table, then an entertainment unit with a TV, a stereo, and more pictures of Carlene. On the very bottom shelf was what appeared to be a complete set of Britannia Encyclopedia.

Wayne wasn't sure where to sit so he stood looking around admiringly until Carlene came beaming towards him carrying a glass. "Ah hope you like limeade," she said, offering him a glass beaded with condensation from the melting ice.

How he loved her smile and wanted desperately to kiss her, but he gulped the limeade instead, halving the glass, thinking he needed to get home—his mother would be worried. At the same time Carlene's mother re-entered the living room.

"So Mr. Wayne what big argument you bringing to me?"

Standing in Carlene's home, the almost empty glass of limeade in his hand, which he was certain she had made,—Wayne looked Carlene's mother in the eye.

"Ah asking your permission to be Carlene's boyfriend and to take her to the movies."

"What a way you bold! But Jesus come look what me dealing with!" Again she laughed, a laugh of astonishment. "What you modda name?

"Gloria Green, ma'am."

"She know whe you is?"

"No ma'am. She probably wondering where me is."

"So you like my Carlene."

"Yes, ma'am."

"You the same boy used to pull her ribbon from first all the way through third form?"

Wayne fisted his right hand, covered his mouth and laughed. So Carlene had told her mother.

"Yes, ma'am."

Again Carlene's mother regarded him. "Well, Mr. Wayne, your mother and me need meet one another and me will tell her the same thing me telling you now. You see how Carlene nice, you see how me take care of her? Well I raising her to be a lady, to complete her education, to get a good job so she don't have to struggle like me. And as God is me witness, any boy or man interfere with me plans for me one daughter me will chop him up," Her voice went up at least 2 decibels, "Me will chop him up dead."

"See her there." Carlene's mother strode to where Carlene stood trembling, and, using her middle and index fingers, poked Carlene in the chest as she said "You see how she nice, you see how she bright, you see how she future bright like the sun sitting on the ocean at noon time, you see how much love me put into her; well that is how me expect her to stay until she is woman and can manage on her own."

31

Then turning to face Wayne, her face close to his, her voice calm but threatening like grey clouds seeded with water, Carlene's mother said, "She can be your girlfriend, and you can take her to the movies, but don't go looking for nothing between her legs cause you don't have no business there. And understand me clearly, me machete sharpen and me know how to use it, and me no fraid, me no fraid at all. The only thing me fraid of is ruination."

Wayne counted three distinct beads of perspiration on the crown of her upper lip, before she touched his shoulder and walked out of the room.

Wayne listened to his own labored breathing as well as Carlene's, who stood not too far from him. Wayne knew he should go, but somehow felt he needed to be dismissed. He and Carlene jumped when the lid of a pot fell to the floor, then her mother's voice, "Carlene walk Wayne to the gate. He need to get home and you need to eat dinner, do your homework, and get ready for school tomorrow. Good night Mr. Wayne. Tell you moda howdy."

Released, he grabbed his bag from the floor near his feet, pulled it over his shoulder, and headed for the gate, where he and Carlene said a hurried, "See you tomorrow," almost in unison; and he hurried down her street, an extra bounce in his walk. He felt thankful to be alive, and deeply in love with Carlene.

* * *

Before Wayne was able to act on any of his fantasies, he was thrust from the school, from Carlene's life, from all that was familiar to him. Inexplicably, the father that he barely knew had filed papers for him to emigrate to Canada—although not to join him and his "good" family, but rather to live with his spinster sister and to attend college.

Wayne was shocked. "I won't go!" he shouted at his mother.

He hated his mother for giving him no choice, hated his father even more for bringing him up to Canada but still hiding him at his sister's, visiting monthly to give his sister money for his upkeep.

The first two years he wrote to Carlene weekly, promising he would come and visit. But no matter how much he begged his father to send him home for Christmas or the summer, that did not happen, and when he wrote or spoke to his mother, she claimed she could not afford his return airfare. Miserable, lonely, and feeling abandoned by his mother, Wayne put all his efforts into his studies. There he excelled, winning a scholarship to university the next fall.

Finally Carlene wrote and told him she would not be his girlfriend anymore because it appeared that he was never coming home. She would be going to the University of the West Indies, she informed him curtly, and didn't wish to be one of the many Jamaican women who sat around for years, waiting for lovers who invariably never returned.

Wayne chewed his bottom lip until it bled, and found that sleep became his enemy at nights. Carlene still did not have a phone at home so he could not call her, and although he wrote her long letters, professing his undying love, she stopped replying. He wrote one of his old soccer buddies, who was also attending UWI, and it was from him that he learned that Carlene, whom the friend had always referred to as "too nuff and full of herself," had a boyfriend, who had managed to bring her down to earth.

Defeated, but not willing to concede, Wayne sat down and wrote Carlene one last letter.

"Dear Carlene:

I still remember very clearly that first date we had when we should have gone to the movies, but you suggested we go to the Botanical Gardens instead. What a great choice, especially because, shamefully, I had never been there before. I still consider it one of the best days of my life.

I can still see you in the red pedal-pusher pants and white triangular top tied around the neck. You looked so good, cool like an ice cream cone. We sat under an acacia tree and I told you about my father, that I was his outside child, hidden from the world, and my mother the schoolgirl he took advantage of, who still believes his lies, and was probably still in love with the man, my father whom I hate. And I will never forget you looking at me and saying, "If you hate him you make him more important than yourself."

I was angry when you said that because I didn't understand what you meant, but I do now. I no longer hate my father nor do I feel pity for my mother; they both have to live with their choices.

Then you told me that you too were an outside child, except that you visited your father at his home and knew your three half-siblings. You said you were glad that it was just your mother and you, and that your mother said him being your father was not an accident, anymore than she being your mother; life has both a left and a right foot. I think I am finally beginning to understand.

33

I just want you to know that I am more sorry than you can imagine that I have not been able to come home, and I would not
want you to be one of those women who sit and wait on a man.
You are better than that, and I love you for knowing what you
deserve.

~ Wayne"

The letter sat on his desk for three weeks. Nightly he re-read it, but could not
bring himself to put it in an envelope and mail it. A month later he finally lost
his virginity and the letter was folded and placed in a box with other memorabilia.

* * *

When his undergraduate studies were completed, Wayne decided to stay in Canada, although he hated it, and pursue a doctorate in fishery. He got the news that
Carlene had married two years after graduating. Although he now had money, he
still had not returned home. He dated, and had even gotten attached to a certain
young lady; but when she started to pressure him about marriage, he knew she
was not the one for him.

Occasionally, he still fantasized about Carlene, and after a while he didn't
even try to get her out of his head. She was like the lizard that had lived in his
room behind the bed when he was a boy. Sometimes he saw it and sometimes
he didn't; but it was always there. His mother kept inquiring about when he was
going to come home and get married, but he avoided answering either question.

Then, less than a week after completing his doctorate, a friend sent him
an announcement for a job that matched his qualifications. Not investing much
effort he applied, and was called in for an interview three weeks later. To his
surprise he learned the job was sited in Jamaica, with a Canadian company doing
business there. In less than six weeks after the interview he found himself on a
plane flying home, where he had not been in more than ten years.

Like an owl turning in during the day, he came home, settled into a challeng-
ing job, and resumed his friendship with those of his boyhood friends who had
not migrated. A year passed uneventfully. They played soccer, went for drinks,
and talked politics. It was during one of these political sessions that Carlene's
name came up. By then he had begun living with Patsy, a girl he had bumped
into, literally when leaving work, over a year ago. But he knew he had to end the
relationship because she was not the one. He had come to dread going home, and
she was threatening to trap him with child—with his mother's full support.

Clive, a soccer buddy, said he had ran into Carlene the previous Sunday at the beach and she was not much changed, still had a nice body. He added that she'd had a child with her, a daughter.

"So her husband was there?" he had busted out before he could restrain himself.

"If him was, me neva see him," Clive had replied. Then he had gone silent and scrutinized Wayne. "Don't tell me you still have the hots for Carlene. You better marry Patsy. She is a good woman to put up with the likes of you."

Wayne had gotten vexed and sucked his teeth, "Is who you to tell me who to marry? How I to marry someone I'm not in love with?"

At that Clive had gotten indignant. "Is man like you give good men bad name. Why yu livin wid de woman if you don't love her?" Clive's speech relaxed into nation language. "Tell me dat. Why you nyam up her good years if you don't intend to marry her and have children. You think Carlene thinking about you? She didn't even ask for you. She happily married with a child. You think life is some fairytale and you and Carlene going to come together and live happily every after? Man you is a fool! You betta love who you have and be thankful. Carlene don't give a blood-claat about you."

They had glared at each other and Wayne had paid for their drinks and left without another word. They did not speak to each other for two weeks and when they began again, at a soccer match, neither mentioned Carlene.

Wayne scanned the busy restaurant's lunch crowd to make sure he hadn't missed Carlene. He had finally run into her, at a bus stop of all places. He took it as a sign, a premonition. That morning he had decided to drive to work by a different route, and as he sat in traffic he noticed a petite woman, small-waisted with wide hips, hair in a short natural with large earrings, sitting at the bus stop. He had driven on, but less than a block later Carlene flashed across his mind. Not her, he told himself, but still he swerved and stopped, nervously biting his bottom lip. "It is not her," he repeated, this time aloud, but he was undone. As soon as he was able to U-turn safely, he backtracked, and there she was, standing under the bus shed.

Even from across the street he could tell it was Carlene and he could detect impatience in her stance. Other cars swerved around him, tooting their horns; but Wayne ignored them and shouted across the street, "Carlene, I would think by now you give up bus."

She tilted her head to the side and gazed at him. He thought she was not going to reply, just like all those months when they rode together and she was silent and he was silent, but still they were so deeply connected. Maybe he had changed and she did not recognize him.

"Carlene, is me, Wayne."

She chuckled. "You think I don't know you? So you finally decide to come home."

Wayne let out the breath he had been holding, made another U-turn to get to her side of the street and threw open the passenger side door for her to climb in. Carlene had accepted the ride, and as he took her to work told him that her car had been stolen only two days prior, that she was recently separated from her husband, and that she was sharing a house with a friend who was going through a similar transition. Eagerly, Wayne offered to take her to work every morning, since it was in the same direction of his job, which was not really the case.

After a painful fortnight of restraint, Wayne had asked her out to lunch. He had not missed how she had turned in the car seat that first morning and scrutinized him, agreeing to the daily ride, but adding, "Ah hope you don't think because I am separated and going through a divorce that I am hard up."

He had laughed out loud and shook his head at her forthrightness.

"You haven't changed any," he said to her, realizing that she was still arrogant; and in that instant he determined that he would woo her again and win back her love.

This is what he was thinking as he sat in the restaurant, glancing anxiously at his watch and tapping his fingers on the table. Fifteen more minutes passed before he spotted her petite form striding through the crowd towards him. He rose immediately, and realized that he was smiling foolishly; his shirt was sticking to his chest, his heart was beating fast, and his mouth felt like he had something in it.

"Wayne, sorry. Is like my boss want to kill me with work," she said, not missing a beat and dropping heavily into the chair. "The man knows I go to lunch at noon and here it is 11:45 he coming with something he need for a lunch meeting."

Then she paused and looked at him still standing. "Sit down nah, man. I have to get back soon and complete something because I don't intend to work late. I done tell that man that I have a child, and I have to get home on time and take care of her."

"I can pick you up from work if you want, you know. I don't mind at all," he spat out like something burned his tongue.

"Thanks, but I have a ride home already." She smiled at him, reaching for the menu.

"Sure, no problem," he offered, hating the way his voice came out sounding whiney.

"Why you say it like that?" she asked, locking her eyes with his.

"No problem, man," he offered again weakly.

"Wayne, is a move you making on me?" Her eyes softened and she reached across the table and patted his hand. "Is not a man giving me a ride home, you know. Is my girlfriend. She don't live far and her mother keeps my daughter after school."

He felt the muscles in his face relax. Carlene looked at him and frowned.

"Of course, is not that what I do is any of your business. I'm just coming out from under a man who tried to keep me in jail. You need to know that I'm not interested in being a prisoner or playing games. I'm glad you saw me at the bus stop and offered me a ride. I'm glad we're having lunch. But I can't promise you anything."

That was enough for him. She hadn't said she wasn't interested. She hadn't said she only agreed to lunch out of a sense of obligation. Besides he knew that wasn't her style. She had in fact said she was glad to see him and be with him. That was enough for Wayne.

He had never married nor did he have any children, and now he was glad of that, because if and when Carlene was ready to enter into a relationship again he would be there, ready to commit to her, to state clearly how long and deeply he had desired and loved her.

He would not let anything keep them from being together when she was ready to say, "I forgive you for leaving when our love had just started to grow."

Mattie and Night's Sister

She was a woman who didn't have the good sense to know that fearlessness was not a trait assigned to women and that bravery was an abomination, a real effrontery to all the laws of man. She was what the people in the community despairingly referred to as man-oman, a woman who, never having submitted to the circumferences of womanhood, even out-stepped the boundaries of manhood—totally independent and free of the need for anyone. However, because she was neither ugly, nor tough looking, nor attracted to calamity or seduced by spitefulness, nor known to carry susu—gossip—or harbor malice; because she was never caught stealing another woman's man, or being foolish enough to let any man pull the wool over her eyes—no matter how thoroughly they searched and how deeply they probed, the community could find no social transgressions to pin on her. So, they left her alone.

The only thing she loved more than her own company was the night. It matched her skin; its language echoed her own silence, and whispered to her spine; and its rhythm regulated to her pace. The smell of the night engulfed her, filling her lungs, and the whole land became her stage. Some said she was a duppy, others that she was a witch. None could prove either, so she continued her nightly stroll, her bare feet caressing the soil, her arms saluting the wind. On rare occasions when a member of the community had to be out late, they would happen on Mattie, not seeing her until they were almost upon her. She was always reported to have been alone, very still and peaceful, like a tree, seemingly lost in another world.

She lived inside her head which must have been a happy place because a calm, pleasing look was permanently etched on her face, and this was from birth. Before she was old enough to talk or walk, the people of her village said she was marked. Which baby did you ever hear of who didn't cry or demand attention? Which baby did you ever know who enjoyed her own company, playing all day with her feet and hands? What kind of baby shrieked when adults came around cooing, smiling down, and pinching her cheeks? She wasn't right. That was all there was to it. Something had to be wrong.

As she moved through the stages of infancy, toddler, and girlhood, who did she play with? Trees and rocks my dear, trees and rocks all day. Not a child could persuade her to join in their games. Not her mother scolding and threatening to sting her skinny, always ashy, legs with a tamarind switch could persuade her to seek the company of other children. She kept to herself, talking to trees and rocks. Walking to the river, twice sometimes three times in a day, spending what seemed like hours, returning each time with the front of her dress held like a bag in which she carried small pebbles and rocks.

With these she erected elaborate rock gardens. And whereas most children would never venture outside alone at night without company, many nights Mattie could be found outside; sitting very still, singing to herself. One day her mother got vexed, tired of being the center of the village gossip because of this child she had who was neither pretty nor ugly, neither stubborn or obedient, but who insisted on being different, being herself. Her mother got the rake and scrambled all the pebbles of Mattie's garden, working herself up until she fell to her knees heaving pebbles in both hands, dashing them helter-skelter, demanding that her daughter act right, act normal, be like the others. The mother was beside herself, heaving and shouting until froth bubbled from her mouth. Some of her neighbors had to come to her aid, and threw water on her as they sometimes had to do with two dogs stuck in sexual bawdiness. But that sent her into an epileptic seizure, and everyone present remarked afterwards how Mattie had just stood there, hands wrapped around her own body, eyes closed, rocking back and forth like the branch of a tree.

Daybreak found Mattie, the child, then six, on her knees with concentrated energy remaking the pebble garden, her weary mother beside her, likewise on her knees assisting, offering first one pebble, then a next for Mattie to select and place with tender care. That was the last time the mother demanded conformity, and whenever anyone tried to turn her against the child, whom she passionately loved and secretly admired, she would walk away, but not before kissing her teeth and telling the person, "Kiss me backside, and lef me picknie alone."

By the time Mattie reached adolescence, the community forgot about her, many still choosing to dismiss her as mad or more accurately, fool-fool. They knew she wasn't crazy. They had witnessed enough people go mad from poverty, heartbreak, death, and abandonment to be quite familiar with that state and even to welcome it sometimes for themselves. They knew craziness and they had the utmost respect for it. But she wasn't crazy.

"She just don't care," someone offered.

"Ah tell you duppy walk ova de moda just before she born," said another, for whom duppy was the explanation for all things unexplainable.

39

"She have one foot in dis world and de oda in hell," the religious zealot declared.

"Is nice and nuff-nuff, she think she is," yet another offered.

But as they were unable to arrive at any conclusion, they ignored her and went on with living, which demanded their full attention.

As she came into womanhood with the stamp of a handsome face, clear, penny-clean, dark brown eyes, hair that was fibered yet soft, plaited always like a crown around the base of her head, and ignored all the flirtations of men, they dismissed her saying, "Is gwane nice she gwane nice and stuck up on sheself." The young men squabbled, walking off, heads bowed, shoulders leaning as if to embrace the earth. No rejection from any other woman made its mark on their frail egos more deeply. Without so much as a word her eyes refused them violently, making them feel as if they had lifted up their mothers' skirts and searched her privates; yet Mattie was not related to them. After such a rejection those young men would have to avoid her, because whenever they encountered her thereafter, their meeting left them feeling small and ashamed.

The women who tried to befriend her did not meet with any luck either; she magnified their pretense and desire to be needed, as if being needed validated their lives, made them somehow worthy to continue the cycle of life. So her female peers left her feeling wronged and mocked. Something about the way she looked at them, the gentle manner in which she touched their shoulders or hands, told them to go off to some secluded spot and seek their own company, to love and honor themselves rather than being so eager to give themselves away.

Older people had the good sense to avoid her. They had enough experience to know, "Nuh need seek worries until it find you." She invariably reminded them of something painful they needed to do but kept avoiding, some hurt so old and so deep that they had brushed it aside, buried it in one quick sweep of the hand.

Consequently, Mattie was left alone, to keep company with the night, to make treks to the river and collect pebbles and rocks, to nurse birds and place the beautiful turquoise ground lizard to highlight the intricate designs of her rock garden. In this manner she came into womanhood, not like a Bombay mango, pregnant with juices, its red-orange skin attracting attention, yet not like a bumpy sweetsop, skin easily bruised, looking all bloated. Her emergence, like everything else about her, was almost indiscernible—a fern growing on a hillside in a bed of its own foliage. She blossomed, undisturbed, at least that is what everyone thought, with pity:

"Shame, she nuh have anyone fi tickle she, mek she laugh," some of the village sighed.

"Nutten more sour dan a woman unplugged!" grumbled some of the men.

"She nah go have anyone fi send a shop when she old," chanted the children.

But still Mattie walked, indifferent to whispers and stares. It was as if she wore blinders, and only saw what was directly in front of her. Yet she wasn't anti-social. No one could actually accuse her of not greeting them in accordance with the tradition of the community. She was never rude, didn't appear to avoid anyone, was often quite gentle with drunkards, and generally liked by the children, perhaps because she didn't feel the need to always correct or upbraid them.

So imagine the surprise when her complexion took on a sheen so radiant that even the most beautiful among the young women were jealous. However, when her stomach clearly indicated that something other than fat was the cause of the bulge, the speculation and incredulous utterance waged for well over a month.

"Is who de fada?"

"Me did always know she did wukless."

"You can neva trust dem silent one."

"Good! Now she can't act like she betta dan we."

The condemnation did not seem to in any way affect Mattie, who continued with her life as if she wasn't in fact unmarried, unspoken for, and pregnant. Her mother resigned herself to her luck, not unlike that of many of the women of her community—to have an unmarried daughter in the family way. However, a month before Mattie gave birth, her mother produced a certificate of marriage which she showed to all those gathered at the shop when she went to buy a pound of flour and a gallon of kerosene oil.

Still, no one ever saw this man who had fathered Mattie's child, and who allegedly had married her. Not even after she had Cassie and her mother threw a big Christening celebration for her granddaughter.

Whereas Mattie was quiet and required nothing, Cassie, from the moment she popped out of Mattie, cried out her demands. Her wails were so incessant and pleading that before she was a month old there was hardly anyone who was not intimately familiar with the sound of them. Almost the entire village had to assist—taking turns, holding, playing with, burping, feeding, and tickling Cassie. She soon became known as the village child and spent time in the homes of many of the villagers. Even young children were called upon to act as surrogate sisters and brothers to her, passing her from one hand to the other. Mattie relinquished her daughter with the same even ease she did away with the gossip that always surrounded her life, and quickly resumed her romance with the night.

That was how it happened that one night, long, long ago when the moon was on a rendezvous and the stars were resting. It was the last week in November and the night was particularly cool. Cassie was a little more than two at the time. Mattie was still nursing her, but because she kept no regular schedule and Cassie had been away all day at various people's homes, the sweet mother's milk had soaked through her brassiere, leaving wide circular stains on the front of both sides of her blouse. The night was dark, and for some reason, although she wasn't scared, after walking a few yards from her gate, she retraced her steps, entered the kitchen, and found a box of matches which she tucked in her pocket. She then disappeared into the night.

She seldom followed the road, choosing instead to thread in the undergrowth, meandering in the dense foliage that enclosed the village, but this evening she kept on the road, a heaviness about her heart slowing her steps. Her senses were awakened and Mattie was overcome with a deep sadness. After walking about two miles, she stopped to rest on a rock that formed a seat. Her arms, wrapped about herself, absent-mindedly caressed her shoulders.

That's when she heard a snorting sound. Her body braced, alert; her eyes searched the darkness, but could fix on no person or animal. Afraid of neither man nor duppy, Mattie continued her walk, but found she was dragging as if being pulled by a mighty force. She came to a bend in the road and saw several piglets, bunched together, squealing. She spoke aloud to the night, "Who so careless leave dem pig out dis night?" Instantly, a large sow reared in front of her.

Goosebumps covered Mattie's arms and she felt as if her head was growing and growing until it left her body. In that moment, Mattie knew she was in the presence of Night's sister, an angry mother duppy, from whom she had stolen the fetus that she placed and brought to life within her own womb.

Night, her lover, had told her how to trap his sister. It was he who had reached inside and pulled the fetus out of his hypnotized sister. The sweet milk seeping from Mattie's breasts was what exposed her to the sow.

Mattie stopped in her tracks and glanced around hoping to find a weapon; but it suddenly became so dark, blackness draped her eyes. The sow's snorting increased in volume, revealing menace. "Me and you done step ova one anoder; gwane, done. Mek me pass," Mattie blared, the tremor of her voice floating in the night air. She breathed deeply and moved towards the sow. The sow raised her head and squealed into the heavens, a din so laced with pain it was like a frill skirt going up in flames. Mattie knew the sow was not going to allow her to pass without a fight, but she did not intend to give up Cassie.

How many months, night after long night, had she had to track Night's sister to get the child. Cassie was not just hers, she belonged to the village. Mattie had just allowed her body to be used. "Ah not givin her up! Not a blast!" Mattie stomped her feet and stood about twenty yards from the sow, her arms akimbo. Night's sister was a queen of disguises, but she had adopted the appropriate costume, as a duppy sow was a mother who had died during childbirth.

Mattie clapped her hands in three sharp beats and stepped to the side. The sow moved with her as if they were mirror dancing. Mattie could not think of her name, perhaps she never knew it. If she didn't come up with a plan she knew the sow, a grieving woman in search of her daughter, was going to hurt her. Realizing that she was making no progress, she decided to try to offend the sow-duppy. She cursed, "You bum-bum cloth. You rass-cloth!" She was greeted with a laughter that made her heart skip a beat, and a voice which seemed to surround her taunted,

"Is who you tink fraid bad word. Tink me nuh know how fi curse?"

Again came the laughter that made Mattie's mouth feel dry as if glued shut. Time was a witness, observing Mattie's lack of progress and the sow confronting her at every step. Mattie could feel weariness stealing over her. Then she remembered the box of matches in her pocket. She fingered the box, hoping it would work. "Me nuh know why you standin in me way. You picknie nuh born yet. Betta go home and rest youself til de time right."

The sow snorted, rubbed its snout on the ground, then charged at Mattie who escaped by hurling herself into the bushes by the side of the road. She hit her left knee and bruised her arm, but was able to reach and pull out the box of matches. She broke two sticks before she managed to light a stick. A flicker of light flared up. Instantly, the sow stopped grunting and growling and glared in Mattie's direction. Mattie blew out the match and threw it further in the bushes. The sow took after the extinguished match and Mattie sprang up and ran. She didn't know how long it would take the sow to find the matchstick, but once it did, it would be angrier than ever and take after her.

Before she had run far Mattie heard the sow coming after her so she bolted, moving off the road in the direction of the underbrush where she often walked. Gasping and out of breath, she hoped she had lost the sow. Her chest felt as if it was about to rip open, so she slackened her pace and headed back to the main road. To her dismay, the sow stood in front of her, eyes aglow. Mattie was too tired to even strike another match. She stood leaning forward, breathing loudly through her mouth. The sow blocked her path.

Mattie had to get home. She focused on Cassie. The matchbox was moist and crushed in her palm. Mattie reached for a stick and struck it but lost all but one other stick in the process. Again, as the flicker of light shone in the night air for a few quick seconds, the sow backed away as if blinded. Mattie held the lit match as long as she could, singeing her fingers before tossing it into the bushes. While the sow went in search of it, Mattie swung her arms to her side and her feet flew over the gravel road. She felt as if her chest was on fire. For the first time Mattie knew fear. She tried calling out her daughter's name, but no sound escaped her mouth. However, she kept chanting Cassie's name in her head. She had to make it home, even though home was more than half a mile away and the matchbox had fallen from her hand.

She stumbled forward, too tired to even put out her hands to break her fall. She heard the sow close at her heels. But before her head hit the ground she was dimly aware of the light of a torch just ahead of her.

Cassie's whimpering had caused her to be passed from hand to hand but nothing consoled her. Her grandmother decided to take her on a night stroll, and a few women volunteered to accompany them. One got a torch, a second went for her machete, and a third grabbed a dash of salt and wrapped it in a piece of newspaper.

They walked slowly, the woman holding the baby rocking the infant gently. Though not fearless of the night as Mattie was, and realizing they were heading out of the village, they forced themselves forward in the dark. Cassie was quiet for the first time anyone of them could remember, her eyes aglow in the dark.

Then they heard someone running towards them. The woman carrying the torch held it high just in time to see Mattie fall and to spy the sow at her heels. Spontaneously, in one united voice they shouted,

"Duppy, duppy go back whe you come from. She one of us." Thrice they shouted, each time their voices gaining more authority.

Cassie started to coo and her grandmother grabbed the machete from the woman beside her and trotted ahead. As she got to the sow, she swung the machete and chopped off its snout. The other women were quickly at her side, and the one with the salt sprinkled it around Mattie, creating a protective circle to shield her. The sow took off into the bushes, unnerving them with her squealing, a trail of blood marking her departure.

Mattie opened her eyes painfully, coughed, and felt the burning sensation in her chest. Her lips were dry; sweat covered her body. Mattie heard Cassie cooing just before she swooned.

The women sent up an alarm with the clacking of their tongues and help soon arrived. Mattie was lifted up and carried home. She didn't awaken for four days. At various times throughout her sleep, Cassie was placed to suckle on her breast, and in fact the child was only quiet at her mother's side. When Mattie awoke on the fourth day, it was dark. Cassie was asleep beside her, but no one else was around. She stood up, reaching for something to support her. She managed to make it to the door. The night was soft and comforting, but Mattie knew her romance was over.

After she regained her strength, she continued to create rock gardens, and she spent more time attending to Cassie, who always attracted people to their home.

The villagers, at least the women, now included Mattie into their circle, and although she seldom engaged in their conversations, she felt a part of them. And on dark, dark nights, Mattie stands by her gate singing a song so plaintive the animals cover their ears. She is still singing, this woman whose feet were too big for her own shoes, this Mattie who stole Night's sister's child and finally gained acceptance into her community.

Mattie, a paradox of a woman whose independence caused men to doubt themselves and women to grow mustaches.

Matrimony

Bake-Face returned home two days before scheduled to find her surrogate wife, Ms. Maudlyn, in the match-box of a kitchen, with her hands buried in a pan of fish that she was gutting and cleaning. The glassy eyes of the large, silver-green fish in her hand were open, seeming to accuse her of its death so unexpected. The fish's posture mirrored Bake-Face's sense of unease, so that all she could manage was to nod at Ms. Maudlyn. They were civil with each other, but not friends.

From the kitchen Bake-Face walked to the side of the house where she saw her daughter, Pauline. She was doodling in the dirt with a crooked stick, hunkered down, her body drawn up tight.

Fear wrapped itself around Bake-Face. An image of herself as a girl her daughter's age flashed through her mind. She was alone, with no one to confide in or to console her as her uncle surreptitiously and repeatedly pinched her flat breasts and rubbed his crotch up on her bottom.

A moan escaped Bake-Face's lips as she neared Pauline and squatted in front of her. She recognized the hurt in her daughter's face. Knew it intimately from living with it for most of her life; from the age of ten years old when she was left an orphan. This was not to have happened to her daughter. How did this happen?

Bake-Face circled the child's wrists with her long fingers; the child glanced at her, then pulled free and kept scratching small circles in the dirt as if her mother wasn't there. A hiss escaped Bake-Face's lips and she pulled Pauline into her chest. The child pressed against her, and together they started to rock, clutching each other, Bake-Face trying to press the child's body through her own body, and Pauline wishing that her mother's chest would open up so she could crawl in. They grasped onto each other, refusing to let go. Bake-Face was consumed by guilt; Pauline was consumed by fear and from missing her mother's reassurance.

The sun had traveled over Bake-Face's shoulder before she realized that Pauline had fallen asleep. Using one hand for balance, she hoisted herself up and strode into the house.

To her surprise Pauline's bed, which had always been in her and Ezra's bedroom, was not there anymore. First, she went into the room of Ezra's youngest sons; but it wasn't there either. Her arms were cramped from the weight of Pauline; she shifted the child in her arms and moved on through the house.

She went into the older boys' bedroom, and there she saw Pauline's single bed, pushed up against the far wall, with just enough space for the child to crawl on and off the mattress. Bake-Face placed Pauline on the bed and covered her. She stood looking down at the child, and bit her lips. Was someone...touching her daughter? Was someone making her afraid? Was someone making her hate that she was a girl?

Bake-Face wiped the tears brimming in her eyes. She had failed her daughter. All she had ever wanted was to protect her from the pain, to keep the fear that she'd lived with most of her life from her daughter's eyes. But now Bake-Face thought she saw the same fear staring her down at her through her daughter's eyes. But she wasn't sure if that was what she was seeing; or if the look about Pauline was merely a reflection of her own fear.

"God me neva come home fi do murder, but me go chop up whoever fresh wid me baby," Bake-Face, spoke aloud, her hand balled into a fist. Then she pounded on the wall, hard and harder until the ball that had been lodged in her chest since she couldn't remember when had worked its way to her throat and a wail escaped her mouth, "Wha-oh! Wha-oh!" She spun around wailing, her balled fist hammering the wall each time she faced it. When Bake-Face calmed down she saw Ms. Maudlyn, her hand still covered with fish scales and lime pulp, staring at her from the door.

"Is what? Wha wrong wid yu?" Ms. Maudlyn asked, not venturing beyond the threshold of the door.

"Is who a fresh wid Pauline? Is who a hurt her?" Bake-Face charged.

"Nobody touch you child!" Ms. Maudlyn stiffened, her face clouding with anger. "You go off every year fa five months and leave her, den you a come ask who fresh wid her. Me no put me hand pan you picknie..."

"Some man or boy ah put him nasty hand pan her," Bake-Face declared, staring out the window as if the answer was somewhere in the yard.

Ms. Maudlyn closed her mouth and refrained from saying anything else. She had noticed that Pauline had become a little withdrawn, but had assumed it was from missing her mother. It never occurred to her that someone... She didn't even want to give the idea thought. As a mother she knew all too well the plight of girls and women. She remembered her own adolescence, and how once she had started to develop the same men and boys who before had ignored her became a menace, making her scared to go anywhere alone.

But she made sure Pauline was seldom out of her sight or that of her brothers and father, who were very protective of her. Still, it could happen, Miss Maudlyn knew. Although Pauline was not very talkative, she and the child had a relationship, and Miss Maudlyn felt that as a mother she would know if anything had happened to her. Wouldn't she? She questioned herself silently, uncertain.

"But Pauline is jus' little girl. No bud no start grow pon her chest yet," Ms. Maudlyn said, seeking an explanation more to reassure herself, knowing full well that neither age nor development were deciding factors.

Bake-Face, who had been staring out the window, jerked her head around to look at Ms. Maudlyn.

"Me did flat like board when me uncle start touch-touch me. Everywhere me walk, every corner me hide in, him find me and if him hand couldn't reach me, him eyes nyam me up, chew pan me like cow its cud. Him eyes dem worse dan him hand most times cause when him was a touch-touch me up, me could close me eyes tight and think of me Mama and Papa holding me safe; but me neva could escape him eyes." She sat down at the foot of the bed. She had never before shared her abuse with anyone but her good friend Joyce; not even with Mr. Johnson, whom she loved. And even though Ezra knew, they never talked about it.

"Me didn't know," Ms Maudlyn said, her hand hovering, unsure whether to touch and comfort Bake-Face.

"Most people didn't know; but some did, like me aunt and odda women in de village. But dem pretend like dem didn't know; dem pretend like it was me, it was me who strange. Ezra know. De first time him come, him see and him know and him tek me away. Me will always respect him fah dat, but no matta how me try me neva love him dat way. Me thank him fah rescue me, me thank him fah not pretend like so many others, acting as if dem didn't see what dem did see. Him know.

Me aunty did know too; but she neva once said a word. Fact was, every time she know she husband touch me, she would beat me and say me bad; cause she couldn't say it to him, her husband. But me done wid settling. Me done wid leaving me daughta. Me done wid de shame. Me done wid being fraid-fraid. Me done wid all of it."

The tears streamed unchecked down Bake-Face's cheeks, and Ms. Maudlyn wiped her fishy hands on her apron, placed her arm around Bake-Face's shoulder, and kept repeating in a soothing tone,

"Hush, hush now; today yu done wid it. Hush, hush now."

Bake-Face wept and wailed, and wailed and wept until, exhausted, she crawled onto the bed and nestled beside Pauline. The child, surprisingly, had been sleeping throughout.

Bake-Face woke to the aroma of escovitch fish wafting through the air. Pauline was still asleep. She kissed her on the forehead and stared down at her. Her daughter at eight years old was a smaller replica of herself; tall and thin. All these years, Bake-Face would go off to Noman Estate to be with Mr. Johnson, the man she loved; and she'd never thought about taking Pauline, assured that she would be safe with Ezra, her father. But Ezra, although a loving father, might not have been attentive in that way. Besides, he loved the land and loved working it more than anything else. She knew it wasn't Ezra who had brought fear to the surface of her daughter's face; but she couldn't imagine who might be responsible. She had every intention of finding out.

In that moment Bake-Face decided she was going to take Pauline away and leave Ezra. She wasn't going back to Mr. Johnson either. She would branch out on her own. It was about time.

"So yuh come home."

Bake-Face hadn't heard Ezra approach, but she looked up to see him standing by the door.

"Yes, me come home; but not fah long. Is time you and Ms. Maudlyn live all de time. She tek good care of yuh," Bake-Face said, meeting him eye for eye.

"True. Is true," Ezra replied. "Maudlyn tek good care of me. Me well appreciate her. So what…you go live at Noman Estate?"

"No, me done wid dat too," Bake-Face answered, looking at her hands. "Truth is me no know whe Pauline and me go live; but we go be together."

"You can always stay here; but I don't think that in you plans." Ezra looked above Bake-Face's head and she his. Bake-Face clasped her fingers and she banged the heels of her hands together in nervous agitation. Although Ezra was never able to put into words his feelings for Bake-Face, he cared for her deeply. She had unknowingly cracked open his heart and wedged herself in there from the first moment he laid eyes on her, over ten years ago, when he first met her living with her aunt and uncle. He would go to any lengths to protect and grant her the freedom she craved.

He looked at her now, banging her palms together, and he wanted to pick her up like he did the yams he planted and admired, the labor of his hands. But he had not planted Bake-Face; she was not yam, and he knew that she would not sit quietly in his hand and be admired. His fingers itched to reach out and touch her, but he refrained; he looked around the small room, and then cleared his throat.

"You could go and claim the land and house you Mama and Papa leave you," Ezra said as he walked away to wash the earth of the farm off his hands.

Pauline stirred. Bake-Face turned and kissed her on both cheeks.

"Me no go leave you again, Pauline," Bake-Face whispered into her daughter's ears. "Me gwane take you with me. Me nah leave you again."

Pauline wrapped her hands around her mother's neck and squeezed tightly, a shy smile of gratitude beaming in her eyes.

Bake-Face had forgotten that her parents had owned land, and that, as their only child, it should belong to her. She had never seen any papers, nor was she sure how to begin to claim her inheritance. But she would find out. Yes, she would find out.

While she had never once gone back to see her mother's sister, and the uncle, her aunt's husband, who had repeatedly abused her, she knew they were still alive; and if anyone knew about her parents' land, it would be the aunt.

Bake-Face was resolved, in fact she was eager, to go and see her aunt and uncle—and not just about her parents' land.

When she told this to Ezra he insisted on accompanying her; if not as her husband, then as Pauline's father. "Just to back you up," he said, committed as he always had been. Bake-Face appreciated him more than ever.

Unsure about how to approach the difficult subject, Bake-Face could not think of a way to ask Pauline if anyone had touched her. Yet she felt certain that someone had. She sensed it. However, she decided to give Pauline and her some time to get reacquainted.

Nonetheless, Bake-Face did not hesitate to speak to Ezra about her suspicions. Ezra stared at her, aghast. He assured Bake-Face that Pauline had not gone anywhere alone, not even to the store.

"Many days she come wid me to the ground, the field; cause she like de farming, like me. Sometimes she stay wid Maudlyn when she don't have school. Me know how those things happen even though no one want talk about it." Ezra looked disgruntled. Pauline was his only daughter, and he loved her dearly. He remembered the hurt in Bake-Face's eyes when he first met her, and he was prepared to do anything to prevent such sorrow in his daughter.

"So why Pauline bed in Granvile dem room?" Bake-Face now demanded, bringing Ezra back to the present.

"Well...she could hardly stay in de room wid me and Miss Maudlyn. Besides, Granvile room have more space dan..." A lump rose in Ezra's throat.

His older son had long been a cause for concern. He had dropped out of school, had not been able to keep a job; nor had he been willing to help on the farm. Moreover, on two occasions, mothers from the village had come to Ezra to complain that Granville was forcing himself on their daughters. Ezra had not believed a word of it at the time; he had raised his sons to respect themselves and to respect women. But now a feeling crept over him and cast a shadow over his face.

Bake-Face stared at Ezra and realized why he had paused. She had tried to like Granville, but he always challenged her and more than once she had been certain he had been spying on her while she bathed or changed her clothes in the bedroom. She had never told Ezra this, but she had reproached the boy, who always denied it and accused her of not liking him and wanting to get him in trouble with his father.

"Granville wouldn't hurt him baby sista," Ezra said, louder than he needed to, his head instantly pounding. Ezra thought he could read Bake-Face's mind, but not wanting to believe the worse of his oldest child, he ventured. "Pauline is him little sista. Me always tell him to look after her." Ezra glanced at Bake-Face, a pained look etched into his face.

"Me telling you now," Bake-Face said, staring directly into Ezra's eyes, "me don't know what me go do him, if me find out him touch her." She turned and marched out of the room.

Granville did not come home that night of Bake-Face's return, and when Ezra sent his other sons' to inquire after their brother, all claimed not to know where he was. Ezra asked his other sons if they had touched their sister or if they knew who did, and they all maintained their innocence. He believed them. That still left Granville, whose behavior had increasingly vexed Ezra and pained his heart.

The next day when Bake-Face was giving Pauline a bath, the child blurted out that someone had touched her chocho—her little girl privates—but she clammed up and would not say anymore or tell her mother who. Bake-Face walked to the far end of the yard. There she cried and raged, using the broom stick to beat at the banana tree, as if it were the culprit. Granville had still not returned home, and that convinced Bake-Face that he was guilty.

She strode down to the shop where the idle boys of the village often hung out, but Granville was not there. The three boys liming there said they had not seen him in a few days. Next Bake-Face walked the mile and a half to the river where they sometimes swam and dove and swapped stories, but no one was in the water that day. From there she walked more than a mile to the path leading to the forest, where the boys often congregated to smoke and play dice, but of the four boys holed up there (who fanned away the whiff of the ganja with the branch of a tree they had broken off) none of them was Granville.

Although very tired, Bake-Face's anger had not waned. She stooped and then sat down. The boys watched her as if she had lost her mind. Finally they sauntered off, glancing over their shoulders at her stooping there, using her finger to draw random shapes in the dirt like a child. She sighed finally, stood up, and followed the path the boys had taken. They had not gone far, just out of sight, hoping that she would leave soon and they could return to smoking and bragging about things they hadn't done but wished they had.

"When oonuh see dat Granville, tell him me looking fah him. And tell him, him can't hide from me forever."

The boys stopped, shielded their eyes, and looked at Bake-Face. She walked towards them, and when she was less than four feet away she chided them.

"Me know who oonuh belong to and me gwane tell dem onnuh out here smoking and madding up oonuh head."

The mouths of the boys fell open. In all the years they had known Miss Bake-Face she had never once reprimanded them or demanded anything of them like the other adults in their community. The third boy, knowing the wrath of his father, who had already been threatening to send him away to boarding school, hastily appealed to her.

"Miss Bake-Face, me wasn't smoking, ma'am; please me wasn't smoking."

"See me company, see me too," she growled at the boy and stamped pass them.

Ezra too had gone looking for his oldest son after he took his daughter to the ground with him. For most of the morning he watched her working quietly in the little patch he had made for her. Then he went over and said:

"Pauline, you must tell Papa if anybody hurt you. Alright?"

The daughter loved her calm, quiet father whom she believed to be stronger than everyone. He always kept his word. She nodded and continued to dig in the soil. Ezra continued to watch her from the side of his eye. As they were walking home for lunch, Pauline took her Papa's hand, and in almost a whisper said,

"At nights Granville cover me mouth wid him hand and put him other hand in me panty."

Blood rushed to Ezra's head and he staggered. All he ever did since Granville was born was to love him. All he ever did was want the best for the boy, for him to make something of his life. When he misbehaved, he flogged him, sometimes more harshly than he meant to; but he wanted to beat him good. Where did he go wrong?

He never allowed Granville to get away with anything. After his first wife, the boys' mother, died he'd made Granville look after his younger brothers and help around the house. He'd hammered into him the need to be responsible. How could Granville, a soon-to-be eighteen year old young man, do that to his little sister?

He didn't realize that he had stopped walking until he heard Pauline's whimper ahead of him.

"Papa, me in trouble?"

Ezra looked down and then rushed and scooped the child to his chest.

"You not in no trouble; but Granville gwane feel me hand today. Him no have no right to do dat to you. Him well out of order."

Ezra took Pauline home, but he did not stay to eat the lunch that Maudlyn prepared for them. He walked similar paths to the ones that Bake-Face had taken the previous day, and a few others that he knew of, but none yielded Granville.

By now it was widely known that Granville was being sought by both his father and his step-mother; that whatever he did was very serious, and he was in big trouble. His friends forewarned him; so he stayed away for more than a week until, unable to find refuge any longer, and hoping that whatever he had done had blown over, he headed home. He might have been confident that, as per usual, he would be able to talk his way out of it. With a rag dangling from his back pocket, hungry and hoping to get a good meal, he rode towards home on the broken bicycle he had won in a game of dominoes.

However, he did not make it home on his own. He was accosted, hauled off the bicycle and roughly escorted home by two men of the village, themselves farmers and friends of his father. Ezra was not yet home from his plot when they arrived; but one of his younger sons was summoned to go and get him. Despite Granville's protests and his efforts to shake loose from the men, they held him firmly by his belt as if he were a common criminal who had stolen bread from an old woman in the market. Before Ezra reached home a small crowd had formed.

Ezra was both angry and embarrassed. Now the entire village would know what Granville had been doing to his sister. Ezra was relieved, however, that Bake-Face at least wasn't home. He couldn't face her and Granville at the same time.

Bake-Face had taken the mini-bus into Kingston to go and inquire about her parents' property at the Land Department. Pauline, who often got car sick, did not want to go with her, and Miss Maudlyn had said she would not let Pauline out of her sight.

Ezra stood before his son. Before even addressing Granville he asked Miss Maudlyn to take Pauline to the shop and buy her a soda, a treat reserved for special occasions; and then he ordered his other sons outside. They knew their father well enough so did not hesitate.

While he appreciated his friends' help, Ezra, a private man, was determined to handle Granville alone; the son who looked most like him, and his father after whom he was named. He felt weary and, sensing that, Granville pleaded.

"Papa, please tell Mas Trevor and Mas Len to let me go, sir. I haven't done them anyting. " Granville hoped that by speaking standard English he would impress his father, whom he knew had ambitions for him to be an important, educated man. But Ezra, who was known as a mild-mannered man, walked over and cuffed his son in the mouth, silencing him.

Granville's lips instantly began to swell. Ezra thanked his friends, and without taking off his muddy rubber boots, hauled Granville inside the house and closed the door. Alone with his father, Granville, who had taken to smoking ganja regularly, sat quiet but defiant, eyeing his father guardedly now. In an even-spaced, extremely quiet, voice, his eyes peering into Granville's face, Ezra spoke to his son.

"Wha you do to you little sista?"

Sweat broke out on Granville's forehead. Ezra scrutinized him closely.

"Papa, me...I mean... I have not done a thing to her. She is a liar. Is lie she lying on me," he stammered.

"Why she would lie on you?" the father probed.

"I don't know, Papa. She always gwane like she big...I mean she's always acting like she is big." The boy tried to shift the blame.

"Gwane big like how?" Ezra continued in an even calmer tone. His fingers twitched.

Calculating, trying to figure out what his sister might have told his father, Granville stared at his father, bidding for time. He had threatened to tie her up and drown her in the river if she told, so he didn't think that she had. He studied his father from beneath bowed head, his eyes trying to read his father's gestures. He had never seen his father like this before. He tried to gauge quickly what to say; if not to escape punishment all together, to at least soften the blow. He was sure it must be about touching her.

"Papa, Pauline love to play with her chocho..." Granville could not have anticipated the blow that knocked him clear off the chair. Before he could gather himself, his father was kneeling over him, holding him firmly by the front of his shirt, breathing like fire on his face.

"Is how you know what she accuse you of if you innocent?"

Most times Ezra did not have to beat his sons. Usually all that was required was the sternness of his voice or a look that made them jump at his command; so he had no routine or special belt or stick that he used for punishment. Granville

54

glanced at his father's face and saw in it the sky all pained and ashen before the downpour of heavy rains.

"Papa, please," he begged.

Ezra did not loosen his hold. He shook Granville.

"Now think before yu answer cause lying could cause me fi knock out yu entire mouth of teeth and mek yu swallow dem. Yu undastand?"

Granville whimpered like a dog whose hind legs had been run over by a car, but nodded his head yes; beads of perspiration draped his face.

"Good," his father said, perspiration pouring from his own face onto his son's. "Did you cova you little sista mouth and touch her?" Ezra unconsciously held his breath, peering into his son's eyes. The boy started to cry, fat tears trickling from his eyes. Ezra used the sleeve of his right arm to wipe his own forehead. "Me didn't tell yu fi cry. Me ask yu a question. Now answer."

"Papa, me just was a play wid her."

Ezra's fist slammed into Granville's face again, bruising his chin. "Yu little sista just mek eight and yu touch her down dere and talk bout playin." He hit him again. "Suppose me play wid yu fingers and bruk everyone?"

So saying Ezra let go of the boy's shirt, grasped the four fingers of his right hand in his firm grip and bent them back until the boy's scream cartwheeled like a caged bird suddenly set free and fluttered in the ears of the small group that was gathered by the gate waiting to hear the full story, and listening to learn what punishment was being meted out.

But Ezra was not a mean-spirited man; and although he was appalled by his son's behavior, he did not have the stomach to inflict severe harm. He pulled Granville up and shook him like a dish rag. "And dem two girls whose mother come to me? Yu did mess wid dem too?" Ezra didn't wait for an answer. "Is wha do yu Granville? Is wha do yu? Decent man no do dem things."

But Granville didn't have a chance to reply because Bake-Face burst through the door. She carried a cricket bat that she swung with full force at Granville's chest. And as he bent over in pain, she raised the bat again and thrust it forward like a master batsman connecting with the ball, breaking four of the fingers on his right hand. Again, he screamed. Then she tossed down the bat.

"If yu touch me dawta again, or any oder girl child, me gwane cut off every last one of yu fingers."

Granville cowered on the floor, while his father and stepmother stood above him, their chests heaving. Bake-Face belched involuntarily, but still felt as if gas was on her chest. She had cared as best she knew how for Granville and his brothers when their father took her in. She had washed his clothes, cooked for him, even helped him with his homework; and yes, she had loved him too. So there was no joy or triumph in what she just done to him.

Ezra, for his part, felt only deep sadness and bewilderment. How did his oldest son get to be this way? Was he lost to him? What would become of him? He was not prepared to have him live at home anymore. Ezra opened the door to his house and called for his next two eldest sons.

"Glenford! George! Come tek yu broder to de hospital." Turning back to Granville, he continued: "But as of today yu no live here anymore."

And so saying, Ezra turned into his bedroom and closed the door quietly.

* * *

The following week Bake-Face, accompanied by Ezra and Miss Maudlyn, climbed the path leading to her aunt and uncle's home, the place where she had lived from ten years old until she was almost seventeen. She stumbled as she neared the steps leading to the house, and was surprised that her palms were sweaty. She had thought after her attack on Granville that she was ready to confront her own abuser, but fear like early morning fog threatened to smother her resolve.

"Is alrite," Miss Maudlyn consoled, steadying Bake-Face by the elbow. "Me not go let you fall. Me a do this for meself and me daughters too." Bake-Face's uncle was propped up in a chair on the veranda rocking. He'd had a stroke recently and had lost the use of his entire right side. Bake-Face climbed the steps and stood before him. She was surprised that she felt not only loathing, but pity too. Her aunt emerged from the house at the sound of the car, with two of her church sisters trailing behind her. But she faltered when she saw Bake-Face, Ezra, and Miss Maudlyn. Recovering quickly, though, she beamed as if they were long lost friends come to visit.

"Bake-Face, is you that?" the aunt said walking towards her niece. "What a way you look good. So nice of you to come visit your uncle."

Bake-Face looked at her, stunned, forgetting all the words she had rehearsed in her head to throw at her aunt, to trace her out. And it wasn't until after her aunt walked up and threw her arms around her neck to hug her that Bake-Face found her tongue.

"Tek you hypocritical hands from me!" she spat. "You neva hug me when you husband was raping me. You neva hug me when at night him pin me down and push him nasty ting in me and me cry out. You neva hug me when him come home at lunch time and you send me to serve him lunch and him pull me pan him lap, and grunt and wiggle, pulling me down pan him hard wood while you turn yu back and bang pots in the kitchens. How come you neva hug me den?"

Bake-Face's aunt stood frozen for what seemed a full minute; then she began to sputter unintelligibly.

At which point Ezra took over and asked about Bake-Face's parents' land. Her aunt broke down and cried. But she got no sympathy, neither from her church sisters nor Bake-Face. They had all known, but pretended otherwise.

Nothing was resolved on that visit.

After four more trips to the aunt and many days spent in the Land Department office in Kingston, it was determined that ten acres of land did indeed belong to Bake-Face. Her uncle's cousin and family had been living and farming the land, and had in fact added on and improved her parents' cottage.

They had build an extra bedroom, from concrete and also a proper bathroom and kitchen and installed running water and electricity. As such, they demanded compensation. But a barrister was hired and they were expelled as squatters. However, Bake-Face was grateful for how well they had taken care of the place and the improvements they had made. She offered them two acres that they could register as their own, and told them that they would have cultivation rights of her land as well, as long as she got a third of the products they yielded. Although there was some bickering and bad-feelings, after more than eight months the matter was resolved and Bake-Face and Pauline moved into the home in which Bake-Face was born and had been raised until her parents died in a truck accident.

The new addition was attached to the original one-bedroom cottage built of wood. Bake-Face was partial to the old structure except for the modern kitchen and bathroom. Although some more trees had been added, the land had already been populated with every imaginable fruit tree that was to be found on the island: over twenty different species of mango, six tamarind, guava, neaseberry, ackee, breadfruit, custard-apple, star-apple, soursop, sweep-sop, papaya, jackfruit, guinep, plum, cherry. There was also cane, banana, plantain, different yams, gungo peas, sorrel, callaloo—and so much more that it took Bake-Face weeks to identify it all.

Located in an ideal spot, Bake-Face decided the house was a good place from which to run a business; and, since she liked cooking, she decided to build a tent-like enclosure from which she could sell cooked meals: breakfast, lunch, and maybe even dinner. And so began what turned into a thriving business that after two years required outside helpers to keep up with the demand.

Her most popular drink was called matrimony. It was made from custard-apple, sometimes blended with condensed milk and various spices, sometimes blended with pineapple juice and lime; but always so delicious, it was reported that no one could have just one glass.

Bake-Face kept a close eye on Pauline, who was growing fast, and she had made sure that everyone knew that she would readily commit murder if anyone was fast with her girl-child.

It was not long after Bake-Face opened her establishment that Mr. Johnson arrived in his tired car and stayed for lunch. He asked how she was doing, how Pauline was, and how she liked being back home; but he never once told her he missed her and wished her back, although that was the sole purpose of his visit. But Bake-Face knew this and they did not need to say what was clear to both of them.

Yet, also understood was Bake-Face's rejection of the life she had once lived and her unwillingness to go back to it. She missed Joyce, her best friend at the estate; but strangely enough, although she had vowed not to become close with her uncle's cousins, she found that she had gradually gotten to be friends with the cousin's wife, Stephanie, whom she had hired to help in the shop. They soon were exchanging confidences.

It was while she and Stephanie sat to create a menu of the desserts that Bake-Face made just for the weekends that their conversation turned to personal matters.

"Bake-Face, you know that Natasha say is yu matrimony juice why Ivan propose to her. She say she gwane mek him come and buy some every week just to keep the love strong." Stephanie giggled.

"Is what you saying to me? Me turn obeah woman of juice," Bake-Face cackled and returned to the menu. But after a while she paused. "You know, me didn't think me would ever want to be wid a man again, but lately me been feeling…" She didn't complete her thought.

"Is normal fi woman want to be wid man. Is not all man nasty like Gerald's uncle," Stephanie ventured. They had never spoken about Bake-Face's abuser.

"Me know," Bake-Face replied reflectively. "Me know. Ezra is a good man and so is Mr. Johnson; but neither of them right for me."

"Me know what you mean," Stephanie agreed. "Me luck up with Gerald. We did know we love each other from we twelve." She giggled and then, leaning closer to Bake-Face, spoke conspiratorially. "Me tink there is really something to yu matrimony juice. Me and Gerald wasn't so close no more, but since me start giving him yu juice, him can't keep him hand off me, and him not running off every day fi go play domino and drink wid him friend dem."

Bake-Face regarded her, but said nothing. They completed the menu, and Bake-Face left the cleaning up to her and the other helper and headed home.

Bake-Face could not recall dreaming about her mother before, but that week her mother had appeared to her in a dream, and as clear as water told her, "Don't mind, de waiting done." Bake-Face didn't know what the dream meant, nor was she willing to ask anyone; but she recalled it then, after her talk with Stephanie. It stayed with her throughout the day as she prepared the food for her customers. She took the custard apples that were in a clay bowl, rolled them on the counter, cut them in half, humming as she worked. She opened a can of condensed milk and poured half in her special gourd, adding a quart of water. Next she poured in a pinch of nutmeg, a dash of allspice, a dab of grated ginger, a drop of lime juice, and little of this and that, then stirred.

At one point she felt a presence behind her and looked around. She saw no one. 'Is why Mama must dream me now?' she wondered as she covered the gourd and placed it on the windowsill so the sunlight could get to it. Then she went about making her Cracker-Custard. She took out the currants, the remaining half can of condensed milk, a fresh bag of water-crackers, two eggs to bind it, and spices. She greased the pan, covered the bottom with crackers, then a layer of currants, milk, and—since mangoes were in season and abundant—she put a layer of mangoes; then more crackers and currants until the pan was full.

"No shame in looking nice, yu know. Yu must fix up yuself every once in a while."

Startled, Bake-Face looked around to find the owner of the voice. But she was alone in the kitchen. She knew that voice; it was her mother's.

Even though she had been a little girl when her mother died, she remembered the sound of her voice, quick and light like skipping rope. Bake-Face paused, listening to the voice again, but this time she got only silence. She resumed her activity, poured in the beaten eggs with a dash of rosemary water, and sprinkled brown sugar over the layered contents in the pan. Although she had a modern gas oven, she preferred to bake it the old fashioned way, with hell atop and hell a bottom—in an oven with lighted coals at the top and bottom and the pan in the middle. She felt this made it sweeter.

While the custard was baking, she took a shower. She brushed and replaited her hair; like always parting it down the middle in two thick braids. But rather than putting on one of the shapeless shifts that Pauline had been teasing her about, she took out one of two new dresses her daughter had persuaded her to buy when she'd dragged her along on a shopping trip the week before. It was mint green and fitted to her figure, with two pockets by the hips, an orange border along the sleeves and neckline.

Bake-Face had thought the color combination odd but had liked the fit; and as she looked at herself in the mirror now, she liked the full effect. She did not question why on a Thursday evening, with nowhere special to go, she had decided to wear a new dress.

Returning to the kitchen, Bake-Face checked on the custard, then took the gourd from the windowsill and poured into it the bottle that she had put to chill in the fridge. She stirred, and then heaped a spoonful into her palm to taste. "Just right," Bake-Face said smacking her lips.

She put the Custard Cracker to cool and walked the few yards to her little eating establishment that she refused to call a restaurant. Bake-Face had never sat down on one of the chairs and table to eat, always waiting until she was in the privacy of her home; but that evening, since the place was empty of customers, she did so. Pauline, coming in from school, joined her.

"Mama, you look really pretty in that dress. You must wear pretty dress more often." The girl kissed her mother on the cheek and began to relate details about her day at school.

It was while Pauline was chattering that Gerald drove up and stunned Bake-Face with the announcement that their uncle had died. He had come to get Stephanie to go and assist the family.

Bake-Face surprised herself with how readily she said to Stephanie,

"Take some food carry, and tell Aunty me sorry for she loss." There was no malice or sarcasm in her voice—or in her heart. Stephanie and Gerald both stared at her, and then at each other. They waited for her to continue, but she was done. They gathered some food and then sped off. Bake-Face and Pauline waved from the porch.

Bake-Face's mind flitted over Mr. Johnson and the sweet times they'd had when she had allowed herself to enjoy him. She chuckled.

"Is what Mama?" Pauline asked. She had been sitting watching her mother.

Reaching across the table, Bake-Face held her daughter's face between her palms, then chuckled again.

"Is life, how it sweet even when it sour." Bake-Face observed Pauline's frown and knew she did not understand. "Pauline, promise me that you neva be afraid to love cause is love mek me matrimony juice so sweet." She let go and sat back in the chair. She felt as if she had just told her daughter something very important. Rising to get plates and glasses, Bake-Face turned back and said, "I make a fresh pitcher of juice and I bake custard. Dem on the counter inside, go bring dem so we can eat dem right here."

Immediately Pauline scrambled up because she loved her mother's custard; she dashed the fifty yards to their home. Within two minutes she returned to the table, holding both carefully, but taking long strides. Bake-Face took the pitcher from her, and poured them both tall glasses; then she scooped them each a generous helping of the custard. They ate slowly, savoring each bite.

Although Bake-Face had tried several times to broach the subject of Granville, Pauline had not been ready. But each time Bake-Face told her daughter that she and her father would go to any lengths to protect her. Bake-Face made sure that Pauline knew and understood this, and that she would come to either of them if anyone tried to sexually abuse or harm her again. The fear was gone from her, yes; but now that she was approaching eleven her body was blossoming like a conspiracy. Bake-Face observed it beginning to change, hips pushing out and buds rising on her chest; the mother's heart was heavy with concern about how to keep her safe.

Pauline wiped her mouth and belched and they both burst out laughing.

"Beg pardon," Pauline said after the laughter subsided.

"I guess you enjoyed that," Bake-face smiled. "Is time you go home. Take off you school uniform and do you homework. Me gwane sit here enjoy de evening."

"You want me to put these in the fridge?" Pauline asked reaching for the remainder of the custard and the pitcher.

""No is alright," Bake-Face hastened, holding on to both.

The child skipped home, and Bake-Face's eyes followed her until she was inside. She was so thankful for the relationship that she and Pauline had. She talked to her about everything, including how some men and boys nasty and would try to hurt her, but that she, Bake-Face would always fight them. She was thankful too that Pauline and Ezra were still close and visited frequently. No one had heard a word from Granville, except that he went to live in Kingston. Ezra prayed his son had learned his lesson.

Bake-Face sat alone, enjoying the slight rustle of the breeze. Her life was good now, she thought. Her daughter was happy. What more could she ask for? Then she felt a shadow creep over her, and she rubbed her arms, feeling goosebumps. She stood up and looked out at the street, both ways; but it was empty. Only a lone dog lay in the shade under the cotton tree on the furthest side of the street.

She sat back down and allowed herself to think about her uncle, now dead: the uncle who had stolen her virginity; the uncle who never once said that he was sorry; the uncle she had at one time loved because he spoke softly and always had a sweetie in his pocket for her.

Staggered that only now this memory surfaced, Bake-Face got up and spat over the railing onto the ground. Why had she not remembered that: that initially she had liked her uncle more than her aunt, and that he had once been kind to her. But he took advantage of her feelings and he made them bad. The old anger surfaced, but just as quickly like coal on which kerosene is poured flares up, then wanes, Bake-Face let go of the past. She spoke aloud to herself, to her dead uncle, to the duppies.

"Me hope yu sorry, Uncle. Me hope yu did well sorry. But it don't matter, not really, not anymore. You dead and gone. Me sorry it happen; me sorry it happen to me and me neva had anyone to defend me. But you neva break me. None of oonuh break me. Me fagive you, Uncle, and me fagive you Aunty. Me fagive everybody, including meself fah thinking it was fi me fault."

She stood up and brushed off her arms and dress as if she had just walked into of a tangle of cobwebs; then she sat back down. She poured herself another tall glass of matrimony juice. Although she always tasted what she made before she served her customers, she seldom sat and savored the taste like she was doing now. She drank one gulp, then another, and soon drained the glass.

"It really good fah true," she said to herself, pouring another glass. She scooped out another helping of the custard cracker and put a small bite in her mouth. She chewed slowly. "What a way it good fah true," Bake-Face declared to the air.

She didn't pay attention to the crunching of gravel on the path leading to the establishment, lost in her thoughts until the man greeted her.

"Evening Miss Bake-Face. What on de menu dis evenin?"

Bake-Face started slightly, but then smiled into the face of Mr. Thompson, one of her regular customers. He was a hard working man, without a woman of his own; hence he dropped by for a meal at least a couple of times each week.

"Me close, Thompson. Death in de family." Bake-Face said.

"Respect, Miss Bake-Face; respect. Me sorry fi hear bout yu loss. Is who dead ma'am?" Thompson bowed his head slightly, respectfully, as if in prayer.

Bake-Face opened her mouth to answer, but stopped. It wasn't her uncle's death she was commemorating; it was that the life that had kept her stuck was now behind her. But how could she make Thompson understand that when she didn't understand it herself? But then she decided that it didn't matter whether he understood or not.

"Me past jus dead, Thompson; me pass jus up and dead." Bake-Face looked closely at the man as he nodded his head in understanding; she took him in fully. He stood relaxed under her gaze.

He was the color of two-day old unfiltered cane juice. His arms were muscular, but not big. His hair was closely cropped, sprinkled with a few greys, revealing the full shape of his round head.His knees slightly bowed.

"Thompson, go get a clean plate and glass from de counter and you can have some of this juice and custard before me alone done dem," Bake-Face said, her eyes still scanning him.

Thompson moved to get the plate and glass, then he pulled out the chair opposite Bake-Face, sat down and pushed his plate and glass across the table to her. As she served him, he observed her in his turn.

"Dat is a nice dress you wearing Miss Bake-Face. Ah don't believe ah have seen you in it before."

"Is Pauline pick it out fah me when me tek her shopping." Bake-Face replied.

"She have good taste," Thompson said and then bit into the custard. He ate slowly, aware that Bake-Face was scrutinizing him. As he cleaned the plate, he examined her, taking in—not for the first time—her high cheekbones, her dark brown eyes that always made him think of a deep well, her plaited hair, her lips—he didn't know what to say of her lips except that he'd frequently noticed that the bottom one trembled, even when she was silent. He had on a few occasions wanted to run his finger over and quiet it.

"Miss Bake-Face," he said as if it were a question, as if to make sure that was her name, "You is a cooking woman and a baking woman fah true. Is de best custard dat you eva made. Ah give thanks to you." He beamed.

"Is welcome, you welcome," Bake-Face replied. "So how de juice?"

Thompson picked up the glass in both hands, ran his fingers over the droplets of water from the melted ice, then placed the glass to his mouth. He took a swallow and shook his head in satisfaction. He drained the remainder in one gulp and pushed the glass back across to Bake-Face.

"Fill it up again, Miss Bake-Face," he said, smiling broadly now.

She filled his glass and picked up her own. They clinked their glasses together and drank, emptying them almost at the same time and laughed out loud until tears ran down their cheeks. After they composed themselves, they finished the rest of the custard and juice, sat silently, and watched the night slowly creep in. Eventually Pauline came and interrupted their reverie.

"Night Mama, night Mista Thompson. Excuse me Mama, you going to eat?"

"No sweetie, but you eat. You dinner in de oven," Bake-Face placed her arm affectionately around her daughter's waist.

"Night Mama," Pauline said kissing her mother on the cheek, and before turning to leave, she quickly looked at Mister Thompson from under her eyelashes before saying, "Night Mista Thompson." Neither saw her smile as she hopped into the house.

"That's a good child you have dere Bake-Face; you do well by her. Me like that," Thompson said.

The old fear sprang up, paws ready to strike. Bake-Face felt her hands tremble. Through the darkness of the night that was now fully dressed, she glared at Thompson.

"You eva felt like murdering any man?" Bake-Face asked him.

"No," he said just as pointedly. "But me know that yu did want to murder at least two." He looked at her, and even in the semi-darkness their eyes connected. "If me did have a dawta and a man touch her, me would a murder him, no question," Thompson said. Bake-Face shifted on her chair. "You 'ave me word on that score," he said rising.

"That is how it must be," Bake-Face said, also standing.

They shook hands and Thompson helped Bake-Face pack away the dishes and lock up her establishment. He walked her to her door.

"Miss Bake-Face, thank you for yu company, and thank you for a most delicious meal. Yu must bottle and sell yu matrimony juice." Thompson said, "It well nice, can't done."

"Thank yu fah de complement," Bake-Face said turning in, just as Thompson turned to go, and then both paused. Thompson turned to look at Bake-Face from where he stopped.

"Miss Bake-Face, ma'am, ah would be most honored to know de name you Mama and Papa give you at birth, please ma'am?" he said looking directly at her.

Bake-Face held on to the doorknob more firmly and as she turned and smiled at Thompson, she felt tears threatening to spill down like a welcome July drizzle.

Love's Promise

Friendship, she always felt, was as a flamboyant tree in bloom, red-orange blossoms fashioned into a gigantic brimmed hat. She associated him with the color orange, bulla cake, trees, and the word "yes"—because he always said yes to her. She regarded him as her only true friend, although they were young then, and awkward. They were familiar with each other's families and homes. They had witnessed one another's tears, fights, bruises, spankings, and even deepest shame. Perhaps their lives might have been too intimate for them to entertain feelings for each other, but at a certain point she realized that he was a longing that she had been carrying around until she was lopsided.

* * *

Danny and Lynette had taken the Common Entrance exam to qualify for high school together, and the day the results were published in The Gleaner she was ecstatic because not only had she passed, she had gained acceptance to the school of her choice. That day her father rushed home from work brandishing the newspaper, hoisted her onto his shoulders, and paraded her around the neighborhood, where the people who had known her all her life congratulated her with fruits and small gifts of money. After dinner, her father took her out—just her and daddy—for a banana split, and they talked not like father and daughter, but like friends, she felt. He told her of his first fearsome day at high school, and that he had feared he was not as bright as the other students. But he assured her that she should have no such worries because she was well bright. She confided to him that for the last week she had slept poorly and suffered headaches, worried she might not pass the exam, and disappoint him and her mother. They were silent for a moment before her father reached across the table, patted her hand, smiled and said,

"Eat up. Enjoy your ice cream. You pass already so nothing to fret yourself about."

She then scooped a spoon of ice cream and banana in her mouth and it had never tasted so good. When they finished, just as they got to the car to head back home, her father dashed back to the ice cream parlor remembering to get some rum-n-raisin ice cream for her mother:

"So she don't bite off my head," he had said to her conspiratorially.

Before he reentered the ice cream store, he had paused and shouted to her, "Pity Danny didn't pass again. He's old now; thirteen in a few months."

As she sat in the car waiting for her father to return she felt suddenly ashamed, as she hadn't thought about Danny all day, basking as she was in her own accomplishment. Earlier, during the day, she had heard some of the boys she played with shouting, yonder at someone.

"Dunce boy. Come let we gi yuh a dunce cap. Yuh name not in The Gleaner."

She had giggled self-righteously, not even wondering who they were talking about; but now suddenly her stomach cramped. She never thought about the fact that Danny was two years her senior. Unexpectedly, her eyes smarted and she could taste tears. She glanced quickly toward the ice cream parlor hoping her father would not return and find her upset. She chewed on the palm of her hand until the muscles in her stomach relaxed and her eyes were dry.

The following morning after breakfast, Lynette ran to his house, but only the maid was there. Danny and his mother had gone out, and had not said when they would be back. So she sat on the swing under the large cotton tree almost the entire morning, waiting, refusing to go and play.

Danny had been her very first friend; they met when she was only five years old, and he had wandered into her yard. She had been sitting in the dirt doodling.

"What you drawing?" he had asked stooping to examine her doodle. She hadn't really been drawing anything in particular, but she vaguely remembered that his question spurred her to make up a story because she wanted him to stay. And he began coming daily and they would play, make up stories, and not once in all the six years that she knew him did he ever call her a liar or say she was making up things. Not once did he ever make her feel embarrassed about being a girl or drawing pictures in the dirt or climbing trees, or wading in the canal, or stealing away and going to the alligator pond to poke sticks at the alligators or jumping off roof tops. Not once.

The sun was hot and perspiration pressed her cotton blouse to her back, but still she refused to leave. The maid, whose name was Hortense, came out a few times and told her to go home, but she could not get her feet to obey. Now she watched as the maid walked towards her with a glass.

"Drink dis an guh home. Him nah come back today," she said handing Lynette the glass of limeade, which she loved.

She took the glass, said thanks and drank slowly, all the while aware of the maid, standing, watching her. Draining the glass she handed it back to Hortense.

"You lucky you pass the exam for good school," Hortense said to her. "Danny didn't pass again, and him shame, shame too bad. Him bawl like somebody beating him with a big stick. Him tell him moda dat him gwane kill himself rather than face you. She well worried about him and call him fada at work. Me neva hear wha dem talk bout, but de next ting me know she tell me to pack him clothes, and she pack her clothes, and her brother come for her and dem drive off. Danny still a bawl, long wash-away-river tears."

She didn't realize she was crying until Hortense bent down and wiped her eyes that were liquid pools, saying, "Hush. Nuh cry. Nuteen we can do. Me nuh know why dem ave to put picknie dem name in de paper so de whole world know who pass and who nuh pass." And so saying, Hortense had turned her in the direction of her home and nudged her forward. She stumbled home, her stomach hollow. She climbed into her father's hammock, strung between two mango trees, and slept until it was time to tidy up for dinner.

Although the dinner her mother served that night was her favorite, stew peas and rice, as requested, she was only able to swallow a few mouthfuls. And when her father began telling her mother about Danny, she sat quietly and allowed the tears to fall onto her plate.

"I spoke to Osborne today," her father began directing his remarks to her mother. Uncle Osborne was Danny's father. Although he was neither her father's nor mother's brother, because the two families had become close over the years, the children called each other's parents "uncle" and aunt.

"He said Danny is inconsolable, wouldn't stop crying. They eventually took him to the doctor. They are in Ochi with her sister and will stay there until next week, when they are scheduled to leave for Canada for some cousin's wedding. He says they had been thinking of migrating, so Janice and Danny might just end up staying." They were so engrossed in their conversation that they didn't notice her until her oldest sister shouted:

"Mommy, Lynette is crying and snot is dropping into her food."

She felt all eyes turn to her. Her father sprang forward and used his napkin to wipe her face. He picked her up as if she were a baby and walked out onto the veranda, sat on the rocking chair with her in his lap and rocked.

She remembered hearing her sisters whining that she was a spoiled brat, was always allowed to do what she wanted, and what was she crying about anyway—that barefoot boy Danny that she was always running about the place with, the two of them acting like strayed dogs. Her mother told her sisters sharply to be quiet, and excused them from the table. Her mother then joined her and her father on the veranda, bringing a glass of warm milk with cinnamon sprinkled on top the way Lynette liked it.

* * *

With Danny gone she had no one to play with. The youngest of four girls, she was four years younger than the sister immediately ahead of her. Danny was the youngest in his family too, by six years, with two older brothers. Their friendship had been cemented when they claimed each other; he was the brother she didn't have, she was the sister he didn't have, and they felt that made them perfect siblings and friends.

He was the only boy in the neighborhood who took up for her, who always insisted that she tag along with him and his friends even though the others often teased her, called her tomboy, and tried to shoo her away.

"We don't want no gal follow us. Go play with dolly-baby like the other gal them," they said. But not Danny. He made her the slingshot she used to shoot her first bird, and it was he who insisted that she should be allowed to go with them into the woods, even though she was younger and a girl. It was Danny who climbed the avocado tree with her at the side of her house and would sit with her among the branches, concealed by shiny green leaves. There she would show him the pictures she drew, never of any real thing; but he never laughed at her. He always studied the lines and colors, sometimes tracing them over with his fingers; then he would close his eyes, and would tell her what her pictures made him see, and it was as if he knew what was inside her head better than she knew herself. The stories Danny made up about her pictures took her rafting down the many rivers of her island home. Then he would smile and nod his head up and down as if he couldn't stop saying yes to something as delicious as coconut-drops, which he loved.

Danny didn't return home that week or that month. Lynette drew a picture of them up in the tree together and gave it to Uncle Osborne to give to Danny. Almost daily she went to his house to check; but daily she was sent away without news. It was a long, boring summer. Although many of the boys had long stopped teasing her, she didn't feel like playing with any of them. Her sisters alternately ignored or shooed her, and loneliness crept in like sand flies at night.

Often that summer she had to run to a corner or up a tree to hide and cry; and at those times she hated Danny for leaving her, hated him for not passing the Common Entrance exam, hated him for being a coward and running away in shame, hated him for not saying goodbye. She hated him and wanted to punch him in the nose. She told her dog Timbuktu, who was once his, that if Danny were to come knocking at her door that would be the first thing she would do. She would punch him, hard, and tell him she hated him for leaving her because she had not thought about him that day the results came out, she had only thought about her self and how proud and relieved she was that she had passed.

Danny didn't return when summer was over and school began, when she got her new uniform and was officially proclaimed by her mother to be a young lady. She wanted him to see her in uniform, and admire the fountain pens she had picked out. Even though her mother told her not to waste the ink, the first thing she did was to draw a picture for Danny. Lines were going every which way, and she had written in large block letters, MISSING on top. Evelyn, the sister with whom she shared the bedroom, had walked into the room, seen what Lynette was doing, and looked over her should and hollered.

"Mommy, you should come and see how Lynette has wasted half the bottle of ink for school drawing nonsense!" And, so saying, she had tried to grab the picture, which led to a tussle and before their mother could come, had ripped it. Lynette had punched her, bloodying her nose; but it was Lynette's scream that was loudest. Her tears flowed and through it all she hollered: "That was for Danny, my only friend and he is gone and I am all alone and none of you even care that I am all alone!!!"

Then she had sprung loose from her mother's hold, and run out of the house, out of the yard, down one street after the other, run until it felt as if her chest was caving in, run until her calves burned as if on fire, run until she could no longer see Danny's face inside her head—and until she was completely turned around, lost.

Depleted, she sat down for a long time under a tree, her mind blank. Finally she got up and knocked on a gate and asked the woman who answered for a glass of water. The elderly woman had regarded her in silence for a moment, then motioned for her to step through the gate, directed her to sit on the verandah, and went and got her a glass of water. After she drank and thanked her, the woman asked her:

"Who you be? What's you mama and pappy's names?"

Brought back to reality, Lynette had considered the question but could not at that moment remember the answer.

"I'm Danny's friend," she replied. "Danny's friend."

Then she took off running again, in circles, for the greater part of the afternoon, until in the evening she found her way back home. She was never scolded or punished for hitting her sister, a firm family rule that no one got away with breaking. She did not receive a lecture for walking away from her mother without being excused. And to her surprise, on her bed was the picture her sister had ripped, neatly taped.

She said nothing. She was sweaty, so drew herself a bath and lay in the tub for a long, long time, forgetting that her sisters might need to use the bathroom. She didn't speak to anyone or eat dinner. Before climbing into bed, she wrote Danny's name, in large block letter next to the word missing and watched as the picture slipped out of her hand, and sailed on the floor.

Danny never returned, not even for the Christmas holidays. His father, who was preparing to go join the family in Canada, told her that Danny was adjusting. She didn't know what he meant by "adjusting," but was afraid to ask. However, a few days before Christmas, just before he left, Uncle Osborne brought her a shoebox of Danny's belongings, saying that Danny had asked him to give them to her.

In the box were his slingshot, his precious marble collection, a little red car he had gotten for one of his birthdays that he had carried around in his pocket for more than a year, and a hand-made book from exercise paper, entitled: Love's Promise, The Adventures of Two Friends.

She thanked Uncle Osborne, hugged him tightly, and asked him to tell Danny that she missed him, and that he should come back soon. She had shoved the box in her closet, and had not looked at the contents again or read the story, until the night before school resumed after Christmas break. Then and there she decided that she would never again have a best friend—this way no one could leave her alone to fend for herself. It was all a lie she told herself, his story, Love's Promise, about friendships that endure.

At her first art class in high school the teacher said she was naturally talented and encouraged her. When she ended up winning the top art prize for the entire school that year, she remembered how Danny had always praised her drawings and always saw more in them than she did.

But she worked at forgetting him, and after a while he receded in the mists of her own self-importance, school associates (she never called or thought of them as friends), art classes, and increasing flirtations with cute boys, though this latter preoccupation did not lead to anything as she found herself secretly comparing each boy to Danny, and dismissed them when she realized they were not really interested in being her friend. And although every so often an image of him crept into her head, and some gesture of his flitted across her eyes, she was still too angry with him for leaving to focus on any memory of him.

The summer after her second year in High School Danny finally returned, but in a perverse bit of luck she was away at the time, visiting her grandmother in

Mandeville—and although initially disappointed, she was glad she had not seen him, or she might, or most surely would have punched him and bloodied his nose.

He could have written. Failing the Common Entrance exam did not prevent him from writing. He could have written her a poem. Whenever her mother received a letter from his mother and mentioned anything about him she would walk away. She was determined to forget Danny, and she almost succeeded except every once in a while, when she drew a picture, something abstract that no one else understood and she wished she and Danny could climb the avocado tree like they used to and she would show it to him, and after he spent a great deal of time examining all the details he would close his eyes and tell her what her colors and images made him see, and nod his head up and down like he couldn't stop saying yes. She hated herself for still missing him, and valuing his opinion so much. She was thereafter reluctant to get close to anyone, girl or boy, and she never again referred to anyone as her friend.

Her senior year she returned home from school to find a letter on her bed-side table. Written in small neat letters on the back of the envelope was the name "Danny McFarlin." It had come from an address in Canada. She turned the envelope over and over in her hand, but was terrified to open it. Why was he writing only now, four years later? What if he wrote to say that they had never been friends that he hated her for not coming to find him that morning when the results appeared in the Gleaner? She took off her shoes, climbed into bed, her back pressed against the headboard, her knees bent, the envelope in the fold of her skirt, and a memory she had not allowed herself before descended as a duppie's shadow:

The day before what will forever in her memory be characterized as "that ill-fated day" she and Danny had packed a snack of two bulla cakes (his favorite). These were hard, molasses-with-ginger-flavored round cakes about four inches in diameter. To this he added an entire avocado; two plastic cup containers of limeade, which they both loved, freshly made and sweetened with brown sugar; and a coconut drop to be shared between them. He had all this in a bag slung over his shoulder. She carried a drawing pad, a few loose sheets of exercise pages, four colored pencils, a blue ink pen and a pencil. They had set off, actually sneaked off, after breakfast for some unknown destination, Danny's idea. The neighborhood had not yet fully developed, so there were many vacant lots, a forested area, and rumors that the tail of a river was in the vicinity. They had walked for more than five miles she was certain, and finally after midday, when the sun was directly ahead, had found a shade under a cluster of trees, slicing the avocado, and using a fork to crush and spread it all over the bulla. Danny took a bite of his first and declared, "De-li-cious!" Lynette giggled, watching him smack his lips, and seeing the big smile on his face. After their lunch they were both quiet, she drawing and he writing. They never shared their work with each other that day, but as they walked home the talk was all about the exams results that would appear the next day. She remembered stopping and saying to his receding back,

"Danny, ah so afraid."

He turned, then stopped and walked to where she stood.

"What if I don't pass?"

"Why you worry your head about nonsense? You know you pass."

"But what if I don't? The shame alone will kill me."

"Shame never killed anyone yet."

"I will be the first," she had replied. "I will be too ashamed to ever show my face to anyone. Promise you won't ever talk to me if I fail. I wouldn't want my shame to stain you too. Promise."

He had taken hold of her hand, squeezed her fingers and they had walked home, holding hands, in silence, and they had not said anything else to each other, not even when he walked her home, he had merely waved before she turned and stepped through the door.

The memory impacted her like the sight and sound of a car running over a dog.

Too much time had passed for tears. She had certainly not meant that she would have been ashamed of him if he hadn't passed; she hadn't even been concerned about his not passing, but she had forced him to promise; and although he had been reluctant, he'd said "Alright me promise," and he had kept his word.

She would not open his letter. She did not want to hear his accusation. So she took it—and the other eight letters he would write her during her senior year— and shoved it unread in the shoe box with his other keepsakes.

After high school she left the island to study at Howard University in the United States, where she earned a liberal arts degree in Art and Art History. Then she went on to the Massachusetts Institute of Technology to study architecture, because her father said it was a form of art that was more practical than her drawings, and from which she could get a job that would support herself. And it was there, at the beginning of the second semester, that she experienced the first sense of failure that sent her running home.

She spent a week crying and thinking about how awful Danny must have felt, failing the Common Entrance twice, and everyone knowing that he failed. At least only her parents and professors knew that she was a failure, not the entire island. And the weight of that burden, an understanding of that communal shame that Danny must have felt wore on her so much that she wrote a letter to the Minister of Education, demanding that they stop publishing the results of the Common Entrance Exams in the newspaper, citing the devastating impact it had on thousands of children each year.

Back in Jamaica she climbed their favorite tree and really thought about Danny, and asked him to forgive her. For the first time she confided in her father that she missed Danny and felt as if a part of her life had been amputated.

"I know you miss him. We all know you miss him. Some of your light dimmed and has remained dimmed since he left. Your mother and I were so surprised that he didn't write. Whenever I wrote or spoke to Osborne I asked him to encourage Danny to write to you, but he said Danny said you made him promise not to write. Why would you do that? You two were like bulla and pear."

"Oh Daddy," was all she replied, not wanting to relive that day again and again—and yet she did.

Her parents consoled her, but insisted that she return to finish school. In the end, it was her father's story of his own failure thirty years earlier when he was in England at school that convinced her to tuck her tail and return to complete her degree; which she did, even though it took a year longer than originally planned.

After seven years of school, plus a year at an architectural firm, she'd come home for good, having always felt as if she didn't belong anywhere else. But only a little over a year later she got the chance to study and work in Japan, and opted to do so since she had no strings or serious interests tying her down. She spent two years there, although at times she found the work-driven culture oppressive, yet she rather enjoyed being considered exotic, and was fascinated by many of the young Japanese who were enamored, and even obsessed with Reggae music and other aspects of her Jamaican culture.

It was during her first year in Japan that her mother got word from a friend that Danny's mother had died from breast cancer, and that a year after that his father had had a stroke. That was the last news they had about the family for a very long time. No one wrote or called, and when her mother had tried to find them the last phone number she had was disconnected and her letters were returned. Lynette grieved that Danny was somewhere in the world, probably alone, and she had no idea where. For the last several years, buried in school and work, she had abandoned drawing and painting, but after returning from Japan she resumed with new vigor and began working on a series of painting she entitled 'Friendship.'

Back home she got a job immediately, and simultaneously she began to explore her homeland, realizing how little she knew of its history and places. She decided to explore a new town or parish every free weekend, something she and Danny had talked about doing as children. Though she had not seen him since she was eleven years old nor received a letter from him since high school, he always seemed present, as if alive at the back of her head, looking down at all she did.

Living just outside Negril, mostly working as an interior architect for those awful hotels that were ruining the once tranquil and picturesque landscape by erecting monstrously large, multi-room hotels, a restless dissatisfaction brewed in Lynette. Occasionally she landed the opportunity to design a home or a series of cottages for a local person, which gave her immense satisfaction. However, to her surprise she loved the rural community; especially the people, who appeared free of pretense, but were intensely and unashamedly inquisitive about the details of everyone's life.

Her own life was uneventful, except for the occasional flirtation. Moreover, she lacked confidence in her ability as a painter to present herself among such artists. Her life had become mundane so quickly and so quietly, trepidation stalked all her actions and daily she remonstrated with herself. Arriving home before dusk, she sat on the veranda, where she often sat when she was home, to sip her coffee in the mornings, to do her stretches, to paint, to think, to just allow life to pass her by, as her mother often admonished:

"Lynette girl, thirty is about to smack you on the behind. What you waiting on? You can't go back you know. I'm no psychiatrist, but you have been stuck, and it's way past time you get on with living. Make your peace with the past."

She didn't think she was waiting on anything or anyone, but she did acknowledge, if but to herself, that she was afraid, terrified in fact that if she were to abandon herself to someone, a lover, a man, that he might one day just up and walk off without a word, like Danny had. She knew from therapy that this was irrational, but she couldn't shake it.

Months passed. The Friendship series of paintings and drawings grew. She continued to explore new places throughout the island. A client, for whom she was designing a guesthouse, dropped by her home with his wife as scheduled, but she had forgotten, so engrossed in painting. But all turned out well, call it serendipity as the wife owned a small gallery, loved her series and booked her for a show. Both thrilled and terrified, she called her father straight way with the news and could tell he was beaming even over the telephone. He told her that her upcoming show called for a celebration and that she should drive up for the weekend and he would invite her sisters and she could brag on them for ridiculing her drawings when they were girls.

Imagine then her surprise, when she got to her parents' and her childhood home and her mother rushed out brandishing a package that had just arrived for her, a hour before.

"My good Lord," her mother declared all breathless. "It's from Danny after all of these years! Open Lyn-Lyn; your father and I feel so bad that we have lost contact with Osborne and the boys. Not a word from any of them. We're not even sure if Osborne is still alive since he had that stroke. Please open it."

Standing in the driveway, her mother anxious before her, Lynette ripped open the package to find a collection of poems by Nicolas Guillèn, and when she flipped open the book it was inscribed, "To Net-Net, a special childhood friend whose pictures made me think of stories…" It was signed "Danny" and finished with the note "Love's Promise is in the works."

She clutched the book to her chest, feeling both vulnerable and regretful. There was no letter or forwarding address. Her mother read the disappointment on her face and offered,

"That he sent you the book is a good sign. Maybe he is here in Jamaica; maybe he has returned home and will contact us, you. I am sure that he will."

Did Danny still matter after all these years? she asked herself, surprised at her raw feelings. Every time she thought she was done with him, had made peace with her childhood, something surfaced and she was right back there in that day when she ran to his house and the maid told her he was gone. Where had he picked up the collection of poems by Nicolas Guillèn? Why did he just send her a book and no way to contact him? Her head throbbed, standing there in her parents' driveway, her suitcase and Friendship paintings still in her car. She looked at her mother and felt strange, as if her mother had caught her in bed with a man.

"Mommy do you remember the shoe-box that Danny had left for me? Do you know where it is?" She knew it was someplace in her parents' house, though her room had been converted into a reading room for her mother. She needed to find it, as she was certain the story he had once written about them was called "Love's Promise." And what did he mean "it was in the works?" Where was he anyway?

When her father got home her mother immediately told him about Danny's gift, which prompted her to inquire.

"Daddy, you haven't heard anything from Uncle Osborne?"

"Strange that you should ask. I got a letter from one of his sons, Justin—he is the second oldest if my memory serves me—just yesterday or so, a few days ago the letter arrived…"

"And you didn't tell me?" her mother interrupted.

"Sorry love; it slipped my mind," her father continued. "Osborne is living in Miami and doing much better, although apparently he had some complications from the stroke. I was planning that we should call him this weekend. And Danny is a writer of some sort. Can you imagine that! Boy failed the Common Entrance exam twice and is a writer now."

"Daddy, Danny was a writer from when he was a boy, even before he took the Common Entrance. Remember he would write poems and I would draw pictures."

"You're right about that. The Common Entrance does not always measure the worth of a man or woman."

"But it can ruin the life of a boy or girl," she added. She showed him the book of poems that had just arrived. "This is from Danny; but he didn't include an address or phone number! Someone dropped it into the mailbox and left. Mommy said you packed away the things in my room. Do you remember that shoebox Uncle Osborne gave me with things from Danny? Do you know where it is?" Her father scratched his head and muttered to himself.

"I have to try to remember where I put it." Then, walking towards the back room where stuff was stored, he added, " I don't know why you and your sisters, all of you with your own homes, don't take your stuff. One of these days I'm going to throw all this stuff out and turn this room into a gentleman's sitting room. Maybe with your training you could take this on as a side project." Immediately the idea took shape inside her head and she followed at her father's heels.

"Daddy, that's a great idea, and I won't even charge you."

"Well that is so good of you my child, seeing that all the money I earned I spent on yours and your sisters' education."

Lynette loved the easy bantering that she always shared with her father. Two hours later, having plowed through many boxes, sneezed from all the dust, with dirty hands, they emerged with her precious shoe box, that had been taped shut. She found a cloth and wiped it clean, but decided against opening until she got to her home. She wanted to do this in private, to delve into her childhood and relive a friendship that she had been mourning for more than half her life.

* * *

They all knew that the results would be appearing and she had not been able to sleep, well she had tossed and had stayed awake all week, but had not told anyone except Danny.

"What if I don't pass Danny?" she had clutched his arm, both of them sweaty from trying to out-run each other.

"You worry too much, man. You will pass," he had assured her wiping the bridge of his nose, beaded with perspiration, with the back of his hand.

"But what if I don't?" she has persisted, her stomach in knots.

"You have another chance to take it again."

They had been quiet for a while and she had pondered that possibility—failing and then having to retake it next year.

"But Danny imagine the shame of it. Is why they must print your name in the Gleaner? They just don't have any respect for us children, how we feel, and that if we don't pass everyone knows and both adults and children say how we dunce." She had looked at Danny then, and he had a far away look in his eyes, and she was angry because she thought he wasn't listening to her and that he wasn't worried about failing. She had shouted. "You not even listening to me. You don't care if I pass or not."

"Net-Net," he said, "you not dunce at all, and whether you pass or not you will always be my best friend." And he had gotten up from under the tree where they had been slumped down and run off, ran so fast she couldn't catch up with him.

Was that a dream? When had that scene occurred?

* * *

Lynette took the shoebox into the room and was instantly flooded with memories which made her feel ashamed and stopped her mid-track. She could not open the shoebox. She had been so worried about herself the night before the results were announced that she hadn't remembered that he had taken the exams the year before and failed. She wracked her brain, trying to remember if they ever talked about him failing the first time and how he felt. They never did, but she remembered now that a week before the results he had given her a poem that he wrote that was entitled, "Failing."

She tried to remember one of the lines as he had read it to her three times before he gave it to her. In fact he had memorized it, and had her close her eyes while he recited it; then he told her to create a drawing based on what she'd imagined. That had been the first time he had asked her to draw a picture. Usually he made up stories based on her drawings; but that time the roles were reversed. She got quiet and forced herself to visualize the poem.

Failing

by Danny McFarlin

Some might call me a loser

But I see myself as a cruiser

Some will say what a dunce you are

But I will affirm I am as smart as you are

Do not label or belittle me

I can whittle and sometimes am brittle

I am not a failure

I am an avid learner.

Lynette pulled her feet on the base of the chair, wrapped her arms around her knees, and put the shoebox on the ground, unopened. Friendship was what was missing in her life, and she believed she was ready to redress this.

Her mind traveled to another time when she spent a weekend with Danny's family in Lucea where his grandmother lived. A river ran through the land, and the morning after they had arrived, she and Danny had gotten up early and walked the almost mile to get to the river, then they undressed, except for underwear, and skipped into the cold water and traveled far. They met some older boys who were catching cray-fish and who showed them how, and allowed them to trail after them. The boys had an extra old paint can, which they gave to them, and she and Danny filled it, the cray-fish were so abundant. The sun was well overhead when they waded back, tired and very hungry, neither bothering to put back on their clothes. Weary but elated they had arrived back in the yard holding the paint can between them as a prize.

"But Lawd, look at you, look at you! Where oonuh be all this time? What would I tell your mother? And why you naked? Lawd look on my trial and tribulation!" Danny's mother, Aunt Nicey, ran up to them screaming. Aunt Nicey pulled the paint can from their hands, spilling some of the cray-fish. She reached out and pulled Danny's ear, "I will let your father deal with you." And she marched Lynette into the house, scrubbed her from head to foot, and told her,

"You is a big girl now. You can't be walking all over the place naked like you is a wild little boy."

"But Danny is naked too and we …"

"You back-chatting me," Aunty Nicey interrupted her, holding her face firmly between her hands so she could see her eyes. She knew those eyes. Had seen them on her mother's face and it meant clamp your mouth shut, I am not interested in hearing anything you have to say. All you need to do is listen. She lowered her eyes and bowed her head. Aunt Nicey continued.

"I want you to hear me. I not saying anything your own mother wouldn't say, and she is never going to hear about this; but you are a big girl now, almost nine—and big girls don't run around the place half naked with boys."

Lynette had been hearing this talk from her mother and others and hated it; hated becoming a big girl, hated how being a big girl meant she wouldn't have any fun anymore, but had to stay inside and read like her stuck up older sisters, and learn to bake, and worry about what clothes you were going to wear or who liked you. She vowed she would never, ever become a big girl, no matter what Aunty Nicey or her mother said. She loved being a tomboy, as she was often called, and Danny would always be her friend and they would always run-off and go on adventures.

She had spent the remainder of the day picking peas with Aunty Nicey and Granny and then shelling the peas on a low bench in the back yard. Then she helped them to make grater-cakes, grating the dried coconut, boiling the molasses and brown sugar with ginger and spices, and mixing in the coconut flakes. Every so often she would be distracted when she heard Danny and his boy cousins, shouting in glee, and then she would kiss her teeth, softly enough that Aunty Nicey wouldn't have reason to tell her mother that she was being impertinent and disrespectful, which would certainly earn her punishment—probably another whole day of sitting in the house and reading, or being assigned to the kitchen with their helper to learn to bake or something else useless. For she was never, ever, ever going to be a lady with a house, when there were so many great things outside to do and discover, like catching butterflies, and poking wasps nest then trying to outrun the angry insects to avoid being stung (but getting stung anyway and swelling up and rubbing guava leaf on the sting). Or stripping the leaves form the coconut bough and using it as a string to catch lizards by their tails. Or shooting birds with sling shots. And making kites from old newspaper, with pieces of sticks and scraps of cloth from old clothes for the tail. Or lying flat on your

79

stomach, not caring about the dirt, closing one eye, getting a good grip of the marble in your hand and using your thumb to flick it and knock your opponent's marble out of the ring, winning the coveted tiger-eye marble.

Sitting home and baking could not compare to any of these things, but Lynette sucked in her frustration and dutifully did as instructed by Aunt Nicey and hating Danny for not coming to rescue her or at the least keep her company,

Not even on the drive back home to Kingston did Aunty Nicey let her out of her sight, and she was forced to sit squashed in between her and Uncle Osborne, and so bored with their adult conversation she had fallen asleep. When they got home the adults visited for a little while, her parents being gifted some of the cray-fish; and as she was about to burst out that she and Danny caught them Aunty Nicey gave her such a look that she clamped her hand over her mouth and pulled Danny outside.

He whispered that his father had given him two slaps across his leg and told him he was to watch out for her as she would soon be a little lady. Right, she said, rolling her eyes, and they ran off to see if they could find any peenewales, fireflies.

* * *

Lynette did not go through the shoe box that night or for the remainder of the weekend. She would take it home and unveil it then, which she did eventually; but she worked late all week and found that one thing or the other demanded her time, so she never got to the box.

Then the following Sunday, while reading the Literary Section of The Observer, she saw his name, in bold print, Danny McFarlin, author of "Unexpected," a story about a man whose wife died suddenly from an illness that, if it had been diagnosed in time, might not have killed her. She read the story twice, enjoying it more thoroughly the second time, although she felt she wanted to know more about the character's wife and their relationship prior to her death. However, the pace and reflective nature of the story had a strong emotional appeal and it reminded her of Aunty Nicey, and what she remembered overhearing her parents whisper about her sudden death from a cancer that had gone undetected for too long.

The one-sentence credit said he was a cartographer, with a short-story collection entitled "Love's Promise" scheduled for release next month.

She jumped up and down on the veranda, ran down the steps and danced under the sun. If she could magically make him appear, she would; and they would go hiking or wading over rocks, or snorkeling—she wondered if he snorkeled or had learned to dive like she had. They could go snorkeling. "Danny! Danny! How

I have missed you!" she spoke his name aloud. Her elderly neighbor who was next door watering her garden saw her and inquired, "You feelin okay, baby. Sounds like you have had some news."

Lynette really liked her elderly neighbors who watched out for her, and who knew everything, including the names and short biographies of anyone who passed on the street on any given day. They were always giving her fruits from their fruit trees; and food, when they cooked too much, seeing that she was alone, with no company, and not cooking as they didn't smell any food wafting from her house. They also hoped that since she was skinny and could use a little weight on her body so maybe a man's eyes could see her better, she would take the food they offered and eat it, which she always did, and thanked them profusely.

"Hello Mrs. Thompson," Lynette now said walking closer to the fence that separated their houses. "How is Mr. Thompson?"

"So-so my dear, so-so. We switching up today. I doing the yard and he's in the kitchen trying to fix the faucet. I know I will have to call the plumber on Monday, but I let him fiddle around. A man needs to feel useful." And she laughed a girly laugh and winked conspiratorially at Lynette. Greetings dispensed with, Mrs. Thompson cleared her throat, and spoke softly. "Ah don't mean to get in your business, but it sounds to me like you had some news that sent you dancing off your veranda all the way to the yard in your barefoot."

At close to eighty, Mrs. Thompson didn't miss a thing.

"I just finishing reading a story by a childhood friend whom I haven't seen in eighteen years. He was my best friend." She beamed and heard the joy in her own voice, and felt it throughout her body.

"Huhum, huhum." Mrs. Thompson said throatily, observing Lynette keenly, one hand holding and aiming the hose on the flowers, and the other hand caressing her chin. "So you have writer man friend. Where him be? How comes he don't come visit. You should invite him over and I will cook him a sweet pot of stew chicken. You always say you love me brown stew chicken."

Lynette laughed and thanked her neighbor. "I don't know where he is or I would invite him over."

"Well you must find him. Mr. Thompson's brother was inspector of Police in Montego Bay. He can find anyone you want. What's his name?"

Same time Lynette heard her phone ringing and dashed off, shouting over her shoulder, "Thanks Mrs. Thompson! I will let you know if I need help."

She ran into the living room and grabbed the phone after the sixth ring. "Hallo, hallo," she said breathily.

"Net, what you doing you breathing so hard?" Her mother's no-nonsense voice penetrated her ear.

"I was outside talking to Mrs. Thompson when I heard the phone ring, and ran to answer it."

"How is she? How are they doing? Make sure to tell her hello for me, and thank them for looking out for you. Your father and I don't worry so much you living all the way there without so much as a dog to protect you. Thank God for the Thompson's. And I am so glad she shares a little food with you every once in a while. Nothing wrong with being slim, but maga not going to win a beauty contest or husband." Lynette smiled; her mother was relentless.

"Did you get The Observer?"

"I was reading the Observer..."

Their words collided and they paused and laughed. Her mother had read Danny's story too, and read it to her father, and her father had already made some calls to friends who worked at the Observer to see if they could locate Danny and find out if he was back on the island.

"Imagine that," her mother sighed. "Little Danny, a writer. Remember that poem he wrote? 'I am not a failure/ I am an avid learner.' Pity his mother is not alive to see how he proved everyone wrong. Little Danny! You two were like peas in a pod; nothing could separate you too."

"But something did, Mummy! The Common Entrance! And I never even got to say goodbye."

"I know you been pining for him all this time, but you have to make peace with the past. Maybe now that you know he is successful you can put the past to rest. You never failed Danny, just our archaic system."

Lynette nodded her head although her mother could not see her. Both were silent. No matter what one said, Lynette reflected, the past is an invisible thread that sticks to one's clothes. As if reading her mind, and wanting to shove her forcefully into the present her mother asked, a question she had not broached in almost three months.

"So, you seeing anyone?"

Lynette could not help but smile at her mother's more diplomatic approach and decided to humor her.

"Seeing anyone...Huhum...I am seeing lots of folks, but no one I am interested in seeing more than anyone else."

"You can go on teasing your poor mother, getting up there in age. I only want you to have someone so you not alone in your old age. Is what you really waiting on, looking thirty in the face? While you pick-picking, everyone else grabbing and before you know it, not a man worth having will be left for you to marry."

She hadn't had a relationship in over three year. Affairs, yes, but nothing that made her body shiver like a feather being trailed across the back of her knee, or her mind aroused as clothes on a line fluttering in the breeze. For the first time she realized and was willing to admit, at least to herself, that she wanted someone special in her life; but she would not confess that today to her mother.

"Mommy, I am okay being by myself, really. Besides these are different times."

"So you say, but different or not, it is a basic human need to want someone else. That's all I am going to say on that." Her mother paused, but Lynette imagined her thinking even through the phone. When she began speaking again, her words were spaced and carefully enunciated. "I want you to know your father and I love you, and we don't care who you end up with, man… or… woman. We just want you to be happy."

Lynette burst out laughing, the laughter threatening to choke her. She had to sit down and wipe the tears that lubricated her eyes. Did her parents think she was a lesbian? She found it amusing, especially in light of the fact she had had to practice with one of her own friends how to tell that girl's parents. She remembered sharing this with her mother about a year ago; but didn't think her mother would then assume she, too, was gay—or was somehow using the story about her friend to test the waters.

"Mommy, I am not gay, I just haven't found anyone…"

"Is okay. We don't have to talk about it anymore. Your day will come."

After getting off the phone, Lynette strode to the back veranda, used a butcher-knife to pry open the coconut that she had placed on the table, and drank it greedily, the sweet water dribbling down her chin, wetting her thin cotton shift and trickling down the space between her breasts. Allowing the heat of the day to warm her body, she balanced on the narrow wall that fronted the veranda and allowed her mind to travel forward rather than backwards in time.

What did Danny enjoy doing now that he was a man? Was he short in stature? Was he handsome? Would he like her abstract paintings and nod his head yes when she showed them to him? Would he be as moved by them as he used to be? She realized she wanted his critique, wondered if he would like her Friendship series or think them trite. Where was he? I need to see him to get unstuck.

Sauntering to the front veranda she looked out at the ocean that was many different shades of blues and greens. The day, hot and clear, the wind slight like an old woman fanning herself in church, the crotons rustling, lizards darting. Everything around her was alive and moving; "except me," she thought her sense of longing heightened. For a long time, she stood looking out, but not seeing, until she was again in the avocado tree with Danny—she showing him one of her paintings, and he telling her the story of it and how the colors made him feel. Suddenly she remembered a time, a few weeks before the exam results would be published, he had taken her hand and said, "Me going to be a writer one day. Do you believe me?" Yes, she had replied without a moment hesitation. And then Danny said,

"You want to hear one of my poems?"

She had nodded yes, and he had recited a poem he had written, and had given her a copy, which she read nightly for many months until the words were imprinted on her memory. Now, the words rushed to her head: `in the woods where the birds chirp/like a mother rocking her baby asleep,/ I hear my heart singing to me./ I hear you between the crackle of the breeze. I hear me. I hear us. We are the best of the best/ We are love's promise."

Why had she tried to wipe the memory of Danny out all of these years, to act as if he wasn't the best friend she had ever had, that he had been an important part of her life, that their friendship was as colorful as the vibrant flamboyant petals that came alive and dominated the entire environment from June to September. Now as she allowed her mind free reign she realized she had even broken up with her first "real" boyfriend because of Danny, or rather because her beau was not able to talk about her pictures as Danny used to, in fact had said to her, "I don't think there is any story in all that color." He hadn't known he had sealed his fate with those words, until he called and she refused to even talk to him, and when they passed each other, she walked past as if she didn't know him.

Determined to contain herself after reading Danny's story in the newspaper, she set up her easel, selected a few acrylic colors, gritted her teeth and immersed herself, daubing and painting until her fingers cramped, and the sun, dressed in fiery orange and pink slung slowly on the back of the ocean, before braving a final dive and disappearing—the day gone in an instant. Inside, at the dining table, she spread a mat, got utensils, set out the food Mrs. Thompson had brought over earlier and placed the shoebox to the right above her glass of lime-ginger juice.

She scooped up a forkful and reached for the box, removing the lid, and carefully removing all the contents that she spread on the table before her. Faded and somewhat yellowed was the hand-made book entitled, Love's Promise—the story of two friends. By the time she finished reading the first story, only 2 pages long, she was flooded with tears, sad and joyful at once. Danny had valued their friendship.

Wiping her tears with her arm, she cleared the food from the table, but left the entire contents of the box spread out like a shrine: the bottle of marbles, the two wooden thread reels with each of their names carved on both, the sling shot, the string of fabric that was the tail of one of their kites made from an old shirt of his and her favorite blouse that was stained from guinep and mango and which her mother said was ruined and couldn't be worn anymore, a pencil stub no more than an inch, almost impossible to write with, his little red car from one of his birthdays, a button that she didn't remember from what, but it was white and pearly so must have belonged to one of the many frilly dresses her mother used to insist that she wore, a few poems on loose pieces of paper, and of course the book, which she placed under her arm as she turned off the light and headed for her bedroom.

After brushing her teeth and climbing into bed, as she was placing Danny's book on the bedside table a page fell out from the back. Picking it up, she turned it over, faded over the years, written in pencil, in his neat but small print.

"Dear Net-Net:

"I woke up early this morning, before Daddy and Mommy and went to the gate and got the Gleaner. You will know what day this is, the fateful day, happy for some, but dreaded for others.

"You won't have to worry. I checked your school first, and just like I said, you passed with flying colors. I was so happy when I saw your name, I jumped up and shouted, frightening Timbuktu, who was sleeping with his paws over his eyes on the back step where I was sitting.

"Then I searched for my name, but I didn't find it. I went and washed my eyes and searched again, but still I didn't find it, and I knew in my gut that my name wasn't there and wasn't going to be there.

"Ah feel like me head was going to bust.

"Me shame, me shame so bad me started hollering and wake up the whole house. Me want to get the shame over.

"Me want Daddy to beat me and say how me waste him money for extra lessons and second time and me don't past, the first and only one in the family.

"Me want Mommy to look at me with those mean eyes and tell me she disappointed in me and me should know better, like when

85

you came to Lucea with us and you and I took off and traveled the river, and had such a good time, and we were so proud of ourselves until we got back and you had to stay inside all day, and Mommy said I could not come near or speak to you.

"Me want me brothers to tease me how me is just a little shrimp who love to play with a little girl rather than play cricket with the other boys or kick ball like someone who going to grow up and be a man.

"Me holler because we want all of them to surround me and tell me how me not going to amount to nothing since we just like a little gal and write poetry, and me can't even pass the Common Entrance.

"Me holler so me can get it over with and done, but Mommy just take me in her arms and rock me and Daddy run him hand over him head and spin around; and Cecil, me older brother who always tease me and punch me some times, just kiss him teeth and say is just a stupid exam anyway, but that is what me get from writing poetry and always playing with a girl, and Daddy cuss a bad-word, and me never hear him cuss a bad word ever, and him tell Cecil to get out before him do something him will regret, and all the time me hollering and can't stop, and me tell Mommy just kill me because me want to be dead, and me sorry me bring shame on the family. And same time me start to vomit and vomit until nothing left in me.

"Net-Net, I really wanted to see you, to congratulate you but ah was too shame, and didn't want to bring that shame to you since you and me was friends.

"Ah so glad you pass so you don't have to feel this shame that I feel."

The note ended abruptly.

Lynette's pillow was soaked by the time she'd finished reading it and she fell asleep with soft sobs wracking her body.

Danny stayed on her mind, coming and going freely like a cat, slinking inside for food when it was tired of chasing lizards, or staying gone for days without so much as a meow, distracting her. She called her father who he had no leads, but said for sure Danny was not on island, neither were any of his brothers; and his father had suffered another stroke, was disoriented and his speech was difficult to understand. He said he would keep trying. She languished.

Then, six weeks later, The Observer announced the publication of Love's Promise, a new collection of stories by a promising Jamaican writer who had just returned home to live and work. Immediately she decided that she would drive to Kingston to attend the book launch event, and surely her parents would want to go too. Just as she picked up the phone to dial them, it rang. It was her mother, who was excited and—forgoing the requisite pleasantries—said:

"Lyn-Lyn, Danny has a book! You have to go see him and get his book!" Her words rushed as if they were hot and she had to spit them out to prevent burning her tongue. "Your father and I won't be able to attend the book launch, although I am sure Danny could use the support—and it would be good to see him," her mother added. "Pity, it's the same time as the Sommer's 40th anniversary party, and we surely cannot miss that. Such a pity," her mother ended, with a deep sigh.

Still not allowing Lynette to respond her mother added. "You must make sure to buy a copy for your father and me and have him sign it, and insist that he comes for dinner on Sunday, don't take no. Your sisters and their families will be here, so we will have a little reunion. I think I will invite a few friends that would remember Danny and his family. I am so excited. Danny is vindicated. I am so happy for him, Lyn-Lyn, your old friend. Isn't that wonderful." Her mother paused and she waited not sure it was safe to say anything.

"So can I speak now Mommy? How are you? How is Daddy?"

"So you think it's okay to tease your old mother because I was so excited I forgot my manners. I am fine, as is your father. I sent him to buy a few more papers. I want to send it to friends who knew the McFarlins. Aren't you excited Lynnette? Imagine seeing your best friend after all these years."

"I am excited Mommy, and I am so proud of Danny."

"If only his poor mother, who loved him so, was alive to witness his rise from shame to fame."

"Mommy you are sounding like a poet: shame to fame; it rhymes."

"Maybe I will take up writing in my old age. What do you think?"

They both laughed. Then her mother cleared her throat.

"Lyn-Lyn, I don't want to get in your business." Here it comes. Whatever it was, Lynette was certain her mother had some womanly advice for her, which is how she always prefaced her remarks, 'I don't want to get into your business,' but Lynette knew this only meant her mother was well up into her business; so she braced herself.

"I know you are going to drive up and spend the weekend with us, and I think you should come in early on Friday so you and I can go shopping. I have been wanting to buy you a dress that hugs your body. It will be a change from those loose, one-size-fits-all get ups that you are always wearing so that a man would not know that you have a nice little shape, with curves he can hold. And it really wouldn't hurt for you to put on a little lipstick and one of those beautiful gold chain and earring sets that your father and I saved so hard to buy you, so you could look pretty and like someone's child who is loved.

"And when was the last time you got a manicure and pedicure? I am due one so I will treat you, and when you go to Danny's launch you won't just fade away like those uncomfortable beige chairs in those places, and you know it is mostly women who attend these affairs, and many of them go to seek a husband, and the papers didn't say whether or not Danny was married, and maybe like you he is stuck on the past and seeing you, and you seeing him, you can both finally get on with you life and you could get married and have someone to take care of you when you get old, and maybe even after a child before all your eggs go bad."

Lynette could tell her mother was done, and in that moment her love for her mother overflowed and if they were in the same room she would have hugged and rested her head on her mother's shoulder even though she was a head-length taller than her mother.

"Mommy, I love you too and will be happy for you to buy me a dress, as long as it is the colors of the flamboyant petals." Then she hung up, and gathered up all things that she had left on the table and placed back into the box, including the book that had remained on her nightstand and that she had read from cover to cover, over and over again.

The next week, all the way on the drive to Kingston, her fingers gripped the steering wheel, hands sweated and she had to wipe them on her dress. She arrived at her parents by noon and they ate a simple cabbage casserole her mother prepared; then they left to find her a dress and to get manicures and pedicures. Her mother deliberated over everything, and if others were present she would ask each for their opinion, then assess, looking closely at the stitches, every detail.

They spent an hour in the first boutique, although Lynette said at first glance that she was certain there was nothing there she would like. Still her mother insisted, looking at almost every dress, and debating the color and or style. Luck was on her side at the second boutique, featuring the clothes of a new and local designer that incorporated tropical colors and patterns. She instantly spotted the dress, the exact colors of the flamboyant, one-of-a-kind, tailored to hug the body, a split up the left side to the middle of the thigh, smart and simple. It fit her perfectly, her mother said. The salesperson agreed, as did the other two women that her mother insisted she modeled it for and whose opinion she solicited. The entire purchase took all of 20 minutes, and Lynette forbade her mother to enter another store; so they went directly to the nail shop.

Back at her parents, and in her old room, where she spent time cutting out and pasting items into her various scrap books, Lynette found that sleep eluded her just like the week leading up to the results of the Common Entrance. She tried not to imagine what Danny looked like or how he might have changed, she tried not to run ahead thinking they would resume their friendship as if almost nineteen years hadn't separated them; desperately she tried not to think that they might remember things differently or not have certain memories at all, like she constantly discovered with her sisters. Most of all she told her self repeatedly to have no expectations.

She was glad her parents left for their function before she did. Her fingers itched to paint or draw something. Why had she not thought to bring Danny a painting, something that connected them to the past? She searched through her mother's scrap material but found nothing suitable; her rifle through her father's office yielded a similar result. She walked around the house, like she often did for inspiration. She saw herself as a child, maybe no more than eight years old, running around the house and Danny sitting and watching her, then asking her what she was doing, and she replied, just running, but then she would stop and doodle something and he would come and peer down and make up a story about what he saw. Once she went back inside she walked right to the drawer in the dining room in which she found nice squared paper 5 x 5 and a set of pencils. Her fingers came alive and when she looked up an hour had passed. If she did not hurry she would be late. Dashing out the door, she remembered the bullas that her father had brought at the grocery earlier, having remembered that Danny liked them, and had told her to take to him, and make sure to let Danny know it was from him. She had planned to leave earlier and stop to see if she could find an avocado, even though it was not the season, as she remembered that Danny loved bulla and pear, the Jamaican name for avocado. Her mind ran forward and she wondered if he still liked Jamaican things since he had been away so long. And perhaps he didn't even like these things, she might have been confused or had forgotten, but her father would not forget about Danny liking Bulla.

Just as she turned on the street where the book launch was taking place, there sat a street-vendor selling avocados. On impulse, she screeched to a stop and bought one.

Arriving late to a full room, she had to stand in the back and didn't see Danny until he mounted the podium to read. He was not like she had imagined or even remembered him. His skin was the color of a whole nutmeg intact in its shell, fragrant even from the back of the room. His voice was as confident as an announcer's, and his shoulders were broad although he seemed to be no more than 5' 9". His presence was powerful and alluring and she wondered if others in the room were equally captivated. She noted that the majority of the audience were women in their mid-twenties and a little older, "dressed to kill," or as her mother would say, "ready to snare."

As he read, she closed her eyes and his words traveled over her body, raising goose bumps. She was lost in the sound of his voice, the way his words glided over and prickled her skin; his pauses that caused belly-flips, his pacing that pulled her along to keep pace. After reading, he spoke about the stories, and in response to a question, said his favorite one in the collection was the title story, 'Love's Promise' about two childhood friends, who used to climb trees and draw and read poetry together.

Her body lurched forward and she beamed when he said that. He was talking about her, about them. She felt light-headed and swayed, but luckily, someone sitting on the aisle seat got up and left, so she slumped down in the seat in the back row, a smile bright as Christmas lights warming her face.

Long after he stopped reading and people began talking and moving forward to get him to sign their books, she sat there, with the bulla and avocado in her lap, and the two books she had purchased, one for herself and one for parents. She wanted to stand up and walk towards the front of the room, to the table where he sat, but she could not will her feet to move. People got their books signed and were leaving, except for three women in their late twenties who milled around, every chance they got telling Danny how much they liked his stories. It was clear one woman must have gotten the book in advance and read the stories carefully.

Lynette observed them keenly and snickered. She was certain the Danny she knew and remembered would not be interested in women like those; she was certain they were afraid of lizards and would never lie in the dirt to flick a marble. She still sat as if attached to the chair, trying to get her feet to move her forward. She couldn't will herself to rise, not even after a lilting, female voice called, "last chance to get your book signed." The woman looked towards her, and when she failed to get up, walked up to her and asked,

"Are you okay? Can I help you with anything? I see you have two books. Would you like to get them signed?"

Words would not escape her mouth. She fished in her bag and handed the woman the card that she had made, lines and swirls of color and on which she had printed some of the lines from the first poem he had given her:

"I hear my heart singing to me.

I hear you between the crackle of the breeze.

I hear me.

I hear us.

We are the best of the best.

We are love's promise."

Thrusting the card at the woman, she managed, "Give Danny this for me."

The woman turned from her, but threw a glance over her shoulder to assess Lynette, then scanned the card now held in her hand as she walked purposely towards Danny. The three women where still in the room, now off to the side, closer to the door, waiting as if expecting an invitation. A man stood to the side of the table, getting his book signed. The woman, whom Lynette assumed was the organizer or publicist, waited until Danny shook the man's hand, then handed him the card, with a sideward glance indicating where Lynette sat. She had a direct view of Danny. She saw when he took the card and read it quickly then shouted, "But rawtid! Is you that?" He bellowed, robust laugher spilling as he leapt, chair toppling. "Is really you that?" Stepping quickly away from the falling chair, he strode towards her, words spilling like a busted pipe.

"Is really you Net-Net? You know how many years I imagine this reunion. You know how I prayed you would come, and I could introduce you and tell everyone that all these years, is you, my best-friend, who pass Common Entrance first time and I didn't get to congratulate her because I was so full of my own shame. But is she, you, who kept me writing, hoping that one day, which is today, I would read one of these stories to you and others and you would feel proud of all that we shared."

He was beside her and she stood up and he wrapped her in his arms, and they hugged each other for all that they had shared and all that they never would have. Finally the same woman with the lilting voice, whose name was Monica, said she was sorry to break them up, but she had to lock up.

They separated not even self-conscious about their tear-stained faces.

He held her at arm-distance and, looking her directly in the eye, said "You know how often I think about you, wondering if you're still drawing those complex abstract paintings, wondering how I not so lucky to run into you. Is really you that?" he exclaimed again, his face close to hers, his breath hot, their foreheads connected.

"Danny, is me," was all she could say, with her hands on his shoulders, feeling relieved, feeling finally as if that piece of herself that she had been missing had been reattached. After a long, silence, Monica by now tapping her feet loudly, Danny said to Lynette,

"Congratulations."

"And congratulations to you too on the book." They both smiled. "Daddy send you bulla and I was lucky to find you a pear."

"So we have to find a tree to climb and eat it. You still know how to climb?"

"I bet I can climb better than you even in this dress."

"This I have to see. Let's go find a tree, nuh!"

Laughter erupted from them like the pealing of bells.

Mother Mushet

She was like a white sheet being pulled across the clothesline. The first time I saw her it was just turning dusk and I could have sworn she was a duppy. Then I started to see her almost every evening. Each time she folded in on sheself "like shame-old-lady bush," making her seem smaller than she actually was, her feet always moving like chicken legs escaping the chasing cat. She remained nameless and motherless for a long time. She didn't seem to belong to anyone. No one indicated that they knew anything about her—it was as if she didn't exist. When I inquired about her, blank stares were the only reply. At first I thought I was going crazy, that maybe my anger was nyaming at me,—eating me clean to the bones. Then one day I heard the children teasing her.

"Moda Mushet," they shouted, tossing guinep and tamarind seeds at her, "Mother Mushet, mek yu man jilt yu."

Too shocked to scold them, but also relieved for the confirmation that she did exist, that she had a name, I just stood there and watched as she turned towards the children, stood stoically—maybe even proudly—before erupting, her voice like nails raking over a chalkboard,

"Oonuh little rass a gwane beat oonuh. Just mek me catch yu. Oonuh must behave in school."

Then she charged after them and they fled, legs raising dirt, their voices sailing through the air,

"Help, mad oman a chase we! Help! Moda Mushet ah chase we."

Like a fool I ran after this Mother Mushet as she ran after the children. What a sight it must have been for those looking on. Anyway I didn't catch her. She was faster than I imagined, or maybe I was just slower than I thought.

However, when she turned and saw me behind her, her shriek turned to one of hollow fear and she ran down a lane and disappeared. I didn't spot her again for almost two weeks, no matter how attentively I looked out for her. Again I asked people who she was; but it was as if they had swallowed their tongues. I decided to bide my time. Besides, I was new in the community, not yet three months, fresh from the country—Claredon—and hadn't divulged much about my life so far. I wasn't ready and I suspected neither Mother Mushet nor the community was ready to embrace me.

Image, my Granny who raised me, healthy and strong like lignun vitae branch, just up and died, sitting upright in her rocking chair on the veranda shelling gungo peas for dinner.

It was exactly one month after my mother dropped dead in England, the mother whom I didn't know and didn't even recognize in her coffin. She died sitting on the sofa, watching television, a bowl of flour in her lap that she was kneading to make johnnycakes.

The two of them dead just like that, leaving me all alone with two houses. I was so shocked I couldn't even cry. Even now, three months later, not "a eye-water" leave me eyes. Me put me hands on me head and bawl, but not a sound escaped my throat.

Although I didn't want the house my mother left me, I couldn't stay in Granny's house where I was born and where I spent all my life so I decide to move into the house my mother built, on Princess Lane near the Race Course, intended for when she retired from working in the hospital in England and returned home and settled down.

I hated her can't done. I hated her more than I was afraid of duppy. I hated her so much that when I saw her in the coffin I wanted to punch in her face. I hated her until the saliva in my mouth bubbled and I wanted to spit on her. The damn bitch. Every year she was in England she promised to send for me. Every year. She left me with Granny since me was little-little, just walking, not yet two years old and she never came back and got me. She never even brought me to England to spend the summer with her like she used to promise every year. Not once. She wanted to forget about me. She pretended like I didn't exist. She went to England, married a man and had three more children that she raised. She didn't leave them. She kept them. When I was seven years old she sent the first one, a boy name Everett, to spend summer with Granny and me.

"See yu brother dere; give him a hug, nuh," Granny say to me, but I just look at him, skin the color of sandpaper, then walk off. He wasn't any kin to Granny and me. I didn't play with him, not once the entire summer, and I pinched him when Granny wasn't looking.

Then when I was ten years old she sent that same boy and a little girl that went by the name Rachel, who look just like Everett, for the summer. For the first time I had to share my bed. Every night I kicked them and told them to go back to England to their Mum. The last time she sent them I was thirteen; all three of them, Everett, Rachel and Charlene. I fought them, cut up all their clothes and all the clothes she sent me, and chopped off the girls' hair clean, leaving only patches. I told Granny that if they came back to stay with us, I was going to run away and she would never ever find me. Bitch. The woman who born me, but was never a mother. She never sent them again, my so-called siblings, and all the pictures she sent of them and herself I tore up and burned, except the ones that Granny hid. My life was just Granny and me, and school and sometimes church.

I passed six O levels, but I didn't know what I wanted to do. Granny said I should continue and try for A levels. I passed Biology, English and Math. Granny said I should apply to university and become a nurse like my mama. But I would never be anything like her so I refused. I got a job in an office, but I didn't like it. I worked for six months then I quit.

Next I got a job in a bank because the branch manager went to our church. He and Granny were friends and he knew I was bright. I trained to be a teller and that was okay, counting money. I did my work and without much effort got promoted. Besides work, I was the choir assistant at church, and I visited the sick. I stayed clear of boys like Granny warned, because she said that was what ruined my mother, why she had to leave me and go to England to make her way.

I wasn't going to become like that woman and I wasn't going to have a child and leave her, even with someone as sweet and kind as Granny.

So my life just going, the same, day after day. The next thing I know I turn twenty years old, "almost big woman" Granny said, and I didn't know where I was going with my life.

One evening I came home from work Granny said,

"Yu mama call. She says she well want to see yu. She say she mail yu a ticket to come see her and your brother and sisters in England."

I look at Granny like she was mad, but I don't say anything. A week later, two tickets arrived, one for Granny and one for me. Granny says,

"Child, me not flying in no iron bird. If de good Lord did want me to fly, him would give me wings. But you go. Go and see yu mama, ah beg yu please."

I didn't agree right away, but finally I decided to go—not to see her, but to see the England that we learn so much about in school. I figured I would go and see the blasted queen who used to rule us, and Buckingham Palace, that Granny say is "tief money from our sugar and banana" England used to build it, and Big Ben, and the Museum that full of all the stuff them steal from Africa. Pastor Brown agrees with Granny, and he should know, he visited England plenty times because he has a son and a daughter who live there. So Granny called her—that woman who is suppose to be my mother—and told her that I was coming.

I took time off from work, running around to get pictures for passport and visa and all kinds of things I needed to go and see this woman who was my mama, even though I didn't know her because she left me from I was little-little, and she never ever sent for me, until now that I am a big woman, twenty years old and don't need her anymore.

Finally the day to leave arrived and I was at the airport, assuring Granny that I was coming back, and that I was not going to stay in England and leave her alone in Jamaica, like that woman who is suppose to be my mother; or her other son in Canada, my uncle Lenford, that I did love because he lived with Granny and me until I was ten, and he used to give me piggy back rides, and also used to say, "Who is dark and pretty like the sky filled with stars?"

Uncle Lenford also used to hug Granny around the waist and dance with her and kiss her on the cheeks. But he also left to make a better life, and we didn't see him for five years. Then he came and visited us and he sent for me to spend Christmas with he and his wife and children, but Granny didn't go with me because she wasn't going to fly. And every time Uncle Lenford came to visit Granny and me, he asked me if I wanted to come and live with him and his family and go to college, but I don't want to leave Granny so I always said no.

And Granny other son, my bad-stick uncle Donald, who the woman Granny says is my mama helped to get up to England, and he get in with bad company and was going to be sent to jail, but escaped. The last we heard he was in Germany or somewhere in Europe or who knows because neither Uncle Lenford nor Granny and I have heard from him for over six years now and for all we know he's dead. Granny said he wasn't or she would know, her body would tell her. And although I don't quite know how her body would tell her, she did seem to know everything else, so if she said she would know, I believed her.

So there I was at the airport and Granny on my mind—how she raised all these children to leave her, and I can't help but wonder why it is Jamaica can't keep her children. Seemed like Granny read my mind and said,

"Jamaica just like Africa child, just like Africa. We lose all de strong and lovely ones; but yu and me will keep on."

I told Granny that we will because I was never leaving; I was going for three weeks, and then I would be back. And so we hugged and I got on the plane loaded with all kind of food stuff that I was sure that woman who was my mother didn't even remember about or want.

Bitch. She was so bad-minded she couldn't even wait to die until after I arrived and allow me to tell her a piece of my mind. I didn't even mind the long plane ride because almost the entire journey I was going over in my head just what I was going to say to her.

Everett, who I didn't recognize, met me at the airport, and I didn't understand a word him chat. He hugged me and said, "Welcome Sis," and I was thinking to myself, I don't care what anyone said; he and I weren't related. The entire drive from the airport, Everett talking a storm and I just nodded my head, looking to see what I could in the dark, dreary night. Then I heard him say clearly,

"Mum's really excited, you know mate; she's been planning for this day. Cooking lots of food and even inviting friends over to meet her Jamaican daughter."

Same time I kissed my teeth and looked out the window. The nerve of this woman who left me and forgot about me. But I was ready for her. I was going to trace her out real good.

After almost an hour driving we arrived and just as we parked an ambulance pulled off. Everett got out the car and asked a man who stood by the gate,

"What's up mate? Someone sick or something?"

I was standing by the car so I didn't hear what the man replied. He patted Everett on the back, and the next thing I knew Everett was screaming and running up the stairs, and there were lots of people and crying. Then Everett came down and got in the car and raced off without even taking out my bags and I was left there standing, not sure what was going on, until that same man who had patted Everett on the back came and introduced himself as Mr. Hendricks, the neighbor and a fellow Jamaican.

He took me inside his house and gave me tea, then told me that my mother had died watching telly, while waiting for me to come from the airport.

The saliva in my mouth scaled my tongue and I felt as if my stomach would explode. Bitch! Imagine I came all the way from Jamaica to see her, after eighteen years, and she couldn't even wait until I got there and gave her a piece of my mind before dying.

If I had a knife I would have cut up her body. I would have salted it. I would beat it to pulp. Bitch!

They buried her five days after I arrived. Uncle Lenford came from Canada, but Granny still refused to come.

I stayed with Mr. Hendricks and his wife the entire time. I didn't step into her house, not even the day of the funeral when everyone was over there eating. I only went to the funeral because Uncle Lenford begged me and came and got me. He led me down the aisle of the church to see her in the coffin, but I didn't know who I was looking at and just kissed my teeth. Bitch! I said under my breath.

Uncle Lenford heard and whispered in my ears, "Who dark and pretty like the sky filled with stars?" I didn't feel pretty and I didn't smile and he didn't tickle my sides. The day after they buried her, the woman who was my mama, Uncle Lenford came and took me to see Big Ben and the Museum, four floors filled with African art. He and I agreed that England well thief bad; they weren't satisfied with stealing the people, they also stole the artifacts.

After that all I wanted was to go back home to Jamaica and Granny. I spoke to Granny on the phone and she cried and told me to hurry back and not let England thief me too like it stole her only daughter. I promised her that I would.

The following day Mr. Hendricks took me to see Buckingham Palace because he said I couldn't come all the way to England and not see where the queen lived. We watched the changing of the guards. As I stood there, wrapped in Mrs. Hendricks' sweater, looking at shiny, clean Buckingham Palace, I said to Mr. Hendricks,

"How comes England ruled us for so long and shipped out plenty sugar to sweeten their tea and banana to give them iron to withstand the cold and they never used any of our money or our labor to build something as grand as Buckingham Palace in Jamaica?"

He responded, "That's imperialism my child; that's imperialism."

I felt in love with Mr. Hendricks in that moment, and wished he was my father because I never ever met my father. Granny said he left on a banana boat heading for England after he got my mother pregnant, and they never heard from him again.

Everett, Rachel, and Charlene, my so-called brother and sisters tried to talk to me, but I didn't have anything to say to them. They belonged to England and to her. She raised and kept them. I didn't want to know them. They didn't look or talk like me.

The day before I left, they came and said our mother left a will, and that the house she built in Jamaica that she was planning to live in after she retired, she left for me. I told them I didn't want it, I didn't want nothing from her, that she was a bitch. They started to cry and said how she loved me and kept a picture of me on her bed-side table, and always talked about me and told them her Jamaican daughter was such a good child. I just cut my eyes and told them that talk was cheap. I didn't want to hear their stories of her.

Mr. Hendricks drove me to the airport. He said he and my mama were good friends, and that she always talked about me. He could tell that I didn't want to hear about her, so he shut up and I loved him even more. He hugged me before I went to board the plane and told me that when he and Mrs. Hendricks came to Jamaica next year to live for good after thirty years in England, he would come and visit Granny and me. I promised him we would welcome them.

Granny met me at the airport and I almost didn't recognize her. Her hair had turned completely white, when, before I left, she only had a few streaks of gray;

and she was nothing but skin and bones, mawga like a dog without a home. She must have lost twenty pounds in just three weeks. My heart broke upon seeing Granny and I just held her tight and wouldn't let go, despite people pushing us out the way, begging excuse.

Granny didn't eat much that evening, just looked at me and kept saying over and over,

"Yu come back, England don't thief yu too."

I stayed home with Granny another week before I returned to work. I made her soup and watched to make sure she drank it. We sat on the veranda and swapped stories like when I was a little girl, before we got television. I hugged her around the waist and danced with her like Uncle Lenford used to do. I telephoned Uncle Lenford and begged him to come home and dance with Granny. He promised that he would come as soon as he could get time off.

I took Granny to the doctor although she didn't want to go. I insisted that they do tests but everything come back normal. The doctor insisted that she was physically healthy. I kissed my teeth. What did he know? Pastor Brown visited Granny and told me the problem was that her heart was broken. Miss Evelyn across the street stayed with her while I worked, and her friends, Miss. Esmee, Sister Dorothy, and Aunty Joyce looked in on her from time-to-time.

Then Tuesday before I went to work she told me that she had a taste for gungo peas and that she was going to shell some and make a big pot of gungo rice and peas that would last the rest of the week. As I left for work, Granny sat down on the veranda with the basin in her lap, and she seemed almost like her old self again. I kissed her on the cheek, and she reached for my hand and said,

"Me ears was ringin all last night." She paused as if to catch her breath, then she continued, "Me think me gwane hear bad news today. Me body hasn't been feeling well now for a long time, and me mind on Donald."

My heart dropped down to my stomach and I asked Granny if she wanted me to stay with her and not go to work; she said no. I was feeling awful because I dreamed about Uncle Donald last night and I never dreamed about him before. I hadn't even thought about him, except at mama's funeral when Uncle Lenford spoke of him, saying he had tried to contact him, but didn't know how, and hoped he was alright.

So I went to work, but got really sick so left at noon. When I got home, even before I opened the gate, I could tell that something was wrong with Granny, just by the way she sat stiffly in her rocking chair, a blue airmail letter clutched in her hand. She died before we reached the hospital, even though I begged her to live for me.

They said she had a stroke. The letter she clutched in her hand was from a Stewart Forbes, who said he just found her address, and that he was a friend of Uncle Donald, and he regretted to have to inform her that her son died two weeks ago, in Birmingham, England where he had been hiding out, and that he had been buried, without name or family in the poor-man's plot.

I was too sad and weak to cry. First my mama, who left me all those years, then Uncle Donald, and now Granny.

I vowed never to set foot in England again. It took all that Granny and I loved and wanted. Uncle Lenford and his family came, and he bawled so hard they had to carry him from the grave. My eyes remained dry like an old coconut. Everett came from England too, talking about she was his Granny too. I jumped on him and scratched up his face. They had to pull me off of him. I told him to go back to England, talking like he had something hot in his mouth, and don't try to steal my Granny too. Uncle Lenford begged me to come to Canada with him and his family, but I told him what Granny say,

"If is not England thief we, is Canada or America. Dem keep thiefin the best of we. Who gwane stay to look after little Jamaica?"

I told Uncle Lenford that I was going to stay; I wasn't going anywhere. I was here for better or worse.

After the funeral and everyone left I couldn't sleep. As soon as I fall asleep I would wake up looking for Granny. Pastor Brown watched me losing weight, when I was thin already, and he suggested that I go to Kingston and stay for a little while. That's how I ended up in the bitch's house.

But now I like it so I am going to stay. Uncle Lenford talked about coming home soon and I reminded him that he shouldn't wait until he retired or he might be coming home in a coffin and I was not going to his funeral. He said he heard me, and I hoped he really did.

So I am planting a garden at the house my mother built and died and left me.

* * *

Because I am outside working in the yard all the time I keep watch for Mother Mushet, now that I know her name. I feel close to her. Both of us have been left. She always passes by my house in the evening, wearing all white that's gone beige with age and dirt.

Where does she hole up all day? I wonder. Where is she going when she passes by my gate at nights? Is she angry about being jilted? Did a man really leave her at the altar? What does she carry in her shoulder bag, slung across her breast? Sometimes I find myself chanting her name as I work in the garden,

"Mother Mushet, Mother Mushet, who mess with you? Mother Mushet, Mother Mushet, do you need a friend?"

I know I need a friend. Granny was my only friend. We talked about everything, even mama and why she didn't send for me.

Early one morning, about six a.m., just as I went outside I saw Mother Musket rushing past my gate, in the opposite direction than she took in the evenings. Without thinking, I followed her, leaving the door open for thieves to enter and walk off with what they wanted. I had to jog to keep up with her, yet stay far enough behind so she wouldn't see me. She led me through several alleys, until I was completely lost. Then finally we came to a tenement yard, and she opened the gate, stepped in and was greeted by a large woman with her hair plaited in four thick braids, with one child on her bosom and another hanging onto her leg.

"Morning Teacha," the woman said smiling at Mother Mushet. "Me comin just now wid yu breakfast."

I stood at the half-opened gate, my breath held in, and watched the woman, whom the children had chanted, "Moda Mushet, Moda Mushet, is who jilt yu?" transform from a crabby homeless woman to a teacher. I doubt if many of the children knew what jilt meant or had stopped to think that Mother Mushet's pain, whatever it was, should not be used as arsenal with which to tease her. I watched as Mother Musket straightened her back, climbed up the three steps leading to the narrow veranda and sat down, hands folded in her lap. And in a voice, both proper and sweet, she turned to the woman and said,

"Miss Sadie, I am pleased to have my breakfast now, thank you."

"Coming Teacha, coming. But in the meantime go wash yu hand."

Although Mother Mushet rose up immediately, she said,

"Miss Sadie, how many times am I to correct you on your grammar. It is not yu hand, but rather your hand. I will wash my hands and you will wash yours." Then Mother Mushet walked over to the cistern, soaped and lathered her hands, and kept rubbing them together. Then as if knowing the routine, Miss Sadie who was still indoors hollered,

"Rinse and dry them now Teacha, dem clean, rinse and dry them and tun off de pipe."

Mother Mushet did as she was told, then climbed back upon the narrow veranda and sat where the table was set for her. Not being able to suppress my curiosity anymore, I opened the gate and stepped through. Immediately Mother Mushet started to shriek and holler.

"Mama is headmaster come to ruin me."

At first I looked about, unaware she was referring to me. The woman she called Miss Sadie ran out, brandishing a broom in her hand. Only seeing me, she stopped short.

"Is who yu?" she said glancing at Mother Mushet who was now pressed up against the wall, sheltering her face and cowering. She didn't give me a chance to answer. She dropped the broom, and strode over to where Mother Mushet was crumpled. Gently, she pulled her from the wall, nestled Mother Mushet's head on her shoulder, and spoke to her as if speaking to a baby.

"Hush Mama's Darling. Me gwane beat de headmasta fah yu."

And in that same tender manner, she led Mother Mushet through the opened door just off the veranda.

I sat on the step and waited, more curious than ever. Why did Miss Sadie call Mother Mushet "Teacher," and why would the headmaster want to ruin her? I could hear Miss Sadie humming to Mother Mushet, whose whimpering gradually stopped. After a while, Miss Sadie reappeared, closing the door softly behind her.

"Lady, could yu please tell me what business yu have here?"

I didn't know what to say, so I asked "What is your relationship to teacher?"

"Her moda send yu?" Miss Sadie quizzed.

Realizing that this approach would not get me anywhere, I introduced myself to Miss Sadie, told her where I lived, and that often I saw Mother Mushet, as the children and people in the neighborhood call her, pass by my gate.

It was at that point that one of Miss Sadie's children started to cry and she told me to follow her. I tagged behind while she fed both children, then tended to her mother who was partially paralyzed from a stroke. Then, while I sat in the kitchen and watched from the window, she coaxed Mother Mushet back onto the veranda, and fed her also.

I spent the greater part of the day with Miss Sadie, who I learned had been taking care of Mother Mushet for the last five years after her own mother got a stroke. Her mother had worked with Mother Mushet's family. Now she cared for Mother Mushet, taking her to live with them when she got worse and her parents, especially her father, were ashamed and wanted to hide her away. Although Mother Mushet's family did not come to visit her, they sent money for her room and board. It was close to twenty years it had been like that.

Miss Sadie didn't know the entire story, and said I best hear it from her own mother, when she was up to talking again. I promised to come by daily, to visit and help her care for her children, her mother, and Mother Mushet, whom I was eager to learn more about.

It took more than three weeks for Mother Mushet to get used to me, and not cower and shriek when I entered the yard where she lived. One morning as I entered, she was having her breakfast; she stopped, looked at me, and to my surprised demanded:

"Young lady, just where do you think you are going late for school?"

I faltered. I stared at Mother Mushet, not sure exactly what to say.

"So the cat has got your tongue. Well what is your name, and speak up?"

I fell into the role.

"Gemmeth Grant, Miss."

"Miss Grant, do you know the consequence of being late? No need to answer. You will have to do extra work. Take your seat and I will get to you soon."

I sat on the steps and caught Miss Sadie chuckling from the kitchen. She already told me how Mother Mushet had taught both her and her mother to read and write, and that Mother Mushet was both a good and strict teacher. I had by then seen her teaching Miss Sadie and two other women who lived on the street who had not had the opportunity to get an education when they were young. But now I was the student. After she finished her breakfast, Mother Mushet stood above me on the step where I sat and began her lecture.

"What we need more than anything else in this lovely little island of ours is education. With a good education, we can stand up to anyone; even the queen. Today Miss Grant, I expect you to write a composition on the merits of a good education. You must write this in your best cursive and correct grammar. Begin."

And from the canvas bags that she always had slung over her shoulder she pulled out a smudged and dog-eared exercise book and handed it to me, with a pencil so short there wasn't enough for my fingers to grasp. Surprised I took the book, wondering where Mother Mushet got it. She tapped my shoulder and urged,

"Begin! Begin at once. Don't dillydally."

I glanced at her shadow looming over me, bent my head, and pretended to write.

Although I had not intended it, I took the exercise book home with me, only seeing it after I put down on the kitchen counter the newspaper and fruits I had bought. It fell on the floor when I reached for the newspaper, and when I bent to pick it up, I saw her name, written in small neat cursive, Marcia Elizabeth Hamilton. Miss Sadie had told me that was her name.

I opened the first page, my hands trembling, and the heading read, "The Importance of Being a Lady by Miss Marcia Elizabeth Hamilton." Could this really be Mother Mushet's exercise book? It certainly looked old enough. It was written in fountain pen, and some of the words on the first page were smeared. However, I was able to read most of the 8-page essay, standing there in my kitchen.

I wasn't surprised by what she had written, but it only intrigued me more; made me more eager to learn more about Mother Mushet, whose mother, like mine, had abandoned her during her greatest period of need.

Daily I visited Miss Sadie to see Mother Mushet, trying to win her trust. When I saw her wandering the streets talking to herself, and the children and even some men teased her, I scolded the children and told the men they should be ashamed of themselves. She never seemed to recognize me when I encountered her on the street, except once, as she trotted by my gate I called to her, "Good morning Miss."

She slowed, turned her head, smiled at me and said, "Enjoy your lunch, Miss Grant." Then she was gone again, her small ankles showing from under an off-white, full length skirt that swished in harmony with her fast-paced stride.

Sadie would not give me an address for Mother Mushet's parents when I asked, but I was determined to find them and give them a piece of my mind. If what Sadie said was true, then Mother Mushet was a trained teacher who had attended Shortwood Teachers' College and taught for six years or more at Tinsenpen Elementary School until she resigned due to her pending marriage. But she never got married.

Apparently, the night before the wedding the intended groom married an English woman who had recently come to the island to teach. Hearing this, my hatred for England intensified, and when Sadie had completed the story, I spat,

"Me hate dem England people. All of them thief, and thief, and thief can't done. Dem thief everything from we—our banana, our sugar, our rum, our bauxite. Dem just born thief."

Sadie had to console me, and more than ever, I strived to win Mother Mushet's trust. After more than five months, Mother Mushet was comfortable around me.

The house that I had acquired from the mother I hated was a corner house and so, to dissuade thieves, the side fence that opened into a narrow street had been erected in concrete and at the top broken bottles had been affixed so that anyone attempting to scale the 7-foot fence would be severely cut. The tall fence also enclosed a lively, erratically planted garden. Whenever I wasn't brooding over my hatred for my mother, or missing my darling grandmother, or going to see Sadie and Mother Mushet, I worked in the garden. I relished how physical labor emptied my mind of rancor, and how thrilled I was when I stepped out on any given morning and saw another flower in bloom.

It was on such a pretty morning, the sun inviting, its rays mild, that I strolled around the garden with mint tea in hand. I heard what I thought at first was whimpering, like a sick dog. Then it turned into ear-piercing shrieking. I looked to see where the sound was coming from and saw the hands sticking through the fence, caught on the jagged edge rimmed with the broken bottles.

"Jezampiece!" I hollered, wondering why anyone would choose to break into my yard in broad daylight, and how they could be so desperate. Then I realized that the person was stuck, and the wild shrieking sent shivers through my body. Something about the voice was recognizable. Then I heard a child's voice shouting,

"Come look, come look! Moda Mushet a climb de fence."

I rushed and unlocked the gate and ran around to the side of the house, and there I saw Mother Mushet, hoisted on a large trash barrel that generally stood at the corner.

How she had managed to roll it to the side of my house and turn it over to stand on perplexed me, but that she was stuck I could see. By now her shrieks rang through the whole neighborhood, and a few people appeared, clambering out of their houses to see who was being murdered.

My attempt to calm Mother Mushet was to no avail. I then noticed a man standing looking on, so I grabbed hold of him and demanded,

"Go and help her down, please."

"Me not touching that mad woman. She don't like man. She act like every man jilt her."

By now Mother Mushet screams had turned to crying, and the tears ran down her face. I noticed that her clothes were ripped. About fifteen people were gathered. Someone instructed a child,

"Go call Nurse. Tell her Mother Mushet hurt bad."

I remembered that a nurse lived four houses down from me. I barked at the child.

"Run!"

The child took off like fire was under his feet. Another person said,

"Lawd we ave fi help Moda Mushet before she bleed to death on Miss Gem wall."

"Look how she clothes rip up; a bet yu some wicked man try fi do nastiness to her," a woman moving closer to where I stood next to the barrel offered this theory.

I persuaded the first man that I had approached, with another man's help, to try to ease Mother Mushet down. I stood close to the barrel and spoke gently to Mother Mushet.

"Morning Miss. Could you please come down and help me with my work, please Miss Teacher," I begged like a dutiful student.

And everyone gathered, as if rehearsed, said,

"Good morning Teacha. Present fah school Miss."

Mother Mushet turned the side of her face that had been pressed into the wall, and looked out at the crowd and said,

"Good Morning class, you may take your seats."

And this is how the two men were able to get her down from the wall, carefully pulling out her hands despite the jagged pieces of broken bottle stuck in them. Nurse, who was on her way to work, pulled a small bottle of iodine out of her satchel, and someone else brought water. Nurse did as much as she could, but said Mother Mushet needed to go to hospital. While the women soothed her and continued to flatter her as their teacher, I, who had been in my night shift, quickly changed and got my purse. Someone else found a taxi, and with Mother Mushet in the middle between Nurse and me, we sped off to KPH, Kingston Public Hospital.

Even though Nurse worked at the hospital, Mother Mushet could not be seen immediately as they were short of doctors and more serious cases were ahead of ours: two stabbings, one man's leg barely hanging on due to a slip of the machete, another in cardiac arrest, etc.

Nurse gave Mother Mushet medicine for the pain and a tranquilizer, as she was getting agitated in the crowed space, while I continued to refer to her as "Teacher" and talk softly to her in the language of the schoolhouse.

It was after one o'clock in the afternoon before Mother Mushet was finally attended to by a weary doctor, who removed the broken pieces of bottle from her hands, and applied twenty stitches in all. Although reluctant, I insisted that the doctor examine Mother Mushet to see if she had been raped, and while he said he found no sperm or penetration, there was evidence of bruising around the vaginal area to suggest there was an attempt at intercourse. I corrected him and said attempted rape. At which point the weary doctor, ran his hand over his head, sighed, said,

"Listen I been seeing and hearing about Mother Mushet for years now. The problem is—there isn't enough mental care in this blasted island. Bellevue is full, and if you not off you rockers, then they can't keep you. You know how many mad people walking all over this island daily, just like me and you? There are two

106

mad men downtown Parade, who regularly take off their clothes and walk about the place in front of decent women and children, and nobody does anything. Maybe is one of them try to rape Mother Mushet. We'll soon have nothing but an island of mad people, screwing all over the place." He ended disgustedly. Then, called to attend to more urgent cases, he scribbled two prescriptions for Mother Mushet and left in a hurry.

It was three o'clock before I got the medicine and took Mother Mushet home. Nurse spotted us as we were leaving and ran to us. She looked at the prescriptions and nodded approval, but told me to only give Mother Mushet half the dose of sedative prescribed.

Once home, I had to almost carry Mother Mushet inside the house. Since I had two spare bedrooms I decided I would care for her there. I got her into bed, and undressed her. Then I got a basin of water and began to sponge her down.

As I was sponging her, the image of my mother appeared, and just like that I began to cry. At first softly, thinking it was Mother Mushet I was crying for, but by the time I was through with the sponge bath, and dressing her in one of my own night shifts, my body was wracked by grief and I fell on Mother Mushet and cried out,

"Oh Mama I miss you so much. Why you don't come home?" Over and over I cried, until spent, I crept on the bed and snuggled up right there beside Mother Mushet and slept.

I came awake, and feared that when Mother Mushet woke that she might begin to shriek and try to run, finding herself in unfamiliar surroundings. I also wanted to go and see Sadie and demand to know why she hadn't gone to look for Mother Mushet when she didn't show up for breakfast. Sadie often went looking for Mother Mushet at nights if she did not return, and would lock her in the room before she went to bed, and let her out early as Mother Mushet was an earlier riser and banged and raised a racket to be let out for her regular morning walk.

Could the attempted rape have happened early this morning? I shivered at the thought of the wicked, nasty man. As I was preparing dinner, I heard someone calling my name and knocking at the gate at the same time. I rushed out, not wanting the noise to wake Mother Mushet, and I saw Sadie standing there, her eyes puffy.

"Miss Gem, me sorry fi boda yu, but me need yu help. Two days now me deh hospital, Moda had anoda stroke. Me neighbor keep de children dem, but she sey she no see Teacha two days now. A wonder if yu could just look afta de children dem so me can go look fah Teacha. She mus hunger well bad," Sadie spoke in one rush.

I could see that Sadie was sad and tired so I took Jason, the almost three year boy who was slung over her shoulder.

"Come in, come in. Mother Mushet is here sleeping."

Sadie came in, collapsed on the chair with Mae, her fifteen month old daughter, sleeping in nook of her left arm. I could see she was weak with relief. The children looked unkempt, as did she. As I told Sadie what had happened, tears streamed down her face that she hurriedly wiped away with the back of her hand.

"Is me responsible fi look afta Teacha; and look how something bad happen to her eeh. Miss Gem, ah couldn't help it, Lawd knows me couldn't help it. Me beg me neighbor fi watch out fi her, but she have four little ones of her own and mine two. She seh she didn't ave de time or energy fi go look fah Teacha." Sadie paused and looked around. "Me can see her Miss Gem?" she asked.

Sadie laid Mae on the sofa and I took her in to see Mother Mushet.

Initially, Sadie was reluctant to leave her two children with me, not wanting to burden me anymore since I agreed to keep Mother Mushet, but I persuaded her to leave them so that she would have the time to look after her own mother who was still in the hospital.

And that was how I became the unofficial custodian of Mother Mushet. I also cared for Sadie's children for two weeks. Surprisingly, Mother Mushet didn't seem to object. She began calling me Mama the day after the incident, and she did not venture beyond the gate, as I had feared she would. Instead she spent most of her days in the garden, sometimes pulling up the flowers. I threw away her once-white, long sleeved dresses and had a dressmaker sew her new pastel pink, blue, and green dresses that were simple, but short sleeved, and that stopped just above her calf.

Once Sadie's mother was out of the hospital, she came during the day to help me with the housework and to care for Mother Mushet.

One afternoon while the children slept and the three of us sat around the kitchen table, Mother Mushet writing in an exercise book that I had bought for her, Sadie cutting up vegetables to cook for dinner, and I doing the needlepoint that I had recently taken up, without prompting Mother Mushet filled in the details of her story.

"Mama, please forgive me," she tugged at my arm.

She had asked to be forgiven before, and I had always told her she was. The first time she had made such a request, I was taken aback, and didn't think I had the authority to forgive Mother Mushet. This time she cried and begged, dropping her head in my lap, until Sadie, who had been doing something in the kitchen walked into the living-room where we sat and said sternly,

"Teacha, yu Mama fagive yu. Yu Mama fagive yu," and then Sadie had kissed her teeth, cutting her eyes at me before returning to her chores. After that I readily said "I forgive you" to Mother Mushet, each time feeling as if I was also forgiving my own mother. So this time when Mother Mushet asked for forgiveness, I said,

"I forgive you Marcia Elizabeth," without pausing in my needle-point, but Mother Mushet said.

"Mama, I want you to forgive me for everything," and that was when she related how she lost her virginity, two days before her wedding, because her fiancé had begged, pledging his undying love, and said he only wanted a little touch before the marriage. So Mother Mushet had allowed him to touch her breast, and did not resist when his hand traveled under her skirt, and finally gave in completely. Before they had parted that night, sensing her distress, he assured her that it would be their secret, no one need know since he was assured now that she had saved herself only for him. But the morning of what should have been their wedding, he sent a letter addressed to her parents in which he boasted.

Dear Mr. and Mrs. Hamilton:

Sorry I cannot marry your daughter. By the time you get this letter I will be aboard a plane heading for England, where I have always dreamed of going. I will marry an English girl there and get the opportunity to go to university. Tell your daughter sorry, and that I enjoyed having my way with her.

Sincerely,

Derrick

Mother Mushet's father had read the letter, then he had called her and her mother and read the letter to them. After which he had demanded of Mother Mushet, if she had allowed the scoundrel to have his way with her. When, distraught, she was unable to respond, although she was twenty-five years old, her father flogged her mercilessly, told her she was a disgrace and that he was through with her.

Luckily for Mother Mushet, her aunt who was very fond of her, arrived, was apprised of the situation, and secluded Mother Mushet away. From that day Mother Mushet was never the same. For almost two years no one mentioned that she was to have gotten married, even though family and friends frequently whispered that she was jilted, always said with shame and blame, as if it was her actions that precipitated her ex-fiancé's behavior. When she stopped eating, she was force fed, only surviving on cornmeal mush for a long time. This is why the Aunt who was caring for her began calling her Mush-Mush.

Somehow over the years it became Mushet, and when she began venturing out on the streets, railing at men and admonishing children, someone donned her Mother Mushet and the name stuck ever since. When her aunt could no longer care for her, and her father, with his blind stubborn pride, said she could not return home, her mother begged Sadie's mother who had long worked with the family, to care for her for a small compensation. That was almost twenty years ago, and now Mother Mushet was forty-five.

I took Mother Mushet's hand, and looking at her lovingly in the face said,

"I forgive you my darling, Mama forgives you," and then I patted her face. At which point Mother Mushet said.

"I loved him Mama, I loved Derrick, and he said he loved me."

I sucked in air, and willed away my own tears. I felt as if my own mother was standing over my shoulder, waiting to be forgiven, waiting for me to tell her that I loved her too. I closed my eyes, took a deep breath, then clasping Mother Mushet's hands between my own said,

"I know you loved him Marcia, and Derrick loved you too. He loved you even though..." I didn't know what else to say. Mother Mushet reached over and kissed me on the cheek and for the very first time smiled; then she resumed writing in her exercise book.

I could not continue with my needlepoint. I got up and went into the bedroom, locked the door, and repeatedly mumbled, "I love you mama; I love you." I don't know why I was saying that, but I couldn't stop for long time, over and over, "I love you mama; I love you."

After much persuading, Sadie gave me Mother Mushet's parents' address. I dressed carefully to go and see them, with the intention of giving them a piece of my mind, reviling them with all the things I didn't get the opportunity to tell my own mother. However, when I got there and faced the two old people, who looked as if life had driven a truck over them, my heart softened.

"Good afternoon," I began, in a respectful tone. "My name is Gemmeth Grant, and I just want you to know I have been helping Sadie look after your daughter, Marcia."

When I said the name, I saw Mother Mushet's mother's eyes open wide and I heard the father's breath more labored. I waited, wondering if I should say anything else. Finally, the old woman, after folding and unfolding her hands, asked,

"How is Marcia Elizabeth?"

"She is well, but she asks for you."

"Is she married as yet?" the father cut in.

I ignored him.

"Every day she begs for your forgiveness," I addressed Mrs. Hamilton.

"I forgive her long time. It wasn't her fault. I raised her too good, too trusting, and that brute of a man took advantage of her."

My heart raced.

"It would mean the world to Mother… I mean Marcia Elizabeth, if you were to tell her that," I hastened.

"I told her that years ago, but she doesn't hear me; she doesn't hear anything anymore." And with that Mrs. Hamilton clammed up and her eyes glazed over. I sat with them for another fifteen minutes before leaving. Marcia was their only child. Before I left, I wrote my address on a piece of paper and gave it to Mrs. Hamilton. I told her she could visit any time.

I was not at home the day Mrs. Hamilton came to visit her only child, but Sadie related the details, blow by blow. Sadie was combing Mother Mushet's hair, when she heard the knocking at the gate. She went out and there stood Mrs. Hamilton with her cane, standing in front of the taxi that she ordered to wait on her. Sadie welcomed her and opened the gate for her to enter. Mrs. Hamilton refused Sadie's offer to assist her up the steps, managed by herself. She sat down heavily on the veranda, asked for a glass of water, and looked out at the garden.

"This is a nice place, very nice. Marcia Elizabeth always enjoyed the garden." Mrs. Hamilton spoke to no one in particular. After she finished the water, she inquired, "Is Marcia Elizabeth here? Tell her that her mother is here to see her," she said as if she were a regular visitor.

Sadie wasn't sure what to do. Mother Mushet had not seen her mother in over ten years; she wasn't even sure she would recognize her. Moreover, since Mother Mushet had taken to calling me mother, Sadie was doubly unsure, and didn't want to upset her, since she had been calm for the almost four months since the incident.

But Sadie reasoned with herself that, technically, Mrs. Hamilton was her employer and so she couldn't refuse her either. Mother Mushet appeared at the same time ending Sadie's dilemma.

"Teacha, see yu moda dere come to look fah yu; seh hello to her."

Mother Mushet looked at her mother, smiled and said,

"So you are my new student. Well I am Miss Hamilton. You may take a seat." And with that Mother Mushet turned and went back to sit in the living-room, and remained there until her mother, who never budged from her seat on the veranda, left by the same taxi in which she came. Mother Mushet never mentioned the visit, nor did her behavior revert.

I had recently resumed working, having gotten a job at a bank and had gone to the University of the West Indies to inquire about help for Marcia; I no longer called her Mother Mushet, although the community still did. I was confident that with help Mother Mushet could have an almost normal life. She had resumed her walks, although she always came home before dark. The people in the community, especially the women, were more actively looking out for her, and they threatened their children with spanking if they caught them teasing Mother Mushet although a few persisted. Several of the men also helped to look out for Mother Mushet, and they discovered that when they addressed her as Teacher, she did not curse them out or scream that they were liars and the ruiner of good women.

Mother Mushet's slow but steady transformation not only impacted the community but had a profound impact on me. One day I realized that when I thought about my mother, I no longer felt angry. Most times Mother Mushet called me Mama and other times addressed me as Miss Grant, referring to me as her most diligent student. It was in the role of student that my bitterness was finally shattered.

Once as we sat to eat dinner, Mother Mushet looked at me and said,

"Miss Grant, I am very disappointed in you not doing your homework. I expect your composition on my desk by tomorrow morning."

"Sorry Teacher," I replied and continued eating. When we were through, before Mother Mushet got up from the table she said to me,

"And Miss Grant, remember your essay must have details. I want to know the specific things your mother does that causes you to love her."

My mouth dropped open, and I felt as if food was lodged in my throat, constricting my breathing. I remained sitting at the table for some time, and then I pulled myself together and went and washed the dishes.

That night as I prepared for bed, I went into the closet, reached into the back, and pulled out the small chest that belonged to Granny, and in which I knew there was a picture of my mother that Granny saved. I rummaged through the trunk, found the envelope and pulled out a stack of pictures; some of myself at various stages of my life that I couldn't even remember when they were taken. And then I found what I was looking for: the picture of my mother, taken just before she left for England. She is standing by a tree, holding her bicycle in front of her as if she is about to go for a ride. I peered at the picture and, not satisfied with the light in my room, took it out in the living room and stood under the bright light and studied the image closely.

She had the same unwavering eyes and pouty, stubborn mouth and flat forehead as I did. Tears ran down my cheeks as the memories danced alive in my mind, all those letters Mama wrote, telling me how much she both missed and loved me; the three times she wrote and told me she wanted me to come and live with her in England, but I had been determined to stay with Granny. The second time Mama sent my brother and sister, she had sent a ticket for me to return to England with them. I had torn it up and Mama had written, both angry and disappointed that I didn't want to join her, and swore that she was never going to send for me again—and she didn't. But still she wrote and told me how much she loved me, every birthday and Christmas.

All of this I had allowed myself to forget in my anger, all of it. I clutched the picture of Mama to my bosom, and with my hand over my mouth, I sobbed for all the mean things I said that I would never be able to take back—but mostly for what I would never be able to recover: my Mama's love.

After I cried out my pain, I went and got a thin blue airmail letter and wrote my brother and sisters, asking for their forgiveness, and inviting them to come and visit me whenever they liked, and ending, "After all, we are sisters and brother, from the same mother, and there is nothing stronger than that bond."

I placed Mama's picture on the side-table, intending to buy a frame for it the following day. I realized then that I had a whole lot to learn about love and forgiveness, and hopefully, Mother Mushet will continue to help show me the way.

Then I remembered that I had a composition to write for Teacher that was due the next day. The theme: Why I loved my mother. I hurriedly went in search of paper.

Soup Bones

"When the soup go ready?" Lynton, tone flat and dry like bammy, inquired as he draped the towel around his waist and headed towards the bathroom.

"By the time you finish, I'll have it on the table. You want me to wash your back?" Mazie asked, desire coursing up her legs. It was three weeks since they last made love. She did not understand this change between them she could not decide whether their relationship was a door wedged open or a door nailed shut. Either way the thought caused her arms to cover with goose bumps. Lynton had stopped coming home directly from work in the last three months, but equally worrying was the way he looked at her, rather did not look at her, and that he never touched or kissed her anymore. Mazie couldn't help but reflect on all those Saturday afternoons they spent basking in each other's arms after they made love and their Sundays at the beach, the first year of their marriage—their love rivaled Poui trees in bloom.

Not getting a response, Mazie, hips swishing exaggeratedly, glided towards Lynton, a smile dancing on her face.

"I still know how to wash your back," she said with a laugh, leaning into him.

Lynton sucked his teeth and quickly stepped around her as if she were one of those homeless men in downtown Parade in desperate need of a shower.

Feeling as if a sudden wind had blown dust blinding her eyes, Mazie tried to shrug off Lynton's rebuff as she headed to the kitchen. The way to a man's heart is through his stomach and Lynton loved her chicken-foot soup, she mused. Yet as she stirred the pot full to the brim with dumplings, chocho, scallion, pumpkin, yellow yam, and chicken legs and neck, sadness draped her face like a curtain shutting out the sun. They had been married for just over two years and Lynton had certainly changed. He hardly made love to her anymore. He no longer called her his Sugar-Bun or took her to the movies or invited her to go for a Sunday evening stroll, after a morning wading in the ocean. Daily he used to bring her a treat from work - a coconut-drop, tamarind ball, gingersnaps. But all of that had stopped a little over three months ago.

Mazie racked her mind, trying to think of what she might have done to contribute to the obvious waning of their passionate love. She has not gained any weight. Daily she cleaned the house, everyone who visited said it was immaculate and welcoming. She kept herself attractive, making sure she was bathed and dressed before Lynton came home, perfumed behind her ears, under her arms, around her navel, behind her knees, all the places he loved to kiss, always with the perfume he had bought her that he said he loved. Her hair and nails were always clean and neat. She knew she was still very attractive for whenever she went to the store or some other public places other men always tried to talk to her. She had stopped telling Lynton this because when she first mentioned it jokingly, he was obviously annoyed and remarked, "You just make sure you don't go out wearing tight or revealing clothes," which wasn't her style anyway. She still cooked him delicious meals daily and set the table with flowers, and it was always ready, except for a few times it was late, but that was the first few months of their marriage, when she was experimenting with different recipes. Besides, he never once complained about her cooking and always smacked his lips and told her she had a sweet hand. They didn't quarrel. She washed and starched his shirts like he liked them. She was always ready for love making and melted at his touch. Is what change she kept asking herself?

The first time Lynton came home late, she had run up to him and told him how worried she was when he didn't come home as usual and they had hugged and laughed about it.

"Is what me do?" Mazie had asked Lynton directly, the third time he came home late with no excuse and appeared vexed. He hardly said three words to her, but remembering her mother words, "Don't nag, and if a man don't want to talk, just give him time. The worst thing you can do is carry on carry on, trying to get him to tell you what him don't want to tell you. You will succeed with either pushing him further into his shell, or rile him up so that he walks out." That was her mother's only advice when she told her Lynton had asked her to marry him. So she never pushed and often held her tongue. But over the last three months she did try to find out if it was something she had done why he was withdrawing from her. She had asked him if he wanted her to go and seek employment to help out, even though he was the one who insisted that she be a house-wife before they got married. He had also said he didn't want them to have children for two years or more until he saved to pay down on a house. She had broached that subject too, the second month of the deterioration of their relationship, after she had seduced him by massaging his body. He had flipped her off his back where she had been straddling him, and had made love to her in an urgent way, biting and massaging her skin, a slight pain of erupted pleasure. And afterward, they had laid, their bodies glued together with perspiration, she practicing her kegel,

115

forbidding him to withdraw, she had asked, "So you ready for us to have a baby yet? There's nothing I want more than to have your child, our child."

He had rolled off her then, and before he got up, had said very clearly, with conviction in his voice, "You make sure you stay on the birth control pills until I says so." She had been glad that he went to the bathroom and stayed long because the tears came so quickly so fully, a bucket outside, overflowing its brim, the rain still pouring. When he had returned from the bathroom, he had gotten in on his side, and was snoring less than five minutes later, while all night she tossed and wiped away her tears. That was in fact three weeks ago and she now wondered if he had stopped making love to her because he feared she might disobey him and get pregnant anyway. It had crossed her mind, but she remember even before she got married one day hearing her mother speaking to a friend and saying, "My dear I tell you, women will never learn. They all think having a baby will help them keep a man. If a man don't want you, you could have a million babies, and if he is a dog, he will still stray. That there Thelma is stupid and blind as a doorpost. She have that man breed her then walk. I could have told her he wasn't going to stick around."

Mazie had no intention of raising a child on her own.

Coming out of her reverie, Mazie glanced at the green lizard on the windowsill. The small creature stared at her with a look that seemed to ask, "Why you not asking him what has changed? Why you don't come out straight and ask him if he's messing with another woman?" She rubbed the back of her neck and shoulder, tight with a calcium knot.

* * *

When they met, Mazie had been just out of high school and still a virgin. He had courted her steadily for two years, and during that time she never gave in to his demand for sex. The only consistent thing Mazie had every desired was to be Lynton's wife and the mother of his children.

"You lack ambition," her mother, a successful businesswoman, spat when Mazie broke the news that she did not want to attend university or train for a profession. Lynton, six years her senior, with a degree and a good job had promised that she would never have to work outside the home and that he would always take care of her as long as she made her special soup, his favorite meal. Her mother had slapped her and uttered in her nasal, disgusted tone, "You can't be my daughter. How I could raise a daughter who don't want to have something of her own? Is where you come from? You think man easy? Your father, bless his soul, was an exception, and if he was alive he would tell you the same thing I am telling you.

You can't put all your trust in a man, no care how nice he appears. You think life easy and steady like the tortoise that wins the race? Every woman need to have two pennies hidden in her brassier and three more in a tin can buried somewhere. Feelings change you now. Love's promises change."

Mazie knew her mother did not know everything, so refused to listen to her advice, but now here she was.

Turning the burner off under the pot, Mazie reflected on the conversation she had last month with Judith, a dear friend since elementary school.

"I feel like I'm on a swing with one side unhinged," Mazie, confiding and baring her heart, had said as soon as she and Judith sat down, sipping on tamarind juice. Silence swirled between them like leaves fluttering in a slight breeze. The heat rose, visibly from the ground, shimmering in a drunken stupor.

Mazie realized that she wanted Lynton's complete devotion, for him to keep the promise of their love. Judith, practical in her unhappiness, well into five years of marriage, with two children and tolerating her husband's second affair, pulled her chair around to face her friend, whom she had always felt was too idealistic.

"Girl before you get married it's like drinking a mango-strawberry shake every day. It sweet can't done!" Momentarily, Judith's face had lit up. Then it took on the frozen gaze of a widower mourning the loss of her dear departed husband. "After marriage, it's like putting a cake in the oven and at that very moment someone enters and slams the door causing the cake to fall. You hope it's okay, but after it's baked, it's flat-flat; you don't want to eat it, but you don't want to waste it either, so you pick-pick at it. That's our lot as women," Judith said, her words pungent as burnt toast.

Mazie stared hard at her twenty-three year-old friend and wondered how she had arrived at such a pessimistic, complacent view. Their lot as women! Whose life was she living?

Seeing Mazie's consternation, Judith added, "Lynton better than most. Just be patient."

The visit was ruined, and Mazie never felt like sharing anything with Judith after that.

She had agreed with patience as a strategy, but that was before Lynton came home drunk one night and slapped her, causing her ear to ring.

It happened the fourth time he stayed out without telling her. Worried that something had happened to him, she had several times gone out to stand by the gate and peer down the road. After midnight, when he came home finally, she ran and embraced him. He reeked of perfume and it wasn't hers. Mazie had not suspected or even thought it possible that Lynton was with another woman. Relieved that he was home, but angry at his deception, she had pushed him hard on his chest, and her voice blared, "I am here sick with worry and you out with some woman. You think I am a take whatever you dish out kinda woman. You think I'm going to share you. You think I am some damn woman to play with."

He punched her.

Shocked, she backed away from him, her ears ringing. She tried to find her voice, her outrage. She looked at the man in front of her, trying to see who he was. They had stood staring at each other. A long moment passed. Then Lynton had come to her and grasped her in his arms, saying over and over, "Hush. Hush. Sorry. Sorry. Nothing going on like you think. Is you one I love."

She had gone to bed in his arms, all the while trying to find herself amidst the shame and disappointment she felt.

"Don't ever make any man put his hand on you!" This was her mother's constant warning before she got married. These words reverberated and rotated in her head like wet clothes in a dryer all that night.

Now, standing at the stove, Mazie rubbed away the tears that were seeking escape and poured soup into the bowls.

When Lynton emerged from the bathroom, wearing just underpants, the soup was on the table, steam rising. She sat opposite him; but it was as if an invisible steel wall separated them. He took up the spoon, dipped it into the bowl, and blew on it before his lush, ample lips swallowed the spoon. Her spoon remained heavy in her hand. She counted, twenty-seven times he scooped soup into his mouth without once looking at her. The pain was so deep she could not explain it. It immobilized her and made her dumb. All she wanted was to feel his lips on her lips, on her belly, at the back of her knees. She wanted his hands to wrap her in his arms, to just hold her, to acknowledge she was alive.

What happened to love's promise she wondered. The memory returned fresh, she smelled the sea and heard the gently lap of the waves. It was an early morning, a Thursday of all days. He had told her the evening,

"Go to bed early, I'm going to pick you up before daybreak. Wear you bathing suit." He kissed her on the lips and caressed her shoulders.

"But is not Sunday," she had replied.

"So is only Sunday we can go to the beach?"

She had hugged him tightly around the neck and he had lifted her off her feet, and spun her around just like she had seen couples do in the movies.

His bowl empty except for a chicken bone, Lynton pushed it towards Mazie, then said as, if speaking to someone standing behind her.

"So get me some water, no. You see how the hot soup make me perspire."

Eyes white, she kept her gaze just above his head, then when she felt herself calm enough, got up and poured him a glass of water. He took it from her, careful not to touch her fingers. After gulping down the water in one long swallow, he slammed the glass on the table, pushed back his chair, got up, walked into the adjacent bedroom, and closed the door.

Mazie sat at the table, her soup untouched, feeling like a tight fist was locking her throat. Her left hand kneaded her right palm, she kept pressing harder and harder into her palm, the wrath refusing to lie down and go quietly to sleep.

"Anyone home? Hold the dog, please!" The frantic plea of the boy at the gate jolted her.

She realized that the dog had been barking and rushing to the gate for some time. As she got up from the table she heard Lynton's loud snoring in the bedroom. Her bowl was still full, but the soup cold. Walking outside to see who was at the gate, she tossed the entire bowl into the dog's pan and went to the gate. The fish man's son had brought the fish she was planning to make into fish soup for dinner tomorrow. Truth be told she was tired of soup, wanted some jerk chicken, so hot it watered her eyes even before she bit into it. Lynton did not like jerk as he claimed pepper did not agree with his stomach.

After cleaning the kitchen, Mazie crept to the bedroom door, opened it quietly, and peered in at Lynton asleep diagonally across their bed. She knew that meant he did not want her to lie next to him. Standing at the threshold, she willed him to turn and look at her, but he continued snoring. She left the door ajar and went and sat back around the dining table from where she could watch him across from her sleeping. Not even when the house was covered in darkness did Mazie rise from the chair of vigilance.

Lynton woke about 9 p.m. disorientated, bumping his foot as he stumbled off the bed, simultaneously barking at her,

"Mazie, where you is? You no see it dark. Turn some light on in the damn house."

She didn't move. He turned on the bedroom light and hurried to the bathroom. When he returned, his hands and face, dripping wet, the towel over his shoulder, he spotted her and yelled.

"What do you? Why you just sitting there in the dark?"

She did not reply.

He dried his hands and face, turned back into the bedroom, and began getting dressed. He lotioned his hands then dabbed Limacol on his neatly trimmed beard. Next, he brushed his hair until it was smooth. Satisfied, he put on black nylon socks, the navy pants that were hanging on the closet door, and lastly the shirt, which he handled with even greater care, almost sliding into it so as not to wrinkle it before tucking it into his pants. Mazie's eyes fixed on the new yellow and navy striped cotton shirt that she had saved up for and bought and the navy-blue gabardine pants she had pressed with razor sharp creases. Scrutinizing Lynton, Mazie's saliva tasted like stale hot beer.

Having buckled his belt, Lynton stood admiring himself in the mirror before taking a clean handkerchief from the drawer, which he stuffed into his back left pocket like he always did. Next he took his money off the dresser and put it in his right side pocket. Pleased with his appearance, he walked into the small living-dining room and asked,

"So how I look?"

Mazie had been watching him keenly while sucking on the chicken bone that he had left in his bowl. She couldn't think of anything she had done that would cause him to so disregard her. And his gall! Dressing to go out without her, without telling her where he was going, and now asking her how he looked. Mazie rose slowly, feeling as if a tiara was on her head. She circled Lynton as if on a merry-go-round. Her right palm itched. She paused and began kneading it again.

"I look good," Lynton said glancing at himself in the mirror. Completing the 360-degree inspection, Mazie smiled and her belly bottom flipped.

"You look good. Really, really good. I am proud of how I take care of you. So make sure you tell the woman you all dandy up for that is me, your wife, who bought that shirt that drapes your back and it's me, your wife, who pressed the pants so crisp. And don't come in here after you fuck her."

His fist connected with the side of her head, and she spun then stumbled.

"Don't ever curse at me," his voice a gong, his saliva spraying her face. "You lucky me in a good mood and have to go out or I'd give you an arse whipping."

She made no attempt to rise. This was not nothing. This was beyond shame and disappointment. This was more than a broken promise.

That early morning at the beach, they had hugged each other, and had walked out to where the water came to their waist. They stayed like that for more than an hour, the sea clear and flat as glass and they each shared what they wanted out of life. Three children they agreed on, a house on a quiet street with a big yard where she could grow herbs and vegetables and fruits too, enough to sell, and she wanted a real big kitchen in which she would bake and make huge pots of soup. And just before they went ashore, they had peered into the horizon, the sky somewhat ashen, and Lynton had jokingly said, pointing to a buoy beyond, "our life is out there, too far for us to ever walk it out." Then he told her he loved her. Back on shore, he reached into the bag in which he had brought his clothes, and kneeling in the sand, Lynton asked, "Mazie, please say you will marry me?" And in her memory, at that very moment, the sun broke through and the day was a dazzling glow and she hugged him and said "yes, yes," until they fell in the sand and rolled around, sand matted into their hair. And over breakfast of fish and festival, he said his love's promise, "I will love you, and you only always. I will not hit you nor curse at you. I will always provide for you and our children, and I will make you happy everyday." And he had kept that promise every day until three months ago. "Is what me do?" Mazie wanted to scream but the question stayed in her head, pounding like a hammer missing the nail.

After Lynton was out the door, after she heard the gate clang shut behind him, Mazie pushed herself to her feet. She saw herself rising from the floor. She still felt his fist bruise her face.

She had promised herself, two months ago, when he hauled her off the chair by the front of her dress ripping it, and leaving the whole left side of her face swollen, that if he ever hit her again she would fix him.

"Don't make idle promises." Another of her mother's frequent warnings seemed to echo from the walls.

* * *

Mazie remember when she was about nine years old, and the neighbor's tomcat would slink into their chicken coop and eat their eggs. Her mother pleaded with the neighbor to keep her cat away from their yard, but the neighbor never apologized nor did anything to keep her cat away. When Mazie's pet hen had chickens and the cat ate two of them, she decided enough was enough. When the hen was down to one chicken and Mazie saw the cat chasing it, her head thundered and she began kneading her palm. Then turning all her attention to the cat, with concentrated attention and her eyes tightly closed, Mazie imagined herself squeezing the breath out of the cat. That very evening, they heard the neighbor wailing about her dead cat. Mazie had smiled, but her mother had observed her and said, "The power you have is not to waste on every little thing. There is more than one way to skin a cat."

Not another word was spoken to her on the subject. Her father was still alive then, and that evening as she approached her parents' bedroom to tell them good night she clearly heard her mother say to her father,

"Mazie's power come in harder than steel. Is she do away with the cat."

Mazie held her breath and waited to hear what her father said in response, but to her surprise, he called, "Maze-Maze, come get your goodnight kiss."

Had he seen and known that she was there all along? He kissed her on the forehead like he always did, then pulled her in embrace close to his chest. Then her mother kissed her on her right eye, like she always did, then her lips, then spun her around and pointed her in the direction of the door like they always did, never ever tucking her in, at least not that she could remember. When she was by her room door, she heard her father clearly say,

"Her power can protect her, but it can push her over too. I hope she learn to harness it."

Was he speaking about her? He never mentioned her name, but Mazie was certain that he was.

When she was fifteen, one of the older boys who was always lounging against a neighbor's fence, hollering at girls and women, and speaking loudly about their body parts, was a menace. Almost daily for more than six months he harassed her when she walked home from school, or if she was going to the store, or just walking. He made her feel unclean, and often she had to concentrate very hard to keep from stumbling under his gaze. One evening the lad had crossed the street after hollering at her and had grabbed her hand and touched her bottom. She had pulled her hand free from him and they had stood no more than a foot apart. He reached to touch her breasts, and she slapped away his hand. He was about to grab her again, but he saw the rolling-calf in her eyes and staggered back. The itch in her palm rose to her chest and her head pounded. She closed her eyes, and when she opened them the lad was on the ground, his face twisted. She quickly stepped around him and took, slow, deliberate steps home. The following day when Mazie was doing homework, her mother came into her room and sat on the bed until Mazie paused. Looking her directly into her eyes, her mother said, "That boy yesterday had a stroke, not sure he will ever walk again. You learn him the lesson, but you are a hard teacher." Their eyes locked but Mazie refused to break the stare until her mother looked down, then rose from her bed with a sigh and exited Mazie's room shaking her head as if bewildered.

Mazie did not see the boy for almost a year. She soon realized that none of the other boys who would sometimes catcall, whistle, and seethseeth her along with him did so any more.

Just before she graduated high school Mazie encountered the past harassing lad in almost exactly the same spot. They approached, and she moved to his right, and stopped when their shoulders were about six inches apart. His face was twisted up and he could barely speak, but he mouthed sorry and she could see in his eyes that he meant it. A little too late, Mazie thought, but nodded and continued on her way.

* * *

Moving languidly, Mazie sat back at the table, picked up the chicken bone from Lynton's bowl, fixed his face in her mind, and chewed deliberately. That morning at the beach when he proposed to her, she promised she would love him faithfully, would take care of him, keep a nice comfortable home for them, keep herself attractive, and always cherish and uphold their promises to one another. Mazie reviewed her promises as she sucked on the bone. She had honored then all. She cracked the bone and chewed.

Daydreaming, Mazie relived the sensation of Lynton's tongue gliding over her neck and then she imagined their lips pressed together. How it made her feel and want to do things she had never imagined. But she sucked and chewed on the bone until the memory and sensation of Lynton's tongue were erased and until only a tiny mound of grounded brown matter remained of the bone. She kneaded her palm, kneaded until the pounding inside her head was a hum.

She could see Lynton clearly now. He was holding his mouth. Blood was dripping down his chin. He spat and his tongue, chewed to tiny bits, spilled from his mouth. The woman he was with screamed and ran, her chair falling over. People close by stared dumbfounded. The music was blaring, but Lynton couldn't hear it any longer; he couldn't even scream. His tongue had been chewed away.

A rooster cockled in the distance, and the fist that had been choking her broke like a chain and fell. Mazie stepped outside into the cool night air and glanced up at the stars. Love's promise was that she should love herself as much as she was willing to love another.

"A man's love is only as good as it makes you strong." Another of her mother's maxims that made her smile. She went inside, scooped up the mound of chewed up bones from the table, and scattered them in the flowerbed at the side of the house. Then she ambled to the kitchen, filled a glass with water, poured and stirred in two tablespoons of salt, and took a sip that she then gargled before spitting it out.

Mazie hugged herself, using the cool glass to caress her arm. After tossing the remainder of the salted water across the threshold, she locked the door, climbed into bed, and settled contentedly into a deep, sound asleep.

Trio

Growing up me used to hear Old Folks say 'the heart never walks straight' and only now me understand what they mean. They never say a truer thing.

Is you de one me telling cause you don't condemn me, and you're still me friend, probably me only friend; and me really, really need to tell someone and get it off my chest cause it's like a dead horse lying on top of me.

Wanda was not only me one child, but she was me best, best friend. Me pregnant with her when me just fourteen. You know because you are the first one me tell. She was me fifteen birthday present, born on the same day as me. From that first moment me look on her still covered in blood, me know we would be friends.

Me tell you it hurt me too. It hurt me well bad. Every time me think about what me do it feels as if me is shoving a butcher knife in me own belly. God knows me didn't mean to hurt her; me never mean no harm; never know it would go this far, but it go even further. And yet me ask meself if me could do it over, what me would do different? Is how love go wrong? Is how me must make this good feeling wrong? Is how me to say me didn't want him, when me still want him. Me want her too. Me want her to be happy. Me want her to understand and forgive me cause me never know it would go this far, that the heart could contain so much.

She pauses and looks around her room, crowded with clothes she has finished and some still in progress. Piles of fabric, patterns, threads, stacks of clothes to be mended, patched, darned, taken in, let out, made over for someone else into something new. Pieces of many-colored threads stick stubbornly to the floor. Hanging from the curtain rod on hangers are dresses, skirts, pants, and shirts, pressed and waiting to be picked up.

In every corner of the room there is evidence of her labor, vestiges of her handiwork, remnants that testify to her productivity, including the two sewing machines; the Singer with its pedal-driven motor on which she is making a work uniform for a woman whom she knows lashes her tongue about her behind her back. But what is she to do? She needs to feed her sons, and the woman is a reliable customer who always pays on time.

What she care what they say? She must eat. Her sons need books for school. They must live. People can talk; people can talk all they want, as if they are guiltless, as if they have never walked across the street to get one thing, but picked up something else. She drinks water, catches her breath, pulls aside the curtain, looks out, then she looks at the pattern she is sewing and presses the motor.

She hasn't forgotten about me, her friend—I know this—she is merely gathering courage or maybe just reviewing in her mind whether to continue from the tail of the story or from the head. She clears her throat; I lean towards her.

Me mother never married like me. Is she de one me know growing up. Is she learn me to sew. Many nights me go to bed with the sound of the sewing machine, zeezeeing like lullaby, zeezeeing me to sleep. Some mornings me wake up and Mama asleep at the machine. She sew all kind of pretty clothes for people who don't pay on time, and some don't even pay. By the time me was seven me could hem dresses better than her helper and sew on button, and darn so that it looked like design. But Mama say she working hard to send me to a good school so I can have a better life than her, marry a good man, and work in office with air-condition or even turn barrister. Me love Mama and she don't flog me although sometime she shout at me harsh when me do something bad, and then me have to stay inside all day as punishment, sitting quietly in the corner of her sewing room, not saying a word.

Me do good in school and win scholarship to Alfa High School for girls, a good-good school. Mama proud of me. Me happy that Mama proud of me. Me start to fill out and get woman body and Mama warn me about boys. She tell me she don't want me to end up like she: pregnant at fifteen; have to drop out of school and apprentice with a dressmaker, my dream to get big job finish. Me promise Mama that will never happen to me, and me did mean it; me did really mean it. But Mama or no one else ever explain to me how a man could make me feel so good, how me head could be full up of nothing but him, how me would say yes, even though me know me shouldn't, how me wouldn't be able to stop meself or him, even when me know we should stop, how me could feel so, so good, when him touch me that me lose me head, just like them say. Him touch me and every sense fly out me head like bird let out of cage. Jezampiece. Even now, after all these years, me still remember the feel of that man's hand on me, and me tell you the truth, me would give anything to experience that feeling back then. Me body drank up his touch like hot bread sucking in butter.

She stops pedaling, and uses her hand to fan herself. She frees the fabric from the machine, holds it up to the light and examines the stitching. Satisfied, she positions it to stitch the other side. She calls to her helper to bring us juices and crackers and cheese. She uses a small towel and vigorously wipes her face, neck, and upper arms. The day is hot, and a few pieces of thread are caught on her skin, and in the strands of her hair, which is parted down the middle and cornrowed at both sides, joining in one braid at the nape of her neck. I study her—notice the absence of wrinkles, bright eyes that belie her fifty years, and marmalade hue skin, smooth, except for the moles, which are also on her neck and upper chest area. Gold loops adorn her ears, and she is wearing a simple floral blouse that buttons in front, and a gathered-waist, brown skirt that falls below her knees. She is neither beautiful nor particularly attractive, but she is not plain either, in the same manner that red-ginger flower is neither stunning nor alluring—but lovely, nonetheless. I sense that she has accepted her lot, and is not one to complain, taking whatever comes her way with the same equanimity as she accepts the sun or rain. The helper brings juice and crackers on a tray and we thank her as she leaves. I turn in the chair, anxious for her to continue.

Same way we did live in Vineyard Town then, not far from here when me was going to Alfa. Every day me would pass camp, and all kind of soldiers would try talk to me and me friends, but we just giggle and go on our way. Well one day, it rain hard, hard, and soldiers invite us to shelter. That was the first time me see him. Him was in charge of the soldiers dem, and him tell them loud, loud in front of me and me two friends that they better not fresh with us. When rain stop and we leaving, him wave to me. Me neva see him again till one month pass. Me did stay at school to do some work, and just as me pass the camp gate, him was driving out. Him greet me well nice.

"Good afternoon, young lady. How was school today?"

"Good sir," me replied.

"Are you on your way home? I could give you a lift."

Me was well tired. The books in me bag heavy, and me did well hungry cause me neva had lunch. Mama didn't have any money to give me. She sews but her customers don't always pay.

"I would be thankful, sir," me said quick-quick. Him lean over and open the car door for me. Me hop in like people offer me ride everyday. We drive a little ways and see a man selling coconut water by the road. Him say him well thirsty and going to buy one and would I like one. Me too shock to answer, but me nod me head yes. The jelly-water never taste so sweet. Afterwards him drop me home, nice-nice; him didn't even try to fresh with me.

After a while me notice that me seeing him all the while and him taking me home, and him buying me soda and pattie with coco-bread, and him always asking me about school, and encouraging me to do good and take me lessons seriously. Him also ask me about me life with mama so that after a while me take him as me friend, and would tell him anything. Him talk to me about boys, and tell me to tell him if anyone get fresh with me. Me tell you me love him bad before me realize me fall in love with him. But still him no bring no argument to me, although me can see how him looking at me, especially when him think me not looking.

Then one day him ask if me want to go to Boston Beach with him and spend the Saturday. Me say yes even though me know Mama not going to let me go, but me have a plan. All week Mama ask me why me acting like is me birthday. Me don't tell her about Hilton, me soldier friend, and when Saturday come me lie and tell her me spending the night at your house; you Patsy, my best friend, who I knew would cover for me. Me take the bus and meet Hilton at Crossroads, and we drive to Boston Beach. Me feel like big woman with man with car. Me feel important, even though him is not me man, but me want him to be me man. Me never know me could have those feelings at fourteen, but me did.

We spend a nice day at Boston Beach, and that was the first time him kiss me. Him say him couldn't help himself and ask me to forgive him. Me throw me arms around him neck and him kiss me again and again, and is so me and him spend the night. Him take me virginity, but him was sweet and gentle. Me know him is big man, probably old like Mama so me don't say anything to anyone but you, Patsy, who cover for me with mama. Remember how you warned me to be careful. You asked me why me want be with such an old man. Me told you him don't seem old to me, and him is really, really nice to me. Me and Hilton, that was his name, start carry on, sometime even during the week; me lie to Mama and tell her me have to stay late a school, but is him me meet, and we even go to hotel. Him give me money so me always have lunch, and is him buy me the first dress that Mama didn't sew for me. Me feeling so happy, like big woman, better than Mama, with my store bought dress. Him carry me around some of him friends them. Him rent a room and say is our special place.

Six months we know each other, then me period stop. One month me don't get it. Me was so afraid to tell him or anyone. Next month nothing. One day, during lunch time at school, me cry on you shoulder, remember. You encouraged me to tell him, maybe he can take me somewhere to get rid of it. Me love him so much me never want to get rid of his baby. Me love Mama and me know she going be disappointed in me. Me love school and me know school done for me now if me with baby.

That day when Hilton picked me up after school, him could tell that something was wrong. We drove out to airport way and park and me tell him. Me think him was going to be mad, but him hug me and say, is alright. Him say it's been a long time he's been wanting a son, and how me make him happy. Me tell him Mama go be mad, and she might put me out. Him say not to worry, me can move into our special place that him rent where we make love. Me happy, but me worried about school. Me really like school and want to finish and get nice office job like Mama always want for me, but me afraid to tell him about my dream. Him tell me not to tell Mama anything until after he arranges everything for me to move. Me don't feel good about this, but Hilton make me swear so me listen to him.

"Don't I always protect and look out for you?" he asked me.

I nod my head because is really true. He is the first man to love me and he never once shout at me or make me feel stupid.

Two weeks later, he moved me out of Mama's house; he bought me everything I needed so I didn't have to take much. Me feel bad cause Mama work so hard to put me through school; but me can't explain how all I can think about is Hilton. Him alone full up me head, and when him touch me, me melt. When Mama find out, she cry and ask me why me want to ruin me life like hers. Me tell her me life not ruin; me have a man that love me. That is when she say:

"If him love you and mean to do right by you, why him didn't come and ask me for you proper? Why him don't marry you?"

Me couldn't answer Mama, but me think about what she say, and me mean to ask him just that, when me get the chance. Even though him want me to drop out of school right away, me tell him me want to stay till term end because me not showing and no one know, except you. Him promise me that after me have his son, him will pay for me to go to night school and take me exams. Me just throw me arms around him neck and kiss him all over his face. And is so me begin living with man and keeping house for him when me just fourteen years and three months.

Him didn't stay with me all the time cause him say him have to be at Camp to give his soldiers orders, and him warn me not to come up there because some of the soldiers like to fresh with young girls; and me so pretty they bound to try and fresh up with me and him would have to kill them. Me don't want him kill anyone, so me promise not to go up there.

After term finish, me home all day with nothing to do. Next term begin, but me showing already. Sometimes you came by and taught me what you learned. Me liked that a lot. Most weeks, Hilton only sleep with me three nights, and never on Sundays. Him always on duty on Sundays. Sometimes me very afraid during those long nights, and me always lonely.

"Soldier life not easy," him say, wrapping me in his arms and rubbing me belly. "How me son doing?" Him kiss me belly.

I pray is boy I have since his heart is so set on having a son and I want him to be happy; but deep down I want a little girl just like myself to dress up and comb hair.

As it get closer to me having baby, me miss Mama more and decide to visit her and try and patch things up. She hug me and say she still love me; she will always love me. After that everyday me go by Mama during the day and help her with the sewing. And that's how she get to meet Hilton.

One evening him come pick me up, and blow the horn at the gate for me to come out. Just as me getting up to go, Mama grab a hold of me hand and push me back in the chair.

"Him must have manners. Mek him come knock at the gate and ask for you. Mek him come introduce himself to me and show me that him is a man."

Me shock. Him blow the horn again. Me look on Mama; her eyes tell me to sit down and don't move. Me sit down. After a while me hear knocking at the gate. Me peep through the curtain and see him standing by the gate. Mama peeping at him too, then she click her tongue and say.

"Lawd, is big man that; is big man. Him look older dan me. Lawd, look how big man come right unda me nose come thief me one daughter." Mama's voice sounded teary. But she get up, walk to the front door and, in a proper voice, she say:

"Hello. Who there? Can me help you?"

"I'm here to pick up Juanita," me hear Hilton replied.

"Ooooh," Mama says. "You must be the man that tek me daughter from me house. Please step through the gate so me can meet you. No dogs here to bite you."

Me still sitting down but me heart beating like truck engine. Me watch Hilton open the gate and walk down the path, and Mama stand same place. Me want to get out me seat, but me can't. Him walk up to Mama and extend him hand, but she don't take it.

"Me daughter tell me you gwane take care of her and the baby. Me glad you come to speak to me about the wedding, cause she must marry before the baby born. She can marry right here in this house and me will make her dress. She is a minor and you are a big man so you must do the proper thing." Mama says looking Hilton up and down. Me glad she mentioned wedding to him cause me been waiting for him to ask me to marry him, but him didn't ask yet. Me stand up, grinning from ears to ears expecting him to ask Mama for me hand, but instead him just say.

"I'm here to pick up Juanita. Please send her out if she is here." And then him turn around and walk back out the gate. Is like me feet glue to the ground. Sweat cover me. Me feel weak. Me feel like somebody hold me up and thump me in me chest.

"You is a damn thieving old dog," Mama shouted and tossed one of the potted plants from veranda after him. Me hear him slam the car door. Mama is still standing by the door. Me want to go to him, me want Mama to hug me too. Me want Hilton to come back and ask Mama for me hand, but him drive off and leave me right there. Me couldn't even cry. Me just hug me belly all evening and rock in the chair. Me and Mama don't say one word to each other.

Next morning Mama asks me his name. Me tell her it's Hilton Thompson. She gets dress and leaves the house. She tells me she's going up Camp. Me lay down all day, can't eat, can't move. Me just hug me baby in me belly and moan.

Mama gone all day; she don't come back until way in the evening, after darkness falls. She comes in the room where me lying down and she takes me head in her lap. Me look at her face and see that it look like de sky ready for heavy rain.

"Mama, you see Hilton? Him going to marry me, right?"

Mama humming and rubbing me head gently, just humming and rubbing me head. She makes me hot Horlick and tell me to drink it. She talks to me as if me is a baby. Then she turns off the light and kisses me on the forehead good night. For the rest of the week Mama doesn't say anything, but she refuses to let me go back to Hilton. Me keep hoping Hilton will come and get me, but him don't come. Mama says if she has to tie me up, she will, but me not going back there unless he marries me.

Sunday me get up and me start having contractions. By noon, me hollering and begging Mama to hold me, to take out the baby, to stop the pain. Me never know it could hurt so much. It hurt so bad me thought me was going to die. Two o'clock, Mama hired a car to take me to the hospital and by seven at night, me have me daughter, Wanda. Mama was there with me the whole time, even though the nurse said she was to leave. Me was so grateful for Mama, how she hold me hand tight, and kept saying, "Look how me little girl turn woman under me nose, lawd oh."

When the nurse put me daughter in my arms, me and Mama hold on to each other and bawl, fat tears running down our faces, wetting the baby, both of us happy that she is so pretty and healthy; but sad too, me that Hilton her father wasn't there, and Mama that my life was taking a path similar to hers.

Tuesday Hilton comes to the hospital and me is beside meself with joy. Mama doesn't say anything to him. When he say he taking me home, to our place, him and Mama have a staring down match that only the nurse interrupt when she turns to Hilton and said,

"So father you are here to take home your daughter and grandchild."

None of us said a word. Not Hilton, not Mama, not me. It was the first time since I was with Hilton that I felt shame; that maybe what we were doing was wrong.

Mama left without saying goodbye and Hilton took me home but still didn't say anything about marrying me. Me keep quiet, but from that night I began praying that Hilton would marry me.

The first month home from the Hospital, Hilton acts like him was happy, although him won't pick up Wanda or play with her. Him tell me she's so small and him afraid he might drop her, but him add:

"If it was a boy, if you did have my son, I wouldn't be afraid to hold him."

Then him kiss me and say, "Next time I'm going to make sure to put a boy in your belly."

Even though me beg Hilton, tell him that the nurse warn me not to have sex for at least two months, him force me and rip me open. Then him wouldn't take me to the hospital. Him say is my fault for being so pretty him couldn't resist me. Me cry and cry, and the baby start cry and wouldn't stop, and me ask Hilton to go and get Mama to come and help me. Him get in him car and leave and me don't see him for three weeks straight.

Me worry that me drive him away and him not coming back. Me don't have food, but me afraid to go and ask Mama. Everyday me sit down and listen out for him. Me can't sleep. Me don't even have enough breast milk for the baby. Mama come and visit and look in the kitchen and ask me what me eating. Me lie and tell her Hilton arrange for someone to bring food for me. Me want her to stay with me, but me want her to leave so she don't find out that me lie.

That evening when hunger was licking my shirt, I hear knock on the door, and is Miss Lizzy, Mama's helper, with a large pot of my favorite soup, red peas, and two cans of formula for Wanda. Miss Lizzy fix the formula and feed Wanda while I drink the soup, trying not to gobble it down. After she left me worry that Hilton might be hurt from a car accident and can't get to me. All night me head hurt like someone hammering inside me head and it don't stop.

The next morning bright and early Mama knock on the door. She see that is me only and Wanda, but don't say anything. She take Wanda from me and kiss her all over like she used to do to me. She blow on her belly, she kissed her feet, she kissed her hands, she kissed her cheeks loudly, she hold her in her hands and rock her like her arms were swings; she tell her she is pretty and better than her

131

circumstance, and that she's going to be better than her or me because three is a charm. Mama bathe her and put on clean clothes that she sewed and brought her. After Wanda fall asleep, Mama tell me to come with her in the kitchen, which is no bigger than a closet.

"Watch me and don't ask any questions," she ordered.

She got a pot, filled it with three cups of water that she put to boil. Then she opened the paper-bag she brought with her and took out a handful of bush, dried brown and green leaves, which she pounded. When the water began boiling she poured in the bush, and we stood watching it boil for five long minutes. Then she turned off the stove, got a cup, poured a teaspoon of coconut oil in it, filled it with the liquid from the pot, stirred then handed the cup to me.

"Drink all of it, as hot as you can. Me know it taste as nasty as it smell but drink it."

She watch me sip it. She watch until me drain the cup. Me know the smell, but can't remember from where. About an hour later me ran to the bathroom. Stuff was coming from top and bottom. Me whole body break out in sweat. Me call to Mama, but she ignore me; only talking to Wanda like me was not there. For two hours me in the bathroom. Me don't know how I don't pass out all me insides.

After I lie down and Mama cover me up and give me water with lime to drink I remember where I first smelled that bush. It was when me was about four or five years old and mama had been vomiting and her good friend whom me call Aunty Flow, came and boiled her this same bush, and she was in bed all day, then the next day she was better. And there was another time that Mama boiled it on her own and drank this same bush, when I was about nine years old. Mama stay with me the whole day and feed Wanda formula and only give me water with lime to drink. Just before she left to go home that night she took me face in her hands, stared straight in me eyes and said.

"Don't mek that man breed you again. Me know it hard sometime fi resist the tenderness of a man, but don't mek him breed you. Him ruin your ambition already but don't mek him ruin your life." Her eyes were dancing in tears, and mine sprung too. "You understand what me saying to you, you understand?" I couldn't speak, but me nodded me head up and down and said inside me head, "Yes Mama, yes, me understand."

She kissed me on me forehead, then turn from me. As she stepped out the door, she turned and said,

"Me leave some in the bag on the counter. Wrap it tight and put it in the back of the cabinet so you have it if you need it. Remember what me say. Miss Lizzy will bring you some fish soup tomorrow to build back up you strength. Drink plenty of water and juice so you can make milk fa Wanda."

And Mama was gone into the night.

Almost a week after Mama's visit, one Tuesday night, about eleven o'clock Hilton come, with three bags of groceries, formula for the baby and ice cream for me. Me so happy to see him, even though it hurt a little me let him have him way with me. Me tell him we was worried that him might be hurt. Him tell me that him was in accident, almost dead, and is thinking about me why him still alive. Me so happy me hug him tight.

Wanda just four months and me pregnant again. Me ask Hilton about going to night school. Him say me to wait until Wanda is at least a year, and him not going to discuss it anymore. Me know if me have another baby me will never go back to school, and Mama will never talk to me again. Me confide in you again, although our friendship strain. I remember exactly what you said.

"Juanita. You are being a damn fool. That man is going to keep breeding you until you have six sons for him and you are of no use to anyone. Don't let him take away all your dreams. I will help you to get an abortion."

Me afraid. Me don't know what to do—what is right for me, for Hilton, for me life? What if me pregnant with the son Hilton has been wanting? What if Hilton finds out and leaves me? Me decide to take a chance and talk to Mama. When me tell her she just shake her head and hug herself and rock back and forth like when she heard the news of her mother's death. The following Sunday morning bright and early Mama come for me in a car. She say we are going for a drive. Mama hold Wanda and sing her to sleep.

Then the car stop after a while. Me ask Mama is who we going to visit. She say is someone me know that me need to see. She point to a nice green house, with pretty flowers growing all around, and tell me to knock on the gate. Me cross the street, and just as me about to knock on the gate me notice is Hilton's car. Lawd God, me think, smiling all over. Hilton buy house for me and is going to marry me. Me so happy me don't even bother to knock, me just holler out him name.

"Hilton! Hilton! Is me, Juanita. Hilton!"

A woman comes to the door.

"Can I help you?"

"Yes, me here to see Hilton. Tell him is Juanita," me say smiling.

Me see three little girls peering around the woman's legs. She speaks to them firmly and tell them to get back inside; then she walks towards me at the gate. Me wonder why Hilton hasn't come to me yet. The woman reaches the gate, and something about the look on her face freezes the smile on mine. Suddenly me heart is beating like a horse running race at Caymanas Park.

"Is who you name Juanita coming here hollering out my husband's name after he has worked all night and is tired, and is resting. I don't know who you is or what you want with him, but you best clear out and don't come back."

Me hold on to the gate tight-tight with both hands and steady meself. Me laugh out how me make mistake. Them must have the same car too, me think. This woman's Hilton and mine not the same. Then me feel Mama standing beside me and same time Wanda start to bawl. Me look towards the door, where me see a shadow, and is Hilton me looking at, even though is only part of him face me see.

"Hilton is me, Juanita," me shout.

"Marge, tell that woman we are not buying anything today and come inside," Hilton command, like is soldier him giving order.

"Daddy, the woman called your name."

"Shut-up your mouth and go and finish your breakfast," Hilton said, whacking the little girl on her bottom.

"You don't have any business here," the woman, his wife's voice sounded like a plea.

"Is yu husband breed me daughter," Mama speak up. "She was in school studying to be someone important. Him breed her and ruin her life. Is yu husband daughter dis, his him daughter," Mama said loud, holding up Wanda like a prize.

"Clear away from here," the woman shouted. "Clear away before…"

"Ah can see in yu eyes dat we is not de first one come here calling fah yu husband," Mama said, staring the woman dead in the eye. "Ah can see we is not de first. Ah well sorry fah yu married to a damn, thiefin, lyin dog."

Mama pull me in the car. Me didn't want to believe it. Tears ran down my cheeks like water-fall. Mama tell me that was what she found out that day when she went to Camp, but she didn't know how to tell me. But now that me pregnant again she think me should know.

Me spend the next two weeks with Mama. Three days Mama boil the bush and I pass out my insides, but somehow my heart still intact. Me don't see Hilton for two months, and even though me tell Mama and you that me done with him, when him come, bringing cake and a nice dress for me and clothes for Wanda, and him tell me how him was just helping her, the woman who is his wife, and then she got pregnant, and he wanted to do the right thing by her so he married her, then when he wanted a divorce she got pregnant again, and the second time he threatened to leave, she got sick, then got pregnant again and since she had three daughters for him, he didn't think he could just leave her, but that he really only loved me, and as soon as his daughters were a little older, he would divorce her and marry me, and how he loved me so much, and that he was afraid to tell me because him couldn't stand the thought of losing me.

Me was beginning to hate Hilton and didn't think him was telling me the truth, but him pull me to him, and pressed me to his chest and cry like a baby.

When Mama found out, she suck her teeth and stamp her feet, and pace up and down before declaring,

"If you insist on mekin that damn lying dog of a man mek a fool out of you, den at least protect youself and don't get pregnant again. If you breed another child for him, me will personally push me hand up inside you and pull it out."

The next day she returned with a large brown paper bag with bush tea and tossing it at my feet instructed: "Any month you miss you period mek sure and boil and drink some until you see blood."

Five more years me stay with Hilton, on and off, and me wash away three more bellies. Every time me start night class, him start come round regularly and before you know it me drop out again. Then you Pasty get scholarship and go to Trinidad to attend university there. Me jealous. Me feel good for you, but bad for me. Then you write that you meet a nice boy there, but then me don't hear from you for almost two, three years when you graduate and then get married. After a while me don't hear from you at all.

Me find out that Hilton get another school girl pregnant. By now him can't hurt me no more. Me believe everything him tell me, even though me know is lie. Me know that me life ruin. Me realize that me never going to have a nice job in an office. But me love me daughter and realize me have to provide for her.

Mama help me buy a sewing machine and is so me turn dressmaker just like Mama. Me tell meself me done with man. Once or twice a year Hilton come around. Most times him a try to tell me some story about why him don't have any money to give me to help with Wanda. Me hear that him wife leave him and take their three daughters and living up State side.

Him get a third school girl pregnant, and the girl mother chop him with machete on his leg so bad him had to have operation, and now him walk with a limp. Me tell Hilton that his stories are like old newspapers piled in a corner—useless, waiting to be discarded or burned.

"Listen, Hilton, you can come and look for Wanda, but me don't want hear another word from you no more about anything." Me tell him that so him stop coming.

Wanda growing nicely. Me watch her and me talk to her plain as soon as her little woman visit her. Me tell her that man will sweet talk her, that man will touch her in places on her body and make her feel so good, she might want to forget her head; me tell her there are men who can spot a needy girl a mile away, and play her like dominoes in them hands; me tell her that it's that easy to ruin her life just like me and her grandmother.

Me watch her like hawk, especially after she start high school. Me take bus and meet her at school and bring her home. Me know all her friends, and she can't go to their house; is only here they can come. Me make sure she always have money for lunch and to buy little things so that she not needy. Men can smell neediness on girls. Every day me remind her one turn can ruin her life. Every day, no matter how much me have to do, when she come home we stop and talk with her and we play together, hopscotch and jump rope. Most nights we sleep in the same bed, hug up each other.

Wanda finish high school, pass all her exams and not a man touch her. She is still virgin. Me and Mama shout and holler and dance all up and down; people look at us as if we're crazy, but we know what we know. Three is a charm.

Wanda say she want to study chemistry, and work with canning foods. She apply to the university but don't get in first time. Mama and me tell her to try again, and she get in; but them only give her little money. By this time Mama had saved and opened a little dress store, and she was so proud of Wanda, just like me, she said she would help so she can go to university. Wanda start UWI and me doing lots of sewing. Sometimes me jump out me sleep thinking me at the sewing machine.

Me so proud of Wanda, and before you know it she finish and have degree, and me and Mama happy can't done. We get up every morning and dance for almost a month. Wanda get job with the food company. She still live at home. Me still doing me sewing, but Wanda tell me she making good money so me don't have to work so hard. She take me to the movies. She take me to see play. We go beach together. We go listen to music. Everywhere we go people assume we are sisters.

For the first time me enjoying me life. Me feel young. Wanda take me to Mall and buy me clothes. We dress alike. We pay down on house, in both our names—this same house.

Then Wanda meet Clive.

She call me from work and tell me she has date. She come home late and tell me how him nice and she can't wait for me to meet him. The next week me meet him and like him. Him make me laugh. Him tell me him like me daughter. Me happy for her, but sad too because now me hardly see her. Sometimes she stays over his place. But many times she tell him, she can't leave her Mommie alone; so the three of us go to the movies, we go to see plays, we go for drinks. Me see how Clive look at Wanda and me know him really love her. Almost eight months them carrying on. Then one morning me wake up and hear Wanda vomiting in the bathroom. We ask what wrong.

"I think I'm pregnant."

Me heart skip a beat. Mama and me was hoping that Wanda was going to get married before she had baby. Me feel like crying, but me tell meself, Wanda is grown woman, almost twenty-five years old. She has university degree and good job. She not fifteen like me was when me had her. Me sit down and fan meself. Me consider the situation: she has a nice young man who is twenty-nine years old, not thirty-six like Hilton was when he got me pregnant. Me remind meself that Wanda well smarter than me. She knows where Clive lives and works, so me don't think him married because she sleeps over him house plenty times; we see him every day of the week, and most Sundays him come and take us to the beach and then me cook dinner and him eat with us.

"So what you planning on doing?" me ask her, rubbing me hand up and down on the side of me dress.

"Friday I will tell Clive. He has a special dinner planned just for the two of us, he says. I think he might ask me to marry him. I will tell him then." She said, moving to get dressed for work, no sign of worry or concern.

"I hope you're right. You know that me and Mama want you to get married before you have baby."

"Mommy, don't worry," she said, hearing the anxiety in me voice. "Besides, I'm a big girl now, and Clive and I love each other."

Me tell you Friday was only two days away, but it was the longest it take to come. That night me watch Wanda as she get dressed, and even though me want to hear what she was going to tell him, me bite me lips. While she putting on make-up, Clive call out from the veranda. I walk out to greet him, and see him standing there with flowers in his hand.

"Evening," me say, trying to read what mood him in.

"And good evening to you Ms. Juanita," Clive replied, kissing me on the cheek, then handing me the flowers. "These are for you, a token of appreciation for raising such a lovely daughter."

Me so surprise me mouth fall open. No one ever brought me flowers before, not even Wanda. Same time Wanda come out, and Clive turn him attention on her.

"You look radiant," him says to her, kissing her lightly on the lips. "You're ready?"

She nodded yes, and just before they step out the door, Clive turn to me and say,

"Juanita, don't do anything we wouldn't," he said winking at me.

"That might be giving her too much room to play," Wanda said kissing me on the cheek, then, "Night, Mommy. Don't wait up for us."

After they leave me sit out on the veranda for a long time, looking at the full moon and nodding on and off. A piece of loneliness wash over me, and me wish me had a nice man like Wanda to take me to dinner too. Me just turn forty so me not too old yet. Finally, after midnight, me get up and go in me bed, but every turn me turn, me wake wondering if Wanda tell Clive, and what him say. Me pray him ask her to marry him. Three is a charm I keeping saying until I fall asleep

When the sun bright, me get up and go into Wanda's room to see if she come home and me didn't hear her, but her bed same way, littered with the three different dresses she tried on before deciding on the one she wore. Me pick them up, put them back on hangers, and then hang them in the wardrobe. Me straighten and smooth out the sheets on her bed, me rearrange the perfumes on her dresser, me walk round her room as if me just seeing it for the first time. Me sit down on Wanda's bed and look through the window. Me listen to the bird in the mango tree. Me listen to the dogs barking. Me listen to the early morning breeze playing with the leaves; me listening for Wanda to come, but she don't come, not after me cook breakfast and eat alone, not after me clean most of the house, not after me sit down at the machine and try to make the simple curtains me promise this woman over two weeks now. Wanda don't come and me feel like me heart start to move up to me throat. Me repeat inside me head, Three is a charm, three is a charm, three is a charm.

Just when me feel a scream of desperation bubbling up from inside meself, me hear car stop at the gate, and me look out and is them. Wanda sit down waiting for Clive to get out and come round and open the door for her. They are hugging each other around the waist and just laughing as they step through the gate.

Me pretend to busy meself, dusting the furniture in the living room and acting like me don't hear dem. Me play deaf. The next thing me know Clive pick me up from behind by the waist and swing me around, and Wanda say to him,

"Tickle her Clive; tickle her and hear her squeal."

And Clive tickles me and we laugh so much that me and him fall on the floor and Wanda join us and the three of us crawling around on the floor tickling each other and laughing like children. Me tell you is one of the best memories me have of us as family. Then Clive take me left hand and with his arm around Wanda him say to me, suddenly all serious:

"Miss Juanita, you know that I really like your daughter. The truth is I love her and I hope you will agree to us marrying." Me feel like me heart leave me body and fly way into the clouds.

Immediately me start to make plans for the wedding. Me want to run and call Mama and tell her. Me know she going to be as happy as me, and we both going to plan the wedding, with Wanda of course. Then Wanda stick out her finger and wave it up and down in front of me so me could see her ring.

Three is a charm, Yes! I jump up and shout.

"So Mommie, what do you say? Clive is okay to be your son-in-law?"

It was like him ask me to marry him. Me tell you it was the happiest day of me life, to know my little girl—me best-best friend—getting married. The three of we sit down there on the floor and just hug up each other like new puppies.

Wanda was five months pregnant when she got married. Me and Mama make the dress, and you couldn't even tell that she was pregnant. It was a big wedding in a hall that she rented with catered food. Me don't think me ever had so much fun before or since. Me and Mama was so-so proud of Wanda—married woman with good husband. Wanda and Clive insisted that me live with them. This house here—is me and Wanda did buy it, and we were living in it when she met Clive. But Clive insisted that they get their own house, so we rented this one and me went to live with them in Dunsmair Park. We all lived together, happily for many, many years.

Clive and Wanda work long hours some days, but me cook and keep the house and still do a little sewing on the side so me have me own money Then all too soon she have baby; the prettiest baby girl me ever seen, even prettier than Wanda—and Wanda was a very pretty baby, everyone said so.

They name her Carmen. Then before Carmen was two years old she has Carol, and three years later, Caroline. She had a rough time with Caroline. Wanda sick almost the entire pregnancy, and labored long and hard; she hemorrhage and ended up having a C-section. She was sick for weeks; she couldn't even breast-feed. Me worried bad. Poor Clive worry until him lose weight, and him did skinny to begin with, no matter how me try to fatten him, no matter how much him eat. It took her a long time to recover, more than three months, and after that she said she was done having children, no more. Clive agreed, and laughing said,

"No one man should have to support more than five beautiful women."

We all laughed and me so thankful that him regard me as one of the women he had to look out for. And in truth, from the very beginning, Clive looked out for me and me felt close to him. Sometimes, me would lie down in the bed with Wanda and him and the three of us talked and laughed and just got on like good friends.

Shortly after Clive and Wanda got married, Clive set me up with some of his older friends, once even with his boss. He told me no one believe me was Wanda's mother because me look like a schoolgirl. In fact, after Wanda had the three girls she gained weight, and was big more than me even though we are the same height. Me have the same body me did before me had Wanda. Even Mama say I have a sexy body still. Anyway, I went out with a few of Clive's friends, even dated one for six months before we both lost interest. Me don't know why, but me just wasn't interested in any of them. So after a while Clive don't set me up anymore, and him start to call me his number two woman.

In fact, many times Wanda say me and Clive like two ackee seeds in a pod. We agree on the same things. We loved many of the same foods. We both prefer going to beach on Saturday rather than Sunday. Mostly, Clive and me prefer sitting on the veranda rather than around the table to eat dinner. So whenever Wanda working late Clive and me would take our plates and eat out there.

That and other little things we would keep from Wanda, and me didn't understand why then. Like the pair of gold earrings with my birthstone that Clive bought me for me birthday. The morning Wanda and Clive give me a beautiful gold chain with a pendant, but Clive came and took me for lunch that same day— Wanda was to join us, but she called and said she had a meeting. After lunch Clive dropped me back home, and handed me the box saying,

"These are from me. I just want you to know how much I appreciate you, for everything you do for me and Wanda and the girls. You know you're my very special number two woman and I love you." He kissed me on the check like always, but this time close to my lips and when me look at him me had this funny sensation. We both smile before me stepped out the car. When me went into the house me opened the box and that when me see the gold earring. Me wanted to wear them immediately, but me didn't. Me kept them in me drawer for over a month, and only put them in one day after me went to the Mall. Wanda noticed them at dinner.

"Mommie, those are gorgeous earrings. Where did you buy them?"

And just like that the lie fly out me mouth. "Me treat meself to them today." Me didn't dare glance at Clive. The first opportunity Clive get, him say to me,

"I don't think Wanda would mind if I buy you a separate present for your birthday, you know."

"That's why you slip it to me after lunch in the car?"

His jaw went slack, and me walk away quickly. It was after that, the cat and mouse game start. Me find that every time Clive near me, me heart racing. Everyday me find meself anxious to see him, me gloating over his body. When him walk around the house without shirt, which him did from the beginning, now me find me eyes roving over his body, and me have to remind meself that him is me son-in-law. Him always was touchy-touchy, and always pull on me and Wanda, playfully, pulling we in his lap, hugging me from behind around the waist, dancing with we, but now me find me can't stand when him do any of those thing.

One evening just as me was walking from the living room to go to the kitchen, him reach out and grab me hand. Wanda was sitting there beside him. Him used to do that all the time, but this time something in me just snapped,

"Why the blast you can't keep you damn hands to youself," me shout.

"What get into you lately, Juanita? You just touchy so. All I did was touch you. What's the harm?"

"Touch you wife and leave me the blast alone," me reply and stomped into the room. Me begin to pack me clothes. Me feel like me have to leave. Wanda knock on me door.

"Mommie, Clive's sorry. You're alright?" Then she noticed me clothes and the suitcase me pulled from under the bed. Me read the alarm on her face.

"Mommie! What are you doing? Did I do something wrong? Did Clive?"

"No, me just want to leave, me just need to be by myself."

"But what about the girls? What about me? Why do you want to leave? Why now?"

Me don't reply. Wanda start to cry, and me keep packing.

"Clive! Clive," Wanda hollered like somebody hurt her. "Come here. Come here quick."

Him come in the room and Wanda fall into his arms crying and me feel like slapping her and him. Them happy together and never think about me.

"Clive, please tell Mommie that she can't leave. Please, tell her how much me need her."

Clive looked at me with Wanda crying in his arms, and the words he uttered was not the words him eyes were saying to me.

"Wanda Baby, if Juanita wants to leave, she has the right to have her own life. We will miss her, but we shouldn't try to stop her happiness."

"But she can have her own life and still be happy living with us."

"Maybe she had found herself a man," he said, his eyes penetrating into mine.

Me tell you, me should have left that night and all the rest would have been avoided; but me allowed Wanda's tears to persuade me out of me good sense.

Things went on the same for a while, but it wasn't the same. Me pretend as if me growing feelings for Clive didn't exist. Wanda get promotion again, and working till late at night; she traveling to America, to other islands. Many nights me and Clive and the girls sit down in the house watching TV, doing homework, going to the movies and the beach. The girls call me Mama, and them call Wanda Mommy. Sometimes them crawl in me bed, sometimes me fall asleep in their beds when me read them a story, and Clive kiss all of us goodnight. Soon all the girls in school, even little Caroline, just three years old and start pre-school.

Me feel like life leaving me behind, but me don't know what to do. Me have an ache in me heart. Me find me vex easy for nothing. Wanda saying me going through change of life, but even though me almost fifty me still have me period. All of a sudden, all these years me not interested in being with any man, now me find me eyes start follow man, including Clive. Me shame, me shame so bad. Me thinking, maybe Wanda right, and me should get a man-friend. Even Mama after all these years start live with a man.

Just as me decide to start go out, Clive come down sick. Doctors do all kind of tests. Nothing. Is me one him want nurse him cause him say Wanda too impatient with him. Almost a month he's off work before him start to improve. One morning after the girls in school, and me in the kitchen tidying up, me feel him behind me. Him hug me around de waist and kiss me on top of me head.

"Yu must feel well better," me say without turning, feeling me body going soft.

"Thanks to you," him say, still pressed up against me, his arms around me waist. Me lean into him, push me arse into his groin. Him push more into me. Me body all de way soft. Me not listening to me head. The water running, but me not washing any dishes, just there pressed against him. Then me turn around and say to him.

"Is must tickle, you want me tickle you." And me begin to tickle him, but him grab a hold of me hand, and me look on him, and the next thing we a kiss, then we a roll on the floor, then our clothes off and me a moan, and praying that him keep kissing me and touching me, and pushing into me like that all day. And that is exactly what him do until is time for me to go and pick up the girls.

Wanda come home early that evening for a change, and me tell her me too tired to eat dinner or help the girls with them homework. If shame was a color me was that color. Me could not look at me daughter.

"Mommie, I hope you're not getting sick like Clive," she placed the back of her hand on me forehead.

"Me don't think so; besides, Clive better," I mumbled before turning into my room and locking the door. That night I prayed on my knees and asked for forgiveness and swore that me would never let anything like that happen again with Clive.

The next morning as soon as me come back from taking the girls to school, me knock on him door to beg him excuse. Him say it was his fault, and it won't happen again, but him touch me hand, and me allow me finger to glide over his, and him pull me to him, and me fall in him lap, and we start kissing, and in the same bed him sleep with Wanda, me daughter, on that same bed he made love to me, loved me until me cry. Me never know it could feel so good. And is so we start to carry on, every chance we get.

When him start back to work, him come home lunch time for a quickie. Sometimes, even when Wanda was home, he would come into me room, and with the door wide open, we pretend we playing checkers, but him other hand would be under my skirt. It got so that me couldn't even sleep at nights thinking about him making love to Wanda like him making love to me. Me would get up and tiptoe to their bedroom door and listen. Me heart crumpling when me hear them, but me couldn't stop listening, and me couldn't stop wanting him; me try; we try, but we just wanted each other too much. Me tell you me love him. Was willing to have him when me could. Me know it wrong. We know. Me try to stop. Me pray for strength. Me tell meself me don't want him, but still me want him.

Wanda notice something. One evening at dinner she say,

"Clive, have you noticed how happy Mommie's looking these days. I think she has a boyfriend and isn't telling us."

Me tell you, if me was a white person, me face would turn tomato. Me just look at the food on me plate, but me couldn't eat another bite. Clive act like him don't hear, but Wanda wouldn't leave it alone.

"So Mommie who's the man? Come on tell me. Clive, is it one of your friends?"

"Wanda, why you can't just leave things be and eat your dinner?" Clive snapped. Wanda don't say anything else because the girls looking at her, at them dad, and at me.

Me excuse meself and go into me room, determined to move into me own place and end this once and for all.

They say life isn't lived unless it's full of surprises. Me notice me gaining a little weight, me breasts tender and me tired all the time. One Saturday me sit down at the kitchen table puffing and Wanda bring me a glass of water. Clive had taken the girls somewhere so is just me and Wanda at home. Me tell her me have a taste for some limeade so she make some and we go sit down on the veranda drinking it. It had been a long time since Wanda and me talk and laugh together because of her work, and me and Clive carrying on, life getting in between us. Anyway we sit down and Wanda begin to talk. She tell me how she tired of her work, hours too long, and it not fun any more. Fun! Me didn't even know that work could be fun.

But Wanda in a talking mood so she talk about the girls, and how nicely they were growing, thanks to me; but also she say she want to spend more time with them. Then she got silent, and almost whispered that she and Clive were not close anymore; she feel him pulling away from her. Me don't say anything, but me heart heavy. Me just listening, and hating meself for what me doing to me own daughter that me love as much as life and would do anything for her. But me know no one would believe me if me say that, and yet sleeping with her husband. Wanda was thinking out loud for she said,

"You know what Mommie. I think Clive and I need a vacation, just the two of us. You could keep the girls?"

I am afraid to even look at me daughter. Then Wanda turn to me and say,

"Mommie, you are glowing. Are you happy? Who is your man?"

Right then and there me decide to continue the lie.

"Me going to introduce you to him soon. Is just that him work at nights…" Same time Clive and the girls drive up and me was so thankful.

Well a few weeks later, after that conversation, one night after me showered, me examined me body, and immediately me head start to pound. Next day me make an appointment to see the doctor. The doctor confirmed what me suspected. Me pregnant, four months plus; too late to have an abortion. Imagine my surprise. Here me is fifty years old and pregnant by me son-in-law.

When me leave the doctor office, me sit down at the bus stop. Me too confused to cry. Me get up, walk around until me find phone and call Clive at work. Him come get me, and before me shut the door me blurt out.

"Clive me pregnant and doctor say it too late to have an abortion. What me going to tell Wanda?" Clive reached over and squeeze me hand, but him don't say anything.

Him drive to a little restaurant. We order food; me watch him face knitted. Me well hungry all of a sudden so me eat and still Clive don't say anything. Me trying to decide what to do. Me know me have to move out. Me know me can't tell Mama. Here me is a big woman, with three grandchildren, one as old as ten, and me pregnant by them father. Who would understand? Who would not judge me? Who would forgive me? Me didn't even feel the tears them running down my cheek, until me feel Clive's fingers wiping away me tears.

"Juanita, I am so sorry. I didn't plan any of this. I don't know what came over me, but I don't regret being with you. I love you and I love Wanda and I don't want to lose either of you. I don't want to break up our family."

Me put my hand over his and stare at Clive long and hard. Me could feel his love strong-strong, just like when wave swell up and splash against rock sending water into the air.

"Clive, me shame and me not shame. Me know what me feel for you can't wrong, even though the circumstances is wrong. Yet me love Wanda so and want her to be happy. Is only she one me sad for because as close as we are, me don't think she will understand. If me was in her shoe, me wouldn't understand. Promise me you will never tell her," me say to Clive, tears dripping into my plate.

"Juanita, I love you and want to be with you. I don't want to think about you not being in my life. I love Wanda too, but not like I love you. For a long time now things have been cooling between Wanda and me. It has been a long time now that I've been desiring you as a woman, but I was afraid to act on it. I know everyone will say what we have done is wrong. I know it's wrong, but I can't help my heart feeling what it does. I have tried to stay away from you. I have…" Clive shook his head as if he was trying to shake out and away this situation we find ourselves in. He reached across the table and clasped his fingers through mine, right there in the restaurant where everyone can see us.

Me don't feel comfortable talking there so me suggest we go Hope Gardens where we can walk and talk. Clive called him office and tell them an emergency came up, and it is true—this thing between us is emergency for true.

We walked and talked for almost two hours and still could not agree, except not to tell Wanda and that I should move out. Clive doesn't want me to move, but me tell him, me will start showing soon, and me and him can't keep carrying on like that in Wanda's house. That's when me decide to tell the tenants to move from the house that Wanda and me had bought.

Same day Clive drove me by the house and me gave the tenants one week notice since they were two months behind on the rent. However, the house was in poor condition. It need painting, the bathroom and kitchen need to be redone, major work. Clive said not to worry, he would take care of all the details. But it will take a month or more before the house would be ready. Me say me can bide me time, but it hard-hard, now that me pregnant and Clive and me confess openly to each other how we feel. Nonetheless, we promise and swear that we are not going to fool around anymore in the house. We tried to act like normal, which wasn't normal for a long time now.

Finally, the house was ready and me moved out. Me decided to test out Mama first to hear what she say.

"Mama, me pregnant," me say when me went to visit her. Me decided not to beat around the bush.

Mama laughed. Mama laughed so hard, she held her belly and tears streamed out her eyes, then she said.

"Juanita, me is sixty-five so that must mek you, let me see," she scratched her head, "Fifty your next birthday."

Me didn't laugh with her. Mama looked at me as if she were studying a problem, she sighed and then muttered,

"Juanita, tell me is joke, you joking; tell me nothing go so."

"Me pregnant, Mama."

"But how you to pregnant? You don't have no man, and you is not the Virgin Mary. The only man you fuss about is Clive…" Her mouth flew open and she quickly covered it with her hand.

"Juanita," she says leaning forward, her voice edged. "Juanita, tell me is not Clive breed you, tell me is not true."

Me can't look at Mama; me eyes wander all over the room until she begin to talk again.

"Fah years now me been thinking how you and Clive lovey-dovey not normal, not normal at all for mother-in-law and son-in-law. For years now me been telling you to get your own place, and leave Wanda wid she husband. For years now me been watching you and him hugging up and dancing close at parties and hanging on to each other more than him and Wanda. Now you telling me, you pregnant for you daughter's husband. Lawd Almighty, Juanita! Is what kind of thing this? Is how you mek this go so far? You not fourteen anymore, you know! How you could sleep wid you daughter's husband? Me know you have needs, but why you couldn't go and look man that's available."

"Mama, it just happen. We never plan it."

"Juanita, nutten just happen, not even rain. Me did see it happening, but me didn't think…at least me hope it wasn't happening this way. How many times me warn you: it not natural that Clive and you spend so much time together, lie down inna bed, go beach, him always a hug-up on you. Didn't me tell you it not normal." Mama turned away from me.

There was nothing for me to say because Mama did warn me plenty times that Clive and me too close, but me always replied that he was affectionate with everyone.

Mama's voice cut into me.

"So Juanita, you mean to tell me you and Clive been carrying on all this time; you and him sexing in the house just like him and Wanda? Lawd Juanita. Me shame a you Juanita. Me shame a you. You own daughter husband, you grand-

146

children father. Lawd, Juanita, nothing good can come of this. What poor Wanda say?"

"We don't tell her; she don't know. Me tell Clive we should wait until me move."

"Move! So you moving now? How many years me tell you to move, go find your own place, go find your own life; but you always claim Wanda need you. But now her husband breed you, you moving. Where you go live?"

"Clive fixing up our old house for me to move back to. Me give de tenants notice."

"Clive…So Clive plan to have the daughter in one house and the mother in another. Is not Clive one only who have wood you know Juanita. You plan to keep carrying on with Clive?"

"Mama, Clive and me love each other."

"Lawd, you see the heavy-heavy cross me daughter come bring me to carry today. Me wake up on the wrong side of the bed this morning, but me neva know Satan was in the room." Mama looked around and sucked her teeth. "You and Clive love each other. But him is not yours to love. Is you daughter's husband. Did you forget that?" Her voice was shrill.

"Mama we love Wanda too, but we love one another and we want to be together."

"Juanita, is what this you saying to me?"

"Clive want to leave Wanda and live with me."

"Ah don't want hear no more. No more. Clear out and go home, but know that me on Wanda side, whatever you and Clive decide or don't decide me on Wanda side. Juanita, you too old to have baby, and you too old to be acting this way. You can't even blame youth for your behavior."

"Me not blaming anyone or anything, Mama. Me just know how me feel. Me feel happy and good, not like when me was with Hilton. Me feel like me heart blooming like pretty flowers, like the flamboyant in June."

"Me see you don't learn nutten. Now you is big woman you reaching high bout flamboyant tree. Don't bring the tree into this. Hilton was another woman's husband too. How you heart can be pretty when you sexing your daughter's husband?" Mama turned away from me, and she never talked to me until after me have the baby.

She came to visit me in hospital and she picked up Jason, looked on him, counted his toes and fingers, then glanced at me before saying,

"This is a real miracle baby, real miracle." She hugged and nestled him to her bosom. And although she hardly spoke to Clive, she visited all the time and always brought a little something for her grandson.

But me jumping ahead to happier times. It took over a month before the house was ready for me to move. That same day the doctor confirmed that me pregnant me told Wanda she would need to find a helper cause me would be moving. To my surprise, she didn't beg me to stay. All she said was, "I think Clive has an outside woman; he hardly touches me anymore."

Me have to confess when she tell me that me so happy cause me don't want him sleep with her anymore. Me did tell Clive him have to choose: me or Wanda, but him can't have both of us anymore. Him tell me him choose long time. So me move and still don't tell Wanda, but the second night me in the house Clive come by and we a hug up in the bed watching TV, and Wanda knock on the door demanding to be let in.

"Mommy, Clive, I want to know what's going on between you," she demanded.

Me know the hour come, but me want to let her know no malice was intended, that me love her, so me walk over to where she is and touch her lightly on the shoulder.

"Wanda baby," me say caressing her face, and me couldn't say anymore. Tears start run down her cheeks and she push me away. Clive step forward, and she fist her hand and give him such a thump, him stagger backwards. Before him could regain his balance she screamed so loud me sure the people in the house way across the street, heard it all.

"You're fucking my mother, Clive? You're fucking my mother just like how you're fucking me. You're carrying on with my mother. Fucking your children's grandmother. Who do you like fucking best Clive? Me or my mother?" Then she slumped on the bed and began to cry, then bawl. Clive and I just stood there looking at her on the bed, tears and snot mingling.

Wanda kept asking, "Mommy, why? Why? Why?" And just as she calmed down, the baby kicked and I cradled my stomach. I was wearing a tee shirt and Wanda looked at me, and she saw how big my stomach was. She glared at me.

"Me having a baby Wanda," me say.

She sprang off the bed and pulled up the tee shirt. She looked at me, at my belly and then at Clive.

"Mommie, are you pregnant for Clive? Are you?" Her voice was like a moan.

Me stood like a statue. She walked over to the dresser, looked at herself in the mirror, glared at Clive and me through the mirror, and without turning to face us Wanda said:

"I don't want to see or ever talk to either of you again. Mommy you won't ever see you granddaughters again, and Clive make sure and take all you things tomorrow when I am at work and don't ever come back to that house."

Me didn't say a thing because me know she angry, and me deserve that. Clive spend the night, and although we sad, we also relieve that we can finally be out in the open. Me never want to believe that Wanda meant what she said because even as a little girl she never was mean or spiteful.

The next day when Clive went the house to find most of his things piled on the verandah, covered in bleach and flour; he was able to salvage only a few things. Me tell Clive to give her time because she was hurting and angry, and had every right to be. But me and Clive living together bring out a meanness in her I didn't recognize, and I am not sure even she recognized sheself.

When Clive tried to visit the girls whom he loved dearly, Wanda called the police and lied that he abused her, and said she was afraid for her life. She told the helper if either of us came around to call the police. Both Clive and I missed the girls so much; they were like me own children. Me raised them from them born. We could not talk to them on the phone; we could not see them. Even when Clive tried to see the girls at school, he was warned that if him didn't leave they would be forced to call the police. Clive and me brokenhearted over not being able to see de 3Cs, as we often referred to them. Me missed reading to them at bed time, hugging and kissing them, eating dinner together and hearing about their day at school. Poor Clive suffered; him love him girls, plus Wanda went to his job and created such a scandal, he was almost fired.

Wanda filed for divorce the same week Clive and I moved out, and she made sure everybody knew why. The case even appeared in the Star with the headlines, "Mother Steals Daughter's Husband From Right Under Her Nose." Me so shame for weeks, me don't even go outside, not even to my pre-natal appointments. In court Wanda claimed me and Clive was carrying on from the beginning; how we had sex in front of the girls and that she caught us in her own bed. Worse of all she said Clive and me beat the girls and told them we would kill them if they ever told anyone that we were lovers. Wanda told such lies I didn't recognize her.

Me know me and Clive hurt her; me know she tore up inside; me know she must feel hopeless as she lost her two best friends one time—me and Clive. Yes, we were mother and daughter and husband and wife, but we were friends, also. Still, some of the things Wanda said in court me could never repeat.

Anyway the judge ruled that me can't see my granddaughters, the very girls me care for more than Wanda, the very girls me nursed when them sick, bathed, read to and fed them. The judge stated that Clive and me can't see them, when we both were closer to them than Wanda. The judge declared that we were unfit and should be publicly flogged for our indecent behavior; that we were immoral and could not be allowed to corrupt their young minds with our nasty behavior. But most terrible of all is how Wanda bawled in the court, claiming that me never loved her, that me abandoned her as a child, and always brought men in the house when she was a baby. The things she said I didn't even know who she was talking about. Of course, most people think me deserve whatever she said and whatever happened, and that me get off easy.

All me have to say is, life is like a crooked stick, but love is never wrong. Me will always love Wanda and me granddaughters; and me will always love Clive for opening me heart. Me don't know how Wanda could think because me and Clive together, that me don't love her. How she can think all these years of loving and taking care of her are wiped clean just because me sleep with Clive. How can she call me whore and turn her back on me, when there was never a day that me didn't love her? Me still love her and feel awful about what happened, but me never plan it; me still can't explain how it happened.

Mama refused to talk to me. She said I should not even come to her gate. She disown me. So I lose me daughter, me mother and me three granddaughters.

Me tell you this love thing is one big mystery to me.

So we accept fate, but we don't give up hope. Everyday me tell Clive Wanda will come round eventually; the girls will wear her down, demanding that they want to see us. There is a great gap in our hearts from missing the girls. The gossip and bad talk are crowns of thorn that we wear daily; especially Clive, who was forced to resign from his job. The only good thing during this time was to the doctor's surprise me was having an easy normal pregnancy. No sickness, nothing, except during the last two months me feet swelled badly and me had to stay off them most times. Imagine, at fifty give birth to a healthy eight pounds—seven ounces son. Clive was so happy that the baby and me healthy. The first time he held Jason in him arms he whispered:

"I wish the girls where here to see their brother."

Neither of us had seen them during this time. Turn out Wanda's helper and mine were cousins, so we heard that the girls were crying all the time and not doing well in school. Me tell Clive, me no care what the judge say, me need to go and see Wanda and beg her forgiveness, and beg her to let the girls see us. Why should they suffer when they had nothing to do with what happened between Clive and me?

Me continued to pray and hope that Wanda would come round, but Jason was almost three months and still not a word. So one day me decided to go to her job.

If looks could kill, the way she look at me me would be dead. But me heart cry for her; she was bloated and her eyes looked puffy as if she had been crying morning, noon, and night. Me could tell she was not sleeping well either. Me move to just touch her, but she made the X sign with her hands in front of her and told me,

"Step back and don't ever come close to me. How dare you come here? You're lucky I don't have you throw out." Then she sat behind her desk, pretending to sort through papers. Me didn't know where to begin so me just sit there dumb, just glad to see her and me realized in that moment, from the day she born, thirty five years ago, this was the longest time me had ever gone without seeing Wanda, more than five months, and me hope she was thinking the same, and maybe, she would consider that we had thirty-four years together because in truth, it was only a year since me and Clive started sleeping together. As if she read me mind, she glance up and asked

"What do you want?"

"Me miss you, Wanda. Me miss you. Me miss the girls. Me love you and me sorry that what happened happened. Me didn't mean for it to happen."

"Your sorry is way too late, and the girls and I are doing just fine, and you will never see them again, except over my dead body."

"Wanda we had thirty-four good years, that must mean something."

"Juanita, I hate you. I hate you for what you have done, for taking away the first and only man I love. I hate you for taking away my children's father; I hate you for ruining our friendship and love. I hate you and I want to see you dead and John-Crow eat your body by the side of the road."

Then she sprang from behind her desk and spat on me and spat on me until me entire face was covered with her saliva and she had no more strength to spit. Me sit there and let her because me know we deserve it, and without even wiping her saliva from me eye, I stood up, looked on her and hoping to soften her heart said,

"Know that me still love you and the girls and always will. Me hope you will be able to forgive me and not punish the girls for what me did. The whole time you were growing up. You used to beg me that you want to have a brother, well you have a brother now."

She lunged at me and knocked me to the floor; then started to pelt me. It took her secretary and two other women to take her off me and restrain her. Me face bloody and bruised, me chest in pain. Me guess someone call a taxi and put me in it, and me get home.

When Clive came home, me in bed all bruised and sore. Him mad but him understand, and me realize that this thing between us could not survive under this strain. One month later, a Sunday afternoon, Mama come by the gate and call to me and Clive. She say Wanda's house on fire. By the time we get there, the house burn to the ground, and everything in it, but no one inside.

The neighbors said Wanda and the girls left early that morning with suitcases. Monday we learn that she and the girls took a flight that morning to Miami, and that was the last time we saw or heard about them, ten years now.

Clive turn sick with worry. He had a brother in Miami so he asked him to hire a private detective to track down Wanda. He just wanted to know his girls were okay, and wherever they were, that they were safe. The detective said although they landed in Miami, Wanda must have taken the bus or train to another state, and more than likely she even changed their names.

Things just keep happening. Jason just six months, and me pregnant again. Since Wanda and the girls gone, Mama start talk to me, well mostly she says she come to see her grandson, and that Jesus did say, forgive those that trespass against you, and that she knew I was not too bad a person, because apart from having Wanda at fifteen, and she still was not going to forgive me for that; and apart from sleeping with my daughter's husband and now living with him, and she would never forgive me for that; I was a good person. And besides her grandson Jason should not be blamed for me and his father's sin because when he got old and learned how he was conceived he would judge us enough, so he needed her to love him and provide a balance. Clive and me were grateful for Mama, and little-by-little, I could see that we were getting more relaxed with each other, and I hoped that one day the same thing would happen between Wanda and me.

When Mama learn that me was pregnant again, she joked that me was like Abraham's wife, Sarah, who had her first child when she was more than a hundred years old. Me tell Clive him can't put no more dough in me oven after this second baby. Things a little hard for us, with Clive only working every now and again. Sometimes me worry that him slowly losing his mind worrying about where Wanda and the girls are, and spending every penny he earns to try and find them. So me picked up a little sewing. Clive began an export business, traveling to Miami and New York to buy and sell things; but mostly I know, even though he says that's not the case, hoping to find Wanda and the girls. We managing. Me have another son, and we name him Wayne, which was the name me had picked out for the boy me had hoped Wanda was going to be.

Then Clive get visa and say we must move to Miami. Me refuse. We argue. We fight. Me tired and weary and tell him to go. Him say just for a little while, but me know him not coming back as long as him don't find Wanda and the girls.

Me keep praying. At fifty-three me is left with two little boys to care for. Me so glad Mama is only sixty-eight and still healthy, and love her grandsons. Me have to start back the sewing in earnest.

At first Clive comes home every three months, at least for a week, but in the second year, only twice then him doesn't even come. He sends tickets for me and the boys. Although me don't want to go Mama said me should, we could have a clean start, but I don't like Miami, and don't want my sons to grow up there. Besides, with everything that happened Clive and me not like we used to be…the pain and guilt and shame taller than the Blue Mountains, and most times we don't have the strength for the climb. We're barely hanging on by the fifth year.

Still not a word about Wanda and the girls. Clive is greyer than me, moving like an old man. Me know we over. Yes we still love and desire one another, but we just can't manage the climb. When him come home that Christmas, me say to him as we sit down on the veranda, afraid it seems to me to even hold hands:

"Thank you for the love. Thank you. And don't ever abandon your sons. And sometimes when you think about me, don't think of me as the woman who caused you to lose the wife and daughters that you love; but rather think of me as the woman who needed your love to discover herself. Me will always love you Clive, and me don't feel shame or guilt about our love anymore." Him reach over then and grasped my fingers tight, and I could feel how relieved he was.

He hasn't returned since that Christmas five years ago. He sends money when he can. He calls the boys weekly and twice a year he sends tickets for them to spend time with him. We talk occasionally. He called last week all excited saying he thinks he has finally found a lead; not of Wanda, but whom we hope is Carmen, the oldest of the 3Cs, in a college in South Carolina.

That was the full story, I said raising my eyes for the first time to my friend. She nodded then smiled faintly. As she stood by the door before leaving, she rested her hand on my shoulder and said, "Every river has to carry its share of garbage." I nodded consent, but after she left I wondered…

God's Child

A persistent craving for guava-coconut tarts drove me out the house.

She was walking on the right side of the road, as was usual for that time of day, heading toward Frederiksted, as I approached the Pastry Hut in the direction of Christiansted. Cars were zooming in the opposite direction, so I screeched to a full stop, neglecting to turn on my left turn signal. A courteous driver stopped and signaled for me to make the left turn. As I stopped and got out of my car, she ran up and crouched down in front of me. I glanced over my shoulder to make sure it was her. How could she have crossed the street so quickly?

Stepping back into my open car door, I waved for her to pass, but she quickly and firmly took a hold of my left wrist, slammed my car door shut and, peering into my eyes with fierce determination, said, "Me been waiting long time for you. No time for guava tart."

Her grip was a rubbery manacle, allowing no escape. Easily, she led me from my car and the Pastry Hut parking lot. How did she know that I didn't need to have any guava-coconut tart in this, my second week on a diet, I reflected, but still thought about calling out to someone, anyone, "Don't you see the mad woman leading me away? Help!" It was fleeting. I instead looked around and chuckled, feeling an affinity with my captor.

I had to trot to keep pace with her. I noticed the flamboyant trees lining the road were in blossom and suddenly I wanted nothing more urgently than to see their fire-red petals. I glanced down and realized she was barefoot, her soles black as tires. My breath caught, as if I had swallowed a fish bone. She smelled like parched soil after a sudden shower of rain. "You are not really dressed for the journey," I thought I heard someone say, but realized it came from my own mind. I tossed my head from left to right and dismissed the thought. Don't throw a lit match on kerosene. The wind was indifferent. My two-inch heels crunched yet were comfortable, but my starched cotton peach blouse and straight tan skirt, while ideal work attire, were not intended for a fast-paced walk.

After I had loped behind her on Queen Mary Highway for about three hundred yards, she turned to me, eyes dusky as a sunset, and sneered, "You think you know me, but you don't see the man on me back."

She was a crazy woman. The entire Frederiksted community knew of her—crazy for years—one of the known crazies on the streets. I had been following her for months, asking others about her, trying to find out where she lived, who sewed the eclectic clothes she wore, wanting to uncover the genesis of her mental illness. She was ill. Some might also think me ill. Obsession was an illness. I wanted, no, needed to know her. She mumbled something I did not catch. She laughed, sweet and deep, then spoke clearly, as if delivering a lecture.

"You and me is one, but you don't see that yet. Time will tell."

The clouds suddenly greyed over, and the air smelled wet. There would be a brisk afternoon shower, disappearing as suddenly as it appeared. Drizzles as soft as a lover's touch covered my skin. She stopped, her head back, face to the sky. She had a beautiful mouth, I realized—full, smooth lips, almost mauve colored, and her teeth, surprisingly white. I followed her gaze, trying to see as she saw.

"Me is God's Child," she said, returning her gaze to the road and shaking my left hand with her right. She still held me firmly around my left wrist with her slender, strong, earth-brown thumb and middle finger.

"I am pleased to meet you, God's Child," I replied, bowing my head. "I am She Who Answers the Call," I replied mischievously.

"Me know," she said, a smile flitting across her face. "That's why me go tell you a story. Is right here, on this spot it began." She stood, a tree planted.

I looked around as if seeking evidence, a marker that would indicate a catastrophic event occurred here, but nothing stood out, except maybe two conch shells buried facing tip to eye, pointing east to west, with their pink interior showing. I could feel her eyes, like torches, flaming my skin. I nodded for her to continue.

"Walking helps me forget what I always remember." She paused as if allowing me to take in the full impact of her words. I searched for something meaningful to say, but coming up with nothing, I remained silent. She didn't seem to mind, and I sensed, if I was quiet, she would tell me what was on her mind. There was a Thibet tree stump on which she leaned, while I stood before her, a child being scolded. I was listening to my strained breathing, when her voice, like a wisp of wind, nudged me.

"Is not me alone someone lie to. I know this to be the truth of truths. And me is not the first person who love someone, and the very person you thought was your friend, who love you too, took what you love without so much as a sorry. She was me cousin. Well, she is still me cousin, and me still love she. She knew me love he. He wasn't me first, but me love he in a way that did spell danger. Me love he until me thought he was mine."

155

I knew what she meant. I had loved beyond love, if that is possible. I knew about loving someone so much that if another person got in the way . . .

"So listen, nuh," she said, pulling me back to her story. "When you love someone more than you love yourself, it easy for another person to raise a cutlass and slice up the love, just chop it up." She threw back her head, and a strident anguish that stopped a bird in flight spilled from her throat. Then she shoved me and I stumbled down. When I had regained my balance and dusted off my behind, God's Child was way ahead, dancing up the street. She waved at me and shouted over her shoulder.

"Forget the diet. Catch you later." Her voice echoed.

I didn't know if I should walk back to my car or follow God's Child.

The Living Roots

Dusk skipped in like a woman in haste to meet her lover. The sun, hiding behind the mountain, was the only witness as Essence's head emerged flat from the side of the cotton tree. She knew as soon as the air hit her face that she should have waited until night had crept in like a man returning from a clandestine affair, but she was impatient.

She had told Tuba, who claimed the Maroon leadership after her father died, that they had been too long underground That Piliferous Layer, although a safe haven for them, was only meant to be temporary. He saw her advice as a challenge to his authority. He believed that perhaps Essence, as daughter of the past leader of one the most formidable Maroon colonies, felt she should be the heir. But Essence was only amused by Tuba's masculine insecurity. She loved being a reconnaissance scout and had no ambition to be a leader. She had witnessed firsthand the challenges and sacrifices her father had made, and understood how leading and trying to be everything to everyone had worn him down.

Besides, she fully intended, when she was ready, to woo Tuba to her bed and make him her husband. He had a mind and body that made him as close to an equal that she would get, and it didn't hurt that he titillated her. Perhaps that was why she was on this mission, defying his order, knowing he would come after her and provide her with the opportunity she needed for them to be alone, away from colony scrutiny—especially her mother's, a master strategist.

Before Essence could withdraw and blend fully into the tree, a woman spotted her, and cried out, "How duppy come out so early?" Instantly, the woman dropped the bags in her hands, cupped her palms together, blew in them, then tossed her palms above her head as if throwing something away. Essence smiled. It was not the first time that an enslaved person thought she was an apparition. The woman gathered up her bags loaded with fruits and ground provisions, glanced around at the tree, and moved away swiftly, taking wide strides, her arms swinging vigorously despite the heavy bags that she clutched. Essence was tempted to call out to her, but decided against it, as there was no urgency. Why scare the woman out of her wits? she mused. In due time, she would have the information she needed to report back to Tuba and the colony. Essence stayed connected to the trunk of the tree until night was fully dressed like a bride in a veil.

She separated herself from the tree trunk and wavered in the cool night air—flat, one-dimensional, compressed soil that slowly ballooned out until she was body and flesh. Her waist-length dreadlocks separated from the sap of the tree and Essence coughed and stretched as she acclimated to the slave colony. Then she remembered what she always forgot: that the people of the world she was entering wore clothes, the unnecessary excessive fabric that hid the beauty and sensuality of their bodies. In Piliferous Layer they wore no clothes, had no need for such excess that impeded them from communicating with one another. Everything was through touch and taste, in fact, not to touch or lick another was an indication of animosity towards that person. That was why she knew Tuba was meant to be hers. He tasted like roasted sweet potato. But she had never told him this. Nor had he told her what her taste was.

Essence put aside her reverie as she heard footsteps and squatted behind the tree, making sure she was out of sight of the voices. She had not yet mastered this human form, which she hated, not because it was ugly, but because the enslaved world always infuriated her, with its control of human labor and restriction of their movements: "a complete degradation of the human spirit."

She identified two men, walking slowly, machetes slung across their shoulders, their voices loud and friendly. As they strode past, the shorter of the two craned his neck and glanced at the tree. Essence could feel his eyes scanning the tree and wondered how he knew she was there even though he could not see her.

This had happened to Essence several times in the past when she visited the enslaved world. When she had mentioned these incidents to her father, he told her that even though some of the people were slaves, they were related to the Maroons, and could, if they really tapped into their ancestral memory, escape bondage by submerging below the surface of the earth to live freely as they once did. Essence suspected that this man was related to them and was either a subversive or his memory was damaged by the system of slavery. Still, it was not wise for her to call to him, because with his altered brain capacity, he might think that she was an apparition, or duppy. It was funny to Essence that some of these enslaved relatives of hers were unable to distinguish between the ancestors who had gone ahead and those who were still living in an evolved state among them.

The men moved safely out of sight until their voices were a distant sound like crickets speaking another language. Essence scanned the landscape to ascertain where she might find nondescript clothes in order to move among them without attracting attention. She felt that this time was different than the last time she was here. The air was not as constricted, and she smelled another fragrance—even in the men who had just passed and the woman earlier—that she hadn't smelled in them before. It was like thyme; but she did not know how to read that smell or its meaning. It had been about five years since she had last visited this land they called Xaymaca.

She and the other reconnoiterers had figured out that every one year of their life was equal to five years of their enslaved relatives' lives. Her grandmother had known this from when she was prodded into a ship, pregnant with her first child. That was why in the dark and despair of the hold, rather than surrender to defeat, she had raised her voice, and called out to see who else was in training to be a priestess like she had been. Six other women had responded and despite the vomiting, tears, feces, and the sheer bewilderment that many succumbed to, they had plotted and planned how to transform themselves and escape their fate, paving a way for the life growing inside their wombs.

Essence's mother had told her the story many times about her maternal grandmother whom she had never met, and how the first inhabitants of the underground Maroon colony were all pregnant women, all former priestess-es-in-training who had discovered that pregnant women had the capacity to survive underground and to train their unborn children to do likewise; that the source of their power was in their dreadlocked hair that was like roots that al-lowed them to breathe and receive all the nutrients that they required. That was why all the enslaved people, especially the men, were forced to wear their hair cut short and even the women's hair refused to grow to any significant length because it was being tamed by the enslavers' comb. This was simply another way they were being trained to work for the benefit of others, and more importantly, they were also being trained to dislike and distrust their natural selves. But this was not the time to reminisce. She was on a mission, and if she wasn't careful to adapt to her environment, she could end up like her maternal grandmother: head shaved and doomed to live the life of a captive.

Quickly, she identified a house about two miles from the cotton tree, where she would find clothes and cloth with which to wrap her hair and protect her power. Putting her ears to the ground to make sure no one was walking around in the immediate vicinity, she easily jogged to the farmhouse and found a stack of clothes folded in a corner inside a small room. She selected the simplest sack-like dress, then, digging through a basket, found several pieces of cloth. Selecting a smooth, brown, cotton piece, she wound it around her head, completely covering her thick hair that when left free brushed against her bottom. She was ready to move about, learn how her earthly relatives were making out, and how she and her people might continue to help them regain their freedom.

Morning found her in the market with the other women as they were always the best source of news.

"Howdy!" they greeted each other, their full voices like hampers, baskets, loaded with ground provisions, their gestures free and intimate as the breeze flirting under the leaves of trees.

"Howdy!" Essence joined the women in greeting, quickly scanning their bodies to discern which of them still had active memory. Once again she smelled thyme among them and then she remembered. It was the same fragrance she had detected the night she had wandered into the rebellion that left three overseers dead and several acres of cane-field smoldering. Could it be that these women had acquired their freedom? But how could that be? She did not detect the memory in any of them.

Confused, Essence floundered. She did not know if she could trust herself. This always happened when she covered her hair and wound it tight in a bundle to keep from being easily recognized; she received mixed messages, and wasn't quite sure if the information she was receiving was accurate. Desperate to regain balance, she pushed her way into the midst of a group of women and touched one on the arm. Very clearly she received the answer she sought: "Me neva gwane be anybody's slave," the woman's skin proclaimed. Just as Essence was about to let go and move away, she felt the woman's thumb and index finger circle her wrist.

"Is who yu?" the woman declared, pulling Essence closer to her and jerking up her arm. Essence slowed her heartbeat to synchronize it with the turning of soil as a seed takes root. Instantly the woman dropped her hand.

"Me know yu?" the woman asked, less self-assured now.

Essence looked at the woman and recognized her from the evening before, when in her haste Essence had emerged from the side of the tree.

"You belong to the Starch people, like me," Essence said, spreading her moist calm over the woman. "If you search your memory bank, you will recognize me as a cousin," Essence continued drawing strength from the woman, which allowed her to scan the woman's body more fully. She realized the woman was growing dreadlocks hidden beneath her head-wrap.

"Me see yu before," the woman replied as her mind travelled back in time. "Me se yu before, but yu was different," the woman ended, nodding her head as if to awaken her memory.

"We survive through our ability to disguise and adapt," Essence smiled, touching the woman's hand and immediately drinking in her warmth, like soil being sprinkled with water. "Can we go where we can talk?" she asked, feeling other ears prick up at their conversation.

The woman's eyes bore into Essence, trying to read her in a more obvious way than Essence was trained to do. Then she smiled, satisfied with what she believed she saw and knew.

"We guh afta me get a likkle piece a meat fi flavor de pot," the woman said, turning. Then she stopped and gazed once again on Essence. "Cousin," she said with full meaning, "de people call me Walker because me feets does know where to travel any time day or night; but me other name be Carmen. Carmen de Walker be me preference." She smiled broadly and began to move through the crowd of mostly women haggling over food and prices. Essence kept up, and with her mouth almost touching Carmen's ear, said, "I'm known as Essence of the Starch People."

Carmen de Walker nodded acknowledgment as she weaved with ease through the crowd, occasionally greeting others with both a nod of her head and a salutation which often involved inquiring about other members of their family. After more than an hour of this ritual, Essence deduced that the market was a meeting place to exchange news, shopping was merely the guise. The women's talk was about how sweet freedom was, even though the bacras still had their foot on their backs.

"But we will find a way round dem white people and dem meanness," said a woman selling carrots.

"Me done tell de one me lease land from dat if him keep touching me behind, ah go fall down pan he and squeeze he to death," a rotund woman said with mirth.

"It nah gwane tek much fah you fi squeeze de day-lights out of dat magga, red skin bacra," said another, bearing a bunch of bananas on her head.

The women laughed good-naturedly and moved on. Essence tried to understand their tongue which was slightly different from the language she spoke, but even more, she was trying to comprehend how they could claim to be free, and in the same breath declare that someone had a foot on their back. She listened keenly, trying to sort out all the talk, but always making sure she was close to Carmen's side. On more than two occasions they were stopped, and once a woman who walked with a cane and whose face was filled with lines searched Essence's face and asked,

"Is whe you from, girlie? Haven't seen you before."

161

Essence pondered what to say, trying to bring to her lips the name of other estates over the island that she had visited, but Carmen came quickly to her rescue.

"Howdy Miss Tilda. Yu looking well, today. Dis here is me cousin Es. So what yu buyin'? Yu need any help, ma'am?"

Essence was impressed with Carmen's swift and expert manner in deterring folks. As they moved on, Carmen remarked, "Miss Tilda okay. She mean well, but still one can neva be too careful. If anyone else ask, tell dem yu from Yarmouth Estate. Me 'ave people dere."

This confused Essence, although she did not say anything. If they were free, why did it matter where she was from? All was not what it seemed. There was a great deal more she had to learn before reporting back to Tuba and the Elder Council.

At last Walker purchased a small piece of salt pork and they were on their way to her home, four miles from the market, which they walked in well under an hour. Walker's name was appropriately suited, Essence decided as they made their way to her little round cottage, built with bamboo poles and covered with a thatched roof from coconut boughs and secluded in a grove.

Before they were inside the one-room cottage, Carmen de Walker reached for Essence's hand and said to her. "Yu nuh tell me eberyting. Yu know yu can trust me."

"Are you free or are you enslaved?"

"We claim freedom two years now. Whe yu been hidin out? Yu is one of de Maroon dem?"

So that was why she had smelled thyme. What had her mother told her about thyme? "If you rub thyme into your joints, and behind your knees and under your arm-pits, it will make you invisible to the enslavers and the enslaved." Her mother's words seeped into her consciousness. Now she had to decide how much to tell Carmen the Walker.

"Yesterday evening you saw me at the cotton tree," Essence began, observing Carmen closely. "I was just coming up and had not filled my lungs with air yet."

"Yu is duppy?" There was alarm in Carmen's voice.

"I am still among the living," Essence hastened to assure her. "But you are right about me being a Maroon. There is a whole group of us Maroons who live underground." Before Carmen could interrupt, Essence pulled off her turban and shook her hair, which fell around her like tall, brown grass. "We breathe and survive through our hair. I am a reconnoiterer. I came up to learn what those who are enslaved are doing to gain their freedom. A few of us who came up were

162

captured and enslaved when our hair, the source of our power and transformation, was cut off."

Carmen also pulled off her head-wrap, and her finger-length dreadlocks stuck up on her head. "We is indeed cousin, and me heard oonuh chatting plenty, but me moda tell me me a gu mad cause nu body kyan live inna ground like yam root." Carmen clapped her hands and the balls of her feet tapped the ground. "Yu can neva know how it feel fi know me nuh mad," she said, embracing Essence, who immediately licked her arms in joy. Carmen pulled away.

"Mek yu lick me like puppy?" she asked.

"That's how we greet each other down there," Essence apologized, remembering this was not the way of the enslaved.

Carmen took hold of Essence's hand and pressed it to her stomach. Essence felt the child growing in Carmen's womb. They laughed, then held each other and danced around the small room for a bit, delighted with each other.

After a while Essence yawned.

"Yu tired. Tek a likkle rest while me cook."

Grateful, and sensing she was safe, Essence stretched out on the small cot and pulled the colorful sheet, made from the scraps of many different cloths, up to her neck. Some of her hair, falling to the impacted dirt floor, instantly drank in the nutrients. Her dreams connected her to her grandmother who she saw sitting on a hill looking down on a valley in which people, who appeared to be the size of ants, went about their daily chores. Grandma's grey-roped locks were pulled over her shoulder, still falling almost to her ankles.

As Essence approached her grandmother in the dream, the old woman caught hold of her hand and licked her fingers. Essence returned her grandmother's greeting by licking her shoulder as both a sign of respect for her age as well as a symbol of deep affection. Essence sat beside the elder, who did not avert her eyes from the valley, but spoke as if she was merely continuing a story.

"Your mother has told you how I, along with six others, came to find Piliferous Layer and how I came to lose my claim to it. It has taken more than ten years, fifty in the world of the enslaved, to grow back my hair. Now it almost brushes the ground; this way I am always connected to the soil that sustains us.

"When I was on that slaver's ship, cuffed and chained, bewildered and bereft of hope like all the others, I heard the voice of my great-grandmother saying to me over and over, 'All is not lost, all is not lost.' I was trying to shut out her voice when I raised my own to ask who else beside me was a priestess-in-training. Others replied, and they too were being sustained by their grandmother's voices, telling them, just like my own who had already made her transition from our world, that all was not lost, and together we had the knowledge in our wombs to forge a new way to live.

"I cannot tell you how we did it, except that once the ship docked and we were relieved of our chains, we ran, and to keep from being detected we buried each other; and in our desperation to be quiet, to keep from being recaptured, our bodies transformed and we found ourselves being pulled more deeply into the earth, as if through quicksand, until we sank to a latitude that had a floor.

"From there we learned what we had always been taught, that we could become whatever the occasion demanded, and the season of hostility and geographic realignment slated for our people required that some of us transmute and become one with the yams that had historically sustained us. We grew roots and dug more securely into the ground and gave birth. Then one by one, we rose to the surface to claim men and teach them to live like us.

"Our numbers increased and we learned to slow our aging process considerably because we surmised that this season would be a long one, and our role was not only to be way-makers, but to survive it, as we were the keepers of memory and purveyors of tradition.

"At first we didn't think we would survive, partly because we were ambivalent. Our continent, that would become divided up and renamed Africa, was not perfect, but it was ours. Our needs were met. Like most people, we sometimes fought among ourselves, and often had to contend with kings who wanted to expand their territory, but it was home.

"The tears I shed for that place and the people lost to me are in the ripple of each wave. But every time I wanted to give up, my grandmother's voice would pound inside my head, 'All is not lost. This is a great journey-way that you are making. Go on and make of it something new.' And so I did with the help of Arrora, an Arawak woman, who did not die with the rest of her people, but stayed to help those of us who were coming. She was a mother to me. She had been a high-priestess of her people. She taught all of us how to breathe underground, how to become soil and use our hair like roots. She delivered our babies and showed us how to wriggle like worms to the surface of the earth. Mostly, she taught us the smell of the white man and how to stay safe from becoming one of his slaves. Arrora is your grandmother, too. You are a woman now, soon will be sleeping with a man. You must put water out for Arrora just like how you put water out for me.

"You are as good a scout as I was, better in fact. Once again the wind has changed course, but there are still battles ahead. Always remember that you are a purveyor of memory and tradition. You must always be able to live and survive

164

anywhere. That is our claim. We survived when others did not. I was fifty, the age of your mother now, when the enslavers captured me and cut off my hair. I had been visiting several estates over the years, speaking to the women, teasing out their memory, helping them to set fire to the fields, showing them which herbs to grow to strengthen their and their men's bodies and which to use to weaken the bacras and make them worthless without killing them.

"I was doing well, but then I took up with a man on one of the estates. The woman I took him from got jealous and told the overseer that I was telling the cook how to kill him. I was too wrapped up in this man's love to be vigilant. I was tight in his arms, our legs intertwined, when they caught me, and right there before him, my hair was cut off and my head shaved clean. That was true bewilderment, that and the sting of the whip. Thirty lashes with the cat-o'-nine-tails, but not a sound escaped my mouth or a tear watered my eyes. I knew my responsibility and kept my focus on the colony underground and on our people. I knew I would see them again."

Essence turned on the small cot and the back of her hand wiped the tears that spilled from her eyes. She was still asleep, but mumbled, "Fifty in our years, but 250 in theirs. Oh grandmother, you were such a warrior."

"We all are warriors, child, especially those who were enslaved and did not succumb to death, but kept believing and working to break the chains of slavery. My child, some of the greatest warriors simply kept faith."

While Carmen de Walker hummed a mento and cooked, Essence slept deeply, her grandmother dreaming her the memory she needed to fulfill her duties. She woke after the day had gone to rest.

Her mother had always cautioned her to wait until day was chasing evening before entering the enslaved world. She woke feeling powerful, and immediately her eyes located Carmen sitting just outside the cottage on a low stool and a man standing behind her massaging her shoulders. Essence rose quietly and walked to the door, but even before her feet were over the threshold, Carmen called to her.

"Yu was well tired. Yu sleep sound."

"Yes, your cot is very comfortable," Essence replied, her eyes scanning the man, the father of Carmen's unborn child. She detected that he was safe.

"Dis be Joint, also known as Sammy."

Joint smiled at Essence, and his eyes fastened on her like burr-burr, that thorn-like weed that easily attached itself to cloth.

"Me did know yu," he declared, moving from behind Carmen and walking towards Essence. "Me did know you from another time when memory flowed like river water."

165

"Joint was here before," Carmen interjected. "Him was here two times more dan me, but de both of we been here before."

"And are you free also?" Essence asked.

"Slavery days done!" Joint declared, spittle spewing from his mouth, his nostrils flaring.

A rush of excitement flushed Essence's skin. She wanted to rush back to the colony and tell Tuba and the others that they could come up now, that they no longer needed to live underground; but first, she had to hear the full story. She had to confirm what Carmen and Joint told her, and had to decipher the smell that clung to the colony. Essence walked up to Joint and licked his cheek and then his arm. She had to be sure; taste was the ultimate confirmation. Carmen reared up and Joint brushed Essence away gently.

"Dat's me oman dere," Joint said, pointing to Carmen who had her arms akimbo. "We be family. Me no want no more oman."

Realizing that her action was misinterpreted, Essence hastened to explain.

"It's only through taste that I can verify what you say. It is the language of the Starch people."

"Is who oonuh be?" Joint asked.

"Whe oonuh live fah real?" Carmen followed on the heels of Joint, now insinuating herself between Essence and Joint, and linking her arms with his.

Essence smiled at this gesture of ownership. How would Tuba react if she were to openly declare her intention to possess him by licking his soles and tracing his spinal cord with her tongue at one of their weekly public gatherings? Would he in turn circle her navel with his tongue and lick her eyelids to indicate consent and signal their union?

"Tek me whe yu live," Carmen de Walker demanded, standing in front of Essence . "Tek me; mek me see cause me is one of oonuh." Her voice was determined. Both feet were planted firmly on the ground and her arms were akimbo again. Essence could see that she would not be dissuaded easily, yet dare she take an outsider into their free colony?

"I cannot take you. You do not know how to transform and become a root."

"Me can become whateva me want. Jus tek me and show me how," Carmen de Walker insisted.

Essence knew she was cornered, but her mind quickly reviewed the first tenet of Piliferous Layer: Safety is the responsibility of all, from the youngest to the oldest, and no outsider must be allowed into Piliferous Layer without the approval of the leader, an elder, and two other members of the community. Essence respected this rule and knew that the colony had been protected all these years because everyone, including her great-grandmother who had been captured and made to live like a slave, honored that code. She could not and would not break it, even though she believed Carmen de Walker was one of them, and wanted to show her how they lived.

But before she could explain any of this to Carmen, she felt a cool wind on her arms and legs, and knew instantly that someone else from the Maroon colony was approaching. Almost immediately, she smelled the sweet potato and smiled. So Tuba had come after her as she had hoped.

"The leader of my colony is approaching. You can make your request to him."

Tuba strode into their midst, his skin rich like wet soil, his muscles taut. Essence moved quickly to him and licked his knuckles in greeting as he ambled through the gate. Immediately Joint stepped forward, his hands fisted at his side. With her peripheral vision, Essence glanced at Joint and smiled at the folly of men. Free or enslaved they amused her with their need to always lay claim, to establish their territory. Apparently Carmen was equally aware, because she moved quickly beside Joint and placed her hands over one of his fists, massaging it.

"Him is not here to cause trouble," she said to Joint, although her eyes were on Tuba, drinking him in.

Essence felt like someone was yanking on her dreadlocks and her scalp prickled. She had not experienced this sensation before, but she knew enough to know it was her way of wanting to claim territory, indicate to Carmen that Tuba was hers, even though she had not yet made such declaration to him or the colony.

"Tuba, I am glad that you have come after me. Slavery is over. Everyone is now free. This is Carmen de Walker and her man, Joint. They are free and she is carrying his child." She knew she had said more than she needed to by way of introduction, but she felt the need to establish Carmen and Joint as a couple.

Tuba nodded to the couple, but his eyes were fastened on Essence: she read both irritation and desire.

"I had to come, and for defying your order I will submit to your punishment," Essence said more coquettishly than she had planned. It was the general rule that when the leader was disobeyed, the violator had to spend every minute of two weeks shadowing the leader.

"There is to be no punishment," Tuba replied, smiling at Essence for the first time.

"No punishment?" Essence was incredulous.

Tuba moved closer and licked her neck. "I conferred with the Elder Council before I left. I told them I approved your mission because, like you, I believed we have been underground too long."

Thrown off guard, Essence could only mumble as her mind raced ahead to try and discern if Tuba was laying a trap for her.

"But you always opposed me," she shouted.

"It might have appeared that way, but perhaps I was allowing you to practice your rebellion on me." Tuba spoke softly.

Essence felt as if all the wind and fight had been knocked out of her. Was Tuba more complex than she had thought him to be? He was certainly liked and admired by most, including the Elder Council.

"So Mr. Leader, tek me and Joint so we can see whe oonuh live," Carmen de Walker interjected, jarring Essence.

"First we must experience this freedom that you have gained," Tuba said, focusing fully on Carmen. "My people have been waiting on this day, when they could come up and breathe in the sweet air of freedom. The drums will sound this news when Essence and I return. Then perhaps you can come and see where we live; but of course there will be no need now that you are free. Living in the belly of the earth was how we resisted slavery."

"Well, slavery done, but we still have fi struggle fi get the laws change," Joint said, circling his arm around Carmen's waist. "Some of the bacras dem still want treat we like we is dem slaves. Dem no want give us no land fi grow and plant and profit from we own labor. Dem no want we have any say in how de island fi run." By now Joint was worked up and going at full speed.

"We free, but yet still we not free," Carmen interjected. "Dem still flog people like dem is slave for de slightest ting. Dem nu want pay we what we worth. Dem is true bad-minded people, dem bacra people who chat like hot coal in dem mouth and skin red like wild leaf dat yu boil fi wash sore foot."

The four laughed, feeling a warm comradery.

Tuba was invited to dinner and they ate and exchanged stories about their day-to-day activities in their respective homes. Although Joint and Carmen weren't sure, they believed that slavery had ended more than two years before. They insisted that Essence and Tuba tell them about Piliferous Layer, and they listened to all the details with their jaws agape and their eyes big.

Essence and Tuba also sought more details from them about their new freedom, and the four agreed that they would travel the island over to make sure that everyone now enjoyed freedom. Carmen de Walker said she would lead the way as she had travelled most of the island, and had even witnessed some of the torching of the fields, as well as some killings. Still, she insisted that she wanted to visit Essence's colony and have her unborn child live in a place where the people had always refused to be slaves.

After yawning and declaring her intention to sleep, Carmen stretched out on the ground and pressed her ears to the soil. A smile covered her face.

"Me hear dem talking," she said. "Me hear dem, me always used to hear dem. Me is one of oonuh." She turned on her back and smiled up at the sky sprinkled with stars. Joint and Tuba reached down and helped her up. "Well, me tink we is all tired and must get some shut eye." They started moving towards the cottage.

"Es, you and Mister Tuba can take the cot. Joint and I will pass the night on de floor."

Essence wanted to ask Carmen why she called her Es, but decided now wasn't the time, and besides, she rather liked the sound of Es. And she had no intention of taking her bed and told her so. They argued back and forth for a while, then Carmen proceeded to spread bedding on the floor for Essence and Tuba. With the lamp out, the two Starch people stumbled toward each other, unsure of their next move. They could hear Carmen and Joint settling on the small bed. Suddenly, Essence felt Tuba's tongue circling her navel. Now twice in one day he had beat her to the punch, this time by declaring his affection.

"It does not count," she whispered in his ears.

"It does to me," Tuba rejoined, licking her neck. "When we return, I shall honor you in the appropriate manner, before the community."

Essence pulled Tuba to her and whispered in his ear. "You are my sweet potato."

"And you are my cassava," Tuba said as they fell into a sound sleep nestled together, tongue against skin.

About the Author

Opal Palmer Adisa, Ph.D, is nurtured on cane-sap and the oceanic breeze of the Caribbean. Writer of both poetry and prose, Adisa is an educator and cultural activist, as well as a photographer, playwright and theatre director. Adisa has lectured and read her work throughout the Caribbean, United States, South Africa, East and West Africa as well as throughout Europe.

An award-winning poet and prose writer, Adisa has more than twenty titles to her credit, including *Look! A Moko Jumbie*, CaribbeanReads, 2016; *4-Headed Woman*, Tia Chucha Press, 2013; and *Painting Away Regrets*, novel, Peepal Tree Press, 2011.

She has been a resident artist in internationally acclaimed residencies such as Arte Studio Ginestrelle (Assis, Italy), El Gouna (Egypt), Sacatar Institute (Brazil), McColl Center (North Carolina), and Headlines Center for the Arts (California, USA). Opal Palmer Adisa's work has been reviewed by Ishmael Reed, Al Young, and Alice Walker (Color Purple) who described her work as "solid, visceral, important stories written with integrity and love."

A Distinguished professor of creative writing and literature in the MFA program at California College of the Arts, she has been a visiting professor at several universities including, Stanford University, University of California, Berkeley, and University of the Virgin Islands. Her poetry, stories, essays, and articles on a wide range of subjects have been collected in over 400 journals, anthologies and other publications, including Essence Magazine.

Adisa is the founder and editor of *Interviewing the Caribbean*, an annual journal of poetry, prose, art, and interviews.

www.ingramcontent.com/pod-product-compliance
Lightning Source LLC
Chambersburg PA
CBHW022153260626
47155CB00017B/1861